BLAZER: GHOSTS OF WAR

G.C. HARMON

ROUGH EDGES PRESS

ROUGH EDGES PRESS

Paperback Edition
Copyright © 2021 (As Revised) G.C. Harmon

All rights reserved. No part of this book may be reproduced by any means without the prior written consent of the publisher, other than brief quotes for reviews.

This book is a work of fiction. Any references to historical events, real people or real places are used fictitiously. Other names, characters, places and events are products of the author's imagination, and any resemblance to actual events, places or persons, living or dead, is entirely coincidental.

Published in the United States by Wolfpack Publishing, Las Vegas

Rough Edges Press
An Imprint of Wolfpack Publishing
5130 S. Fort Apache Rd. 215-380
Las Vegas, NV 89148

roughedgespress.com

Paperback ISBN: 978-1-68549-001-0
eBook ISBN: 978-1-68549-000-3

BLAZER: GHOSTS OF WAR

DEDICATION

This book is dedicated to my father, George Harmon. He knows I'm not pretending now.

INTRODUCTION

I grew up reading the pulp fiction adventure novels of the 1970s and '80s, where the hero was frequently a Vietnam Vet. I wrote the first version of this story back in 1997, with the idea that Blazer's mentor, Captain Stanson, was a Vietnam Vet. As time passed and the Vietnam War receded further and further into history, the timing became a problem. But I always felt the story was too good not to share. I found what I felt was a clever way to revisit the Vietnam War, and I made this book a prequel to Red, White and Blue.

Even as the Vietnam War fades into history, we must not minimize the service and sacrifice of those who fought and died there. America shamed herself when some of our politicians turned a blind eye to the plight of the Vietnamese people, and when our youth counter-culture spat upon the veterans returning from the conflict. The sacrifice of those veterans actually means something. We must never forget.

CHAPTER 1

SIX YEARS AGO...

The night was always alive in the city of San Francisco. Inside his unmarked police vehicle, the noise was reduced to background buzz. There were moments when Inspector Steve Blazer found it almost hypnotizing, like now. He was starting to nod off. Busy days of hectic police work were starting to catch up with him. He'd caught a nap at the Tenderloin Precinct earlier that evening, but it wasn't enough. He shook his head to wake up and started taking in the noise around him. Off to his left, just a few blocks to the north, the Bay Bridge began its seven-mile journey across the bay to the city of Oakland. Even at this time of night, there were headlights traveling along both tiers of the bridge, mostly truckers moving their loads to and from the city. A fog was appearing, not rolling in from the ocean, but just sort of materializing around the area. It had started as a gentle mist but was now growing thicker.

A tugboat slid past through calm waters far out in the Bay. Most piers along this section of the Embarcadero, which spanned from the bridge to nearby China Basin, were empty of people this early in the morning. Typically, maritime folk were 'early-to-rise' types, but for most people, four a.m. was just too early.

South Beach Yacht Harbor, which stretched south from Pier 40, was as quiet as the rest of the city. Rows of yachts and sailboats swayed gently in the calm port waters, their masts dancing to nature's quiet music. A mysterious bell from a lonely buoy tolled somewhere in the distance every few seconds.

San Francisco had become famous for its baseball stadium, AT&T Park, constructed in the 1990s to replace the aging Candlestick Park farther down the bay coast. The park had been built right next to the South Beach Yacht Harbor. It had been known as Pac Bell Park and SBC Park until they settled on AT&T Park in 2006.

Their police department-issued Chevy Tahoe was backed into shadows inside a passageway on the north side of the park. The passage was supposed to allow vehicle access to the ball field and it provided a convenient hiding place. The passageway provided them a decent view of the marina parking lot but not much of the marina itself. In scanning the area, Inspector Steve Blazer glanced at his partner for the night. Lieutenant George Cameron was just as engrossed in the tension of the impending bust. In nearly a year that he'd been on Vice, Steve had developed a close working relationship with Lieutenant Cameron. Steve had been in the department nearly four years now, since his discharge from the Army following his involvement in America's new war on terror. As a patrol officer, a "uniform" or "unie," Steve accumulated a lengthy arrest record, and had a special talent for sniffing out drugs. His skill as a cop and a soldier earned him a spot on SFPD's SWAT team. After a year on SWAT, Steve was recommended for an opening on Cameron's Vice Squad.

Looking back, Steve knew Lieutenant Cameron had some doubts about him. Looking through his record, Cameron came up with a few holes in his background. When he asked Blazer about it, Steve offered that he'd been with the US Army's Special Forces but gave up nothing else. In the beginning, he remembered the LT had once described him as "Tough and Aggressive, but Righteous." Steve clung to the "righteous," and wore it like a badge of honor. Every day on the streets, he tried to live up to that, and live up to Cameron's high regard for him. Possibly because of this, he often now felt like he was being groomed for a higher position, such as being Cameron's second in command, or even taking over the squad one day.

Steve pulled himself back to the present, and once again scanned the night. "It's quiet out there."

"I guarantee that will change," Cameron said.

Steve remembered the story Cameron had told him after their previous bust. "This guy really has you scared, doesn't he?"

Cameron regarded the younger cop. Like him, Blazer was dressed casually, in dark jeans and a polo shirt. He wore a leather jacket over his shoulder holster. Knowing the younger hot shot cop the way he did, Cameron suspected Blazer had at least one or two more handguns hidden somewhere on his person. "This son of a bitch put two of my guys in the hospital and almost killed me. You're damn right he's got me scared." Cameron looked at him, eyes wider than they should have been for a brave cop. "You were there, how did you not see him?"

"I was too busy ducking from being shot at." Steve was now getting energized, not from anger at his boss, but from the memory of the shootout two days ago that had wounded two of his fellow cops. "I never got a good look at him."

"I haven't been this nervous since my first rookie shooting," Cameron insisted. "I'm tellin' you, Blazer, if you'd seen this guy the other day, you would be impressed. He moved like a freaking ghost."

Steve remembered the bust, ran through it once more in his head. They had staked out a crack house on the north face of Potrero Hill. The drug operation there was connected to a gang in Little Saigon, a Vietnamese community in the Tenderloin. They had seen a car stop by, presumably to make some kind of drop-off, and Cameron gave the order to move in, to bust the car and the house. Someone from the crack house opened fire from a front window with a submachine gun. He winged one of the Vice cops with the opening salvo, and it led to everyone in the house opening up on the advancing police. The second officer was hit moments later as he tried to retreat to cover.

Cameron was suddenly lost in his memories, recalling his version of the battle. "I'm in through the front door, and I see this big bulky guy going through a doorway into a back bedroom. He tries to slam the door, and I bust through it, but he's already diving out a window. By the time I get there, he's running across the backyard. I knew you were coming up the side of the house, so I started to crawl through that coffin-window. I saw him shooting in your direction. I blinked, and suddenly that MAC-10 is spitting at me. I swear Blazer, I've never been as scared as I was when those rounds were chewing up the window frame around me. I dropped back inside for cover. By the time I got outside, he was gone."

Steve paused for a moment, considering their tactical situation. "With Beckett and Wen still in the hospital, we're a couple guys short."

"Another reason I'm so nervous."

"LT, you've gone up against punks before…"

"Blazer, this is not just another junkie with a gun. This guy was shooting with precision. You saw the vest they took off Wen. There were three holes in a direct diagonal pattern across the upper chest. It's a good thing only one of those rounds actually penetrated the vest. But for the briefest second, I saw this guy. The face was kind of a blur, but the eyes… Only once have I seen eyes that cold. And they were yours."

Steve wasn't sure how to respond, so he let the silence hang for a minute. He did have a reputation with the Department as being one of its toughest cops. He steeled himself for what he suspected was coming tonight. "I guess you're hoping he shows up tonight."

Cameron shrugged. "Hoping he does, hoping he doesn't."

The radio on the floor pleaded for their attention. "Victor one zero, this is one seven. Wake up, boss, we got movement, a car approaching the marina. We've also got a fishing boat entering the marina at the breakwater, south end."

"Where are they?" Steve asked, referring to the police unit on the radio.

"To the north, at Pier 38," Cameron said. "They've got a good view of the marina." Cameron glanced to his right, where the fishing boat would be approaching, but they were too deep into the passageway to see much of the marina.

Steve leaned forward, trying to see around the wall to his right. Through a small stand of trees in the parking lot, branches nearly bare from the fall season, they finally saw the fishing boat slide slowly into view.

As the boat glided among the sailboats moored

to the piers, Steve studied it. It was about thirty feet long, and appeared to be in bad shape, maybe not even seaworthy. It was an industrial boat, one that ordinarily wouldn't find a home in a marina like this. For a moment, he thought he saw a shadow moving at the stern. But then the headlights of the vehicle they'd been warned about swung over the area.

A small guard shack with a pivoting barrier arm had been constructed, but currently no one was inside. The barrier arm was automatic and opened when an electronic key card was displayed. For some reason, right now the barrier arm was left in the up position. The vehicle, a Lexus sedan, was able to drive right in.

* * *

On the boat, a man dressed in black—the shadow Steve had seen—stood at the stern, scanning the shore. He had that old feeling, the hairs standing on the back of his neck. Silently, he directed the pilot to steer close to a fifty-six-foot yacht moored at the end of the pier. He reached up casually as the fishing boat glided past the taller yacht, grabbed a metal bar railing that surrounded the bow and swung his legs up onto the deck. The fishing boat left him behind as he rolled under the railing. He froze in a prone position, facing the city, eyes intently studying the shore. It took him only seconds to pick out the police vehicle parked in the stadium passageway. There would likely be a boat unit, possibly coming up from somewhere behind the fishing boat to try and block its escape. He intended to be nowhere near the boat when that rear escape was closed.

The man in black pulled out his cell phone and

found a number on his recent calls list. "Check your six. There's cops right behind you." He hung up without another word.

The man in black rose and crept across the deck of the boat he'd boarded, slipping down onto the pier on the other side.

* * *

Steve's gaze darted between the Lexus in the Marina parking lot and the south end of the yacht harbor. "Marine Unit should be closing in on the breakwater, are they set?" he asked Cameron. The Lieutenant repeated the question into his radio.

"Negative," a reply came, quiet to Steve's distant ears, "we are not on station yet."

The Lexus had stopped near an electronically controlled gate leading down a plank to the docks. The headlights winked out.

"This is going to be bad," a nervous George Cameron muttered.

"Welcome to my world," Steve muttered.

Steve watched the Lexus. Three men had stepped out, and they were watching the approaching boat. Even from fifty yards away in the dark, Steve could see they were Asian, and they were young. Blazer suddenly noticed the actions of one of the Asians. He was craning his neck, checking their surroundings. Steve could not tell what alerted him, but his eyes suddenly locked on the Chevy Tahoe they thought was hidden so well. Those eyes went wide. "Cops!" he screamed and ducked into the car.

Opposite him, the driver began screaming and waving at the boat. The message was clear: get away.

"We're made," Steve said, then into his radio said, "Go, go, go!"

At Pier 38 to the north, an unmarked police vehicle roared to life and surged toward the melee.

Steve wrenched open his door. They had to take them down now, boat and car, and hope they found some contraband to bring charges for.

The passenger popped back out again, this time with a MAC-10 submachine gun. The weapon swung toward Blazer and Cameron. A tongue of flame darted from the barrel as it burped a quick burst of lead. Steve ducked behind his open door, hearing those rounds whistle past and ricochet off the walls. "Shots fired!" he radioed.

Steve leaned out from his door and opened fire. He drew back as the MAC-10 belched fire and lead again. This time a line of slugs stitched the wall to his right, throwing up sparks. Steve muttered a curse, realizing that for the moment, they were pinned down.

Steve spotted the unmarked cop car approaching from the north.

The Vice vehicle would have had to drive a short distance down the street to make the parking lot entrance. Instead, once Steve had issued the "Shots fired" warning, the driver made a snap decision. Steve watched as the Crown Victoria jumped the curb and cut across a stretch of grass, then bounced over another curb to enter the lot. The vehicle skidded to a stop twenty yards away. The two Vice cops inside were instantly out, aiming their weapons at the Lexus.

The arrival of more cops caused momentary hesitation among the Asians. The two Vice cops began barking orders, and the confusion escalated. To Steve, it looked for a moment like the bad guys were about to give up. He ventured forward from cover, marching across the lot, his gun covering the Lexus.

He saw a commotion at the edge of his vision, off to his left where the second vehicle had stopped. Sensing that danger, he whirled on it. He found Inspector Clyde Chester on the other side of the vehicle, the driver's side, locked in hand to hand combat with…someone. Whoever he was, he had snuck up behind them, and apparently wasn't part of the group from the Lexus… was he? He wasn't friendly, whoever he was. Confused for a moment, Steve trained his gun that way, but he held his fire, lest he hit his partner. There seemed to be nothing he could do to help Chester—he was just too far away. "Let him go!" he yelled, knowing it wouldn't happen.

With brute strength, the stranger had already wrapped an arm around the inspector's windpipe. He leaned back, pulling Chester off his feet. With his right hand still holding his gun, Chester reached back with his left to try to fight back.

On the passenger side, Chester's partner, Inspector Lange, did not see the new player at first. He was alerted to the problem by Steve's warning and turned on the commotion. Steve thought desperately, now with two cops zeroing in on this guy, we still don't have a shot.

The stranger was now grappling for the gun with his right hand, his left still wrapped around Chester's throat. The cop suddenly went limp. From his distance, Steve believed he heard the sound of his neck breaking. The stranger grabbed again for the gun, still holding the cop as a shield. He found the gun, yanked it free. In less time than any of them thought possible, he had aimed the gun at Lange and fired once. That single bullet caught Lange in the eye, boring through his brain.

As Lange went down, Steve surged forward. Men with guns at the Lexus be damned; he had just seen two cops attacked. Steve pumped his legs, trying to get to the unmarked and stop this guy. Even as he ran, he saw the mysterious stranger sliding through the already open door into the unmarked police vehicle.

The shot that killed Lange was the fuse that sparked the next wave of the battle. One of the Asians turned a MAC-10 on the running cop and sprayed lead in Steve's direction. Steve briefly turned his gun on the Lexus, but fire behind him began to pepper the car. Cameron had joined the battle.

Steve remained intent on the Crown Victoria. It was now within reach, just fifteen yards away—

The unmarked Vice unit's engine was still running. Those tires suddenly screeched as the stranger hit the gas. The car careened backwards, away from the scene. Steve opened fire, and actually saw his rounds punch through the windshield, tearing up the interior. Then the driver threw the car into a skidding turn and it sped out the driveway.

Steve felt like a fool for a moment, stopping to stare at the retreating Crown Victoria. Behind him, more gunfire erupted, so he turned and sought the nearest cover, a concrete streetlight base.

Cameron poured a burst of suppression fire at the Lexus, but the bad guys just kept firing back. Seeing the two dead cops now laying in the open, Steve felt a wave of anger rise inside. He popped up, zeroed on the Lexus. The Asian from the back seat was just turning his way. Steve opened fire, and from thirty yards away saw his rounds dig through the man's side into his gut. He jerked, collapsing against the open car door.

His pistol locked open on an empty magazine.

In that moment, he saw the second Asian turn the MAC-10 his way.

That shooter suddenly jerked and collapsed as two more shots echoed across the lot. Steve looked over at his boss—the Lieutenant had finally scored a hit.

Only now was Steve able to put out the message over his radio. "Officer down!" With the group at the Lexus apparently out of commission, he surged into the open again, headed for his fallen comrades. He noted a third police vehicle entering the driveway to the marina. That would be the last two Vice cops, Inspectors Chandler and Green, who'd been posted in reserve on the other side of the stadium. As Cameron ran toward Steve and his dead cops, the car stopped near the bodies.

"Check them," Cameron shouted to the Crown Vic's open window, pointing at the Lexus. The vehicle surged across the lot and stopped just a few yards from the Lexus. Inspectors Chandler and Greene burst from the car and swarmed the Asians with guns drawn. They checked for a pulse on both shooters, then removed weapons from dead hands.

"Talk to me, Blazer," Cameron called out as he closed in.

Steve stood and stepped up to Cameron, stopping him from getting too close. "They're both gone, LT," he said.

Cameron turned away, overwhelmed. He growled, and Steve could see his eyes were tearing up.

A new engine sound reached them, and Steve quickly sought it out—at sea.

The boat.

Steve checked the marina. The fishing boat that had entered appeared to have done a U-turn and was trying to make a getaway, southbound. He heard a new sound, a distant siren. It sounded different from the siren of a police car. It was the Marine Unit patrol boat, finally on station.

Steve stepped toward the marina, craning his neck for a better look. He heard the fishing boat engines rev again, and got a look at what they were doing, pulling another U-turn.

Steve glanced quickly over the marina, searching for a route to—

"LT, we're not done yet," he called to Cameron. Before the Lieutenant could turn and fight through his emotions to see what he meant, Steve was off and running.

Steve found the staircase down to the piers, took the steps two at a time. He was confronted by a gate with an electronic lock requiring a card key. He used a key of his own making, leveled his pistol at the lock and blew it to pieces. He grabbed a handle and pulled, and on the second yank, the gate came open. He darted inside.

Moving down one of the main piers, where the lines of slips branched off, Steve searched for the fishing boat. It was coming abreast of the pier two rows behind him. Steve took the next turn and headed for the end of the pier at a dead run.

On the move, Steve continuously glanced off to his right at the fishing boat closing in. He was wary of the man with the submachine gun on the deck and knew that gun would swing his way any moment. Blazer kept his sprint toward the end of the pier, now just thirty yards away. A large sixty-foot yacht was docked there, but if he got there in time, maybe he could find a good firing position.

The fishing boat passed by the end of the pier. Steve held his pistol trained on that area, but the yacht blocked his aim. He diverted out onto the nearest slip. As he watched the boat power by yards away, he locked eyes with the Asian man clutching the submachine gun. He took careful aim and pumped off a tentative shot. The man on the boat was already dropping to a crouch and answered with a burst from the submachine gun, rattling down the boat next to the cop. Blazer threw himself to the left, dropping and rolling to the edge of the slip, and almost into the water. The fishing boat went on by. Even from his distance, Blazer could hear the push in that engine. It may be a raggedy-looking fishing boat but it had some power in its screws.

As the boat moved on, he took off running again, once more sprinting to the end of the pier. He reached the last slip and kneeled, sighting on the retreating boat. He pumped out his last five shots.

The fishing boat kept running.

Over the ringing in his ears, Blazer heard another boat's engine, and the hiss of the wake it was churning. He looked behind him and found the Marine Unit patrol boat approaching, now two piers away. It had finally entered the marina.

Thinking quickly, Blazer glanced at the yacht and found the stairway attached to the side for passengers to disembark. He bounded up those stairs onto the yacht and hurried across to the starboard side. What am I doing? he asked himself, taking in his surroundings at a glance. He began waving his arms at the approaching patrol boat. Then he holstered his gun and leaped over the railing.

Like an Olympic Diver, Blazer tensed his legs and launched himself out over the water. He extended his arms as he dropped, and he splashed into the frigid waters of the San Francisco Bay.

He cut smoothly into the water and surfaced immediately, taking a moment to orient himself. He turned back to the patrol boat, fast approaching.

"Man overboard," someone shouted from the patrol boat.

"Pick me up!" Blazer shouted, knowing they would. He tread water for the moment, watching the boat. A uniformed officer leaned over the side, holding a white circular life preserver. *Navy SEAL style*, Blazer thought, understanding what the uniformed officer intended.

As the boat drew abreast of him, Blazer hooked his arm into the life preserver. For a moment, he was dragged alongside the boat, and he let the motion position him there. He tried to throw his leg up to hook over the gunwale and pull himself up. His waterlogged clothes conspired against him, but helping hands were waiting to drag him on board. In moments, he was out of the water and tumbled onto the deck.

"Go, go," he shouted even before he was safely on the deck.

The boat surged forward. Steve felt the sudden wind chill from their growing speed, and his body suddenly shivered involuntarily.

"Get some blankets," the boat pilot shouted as he glanced back at the crazy Vice cop, then went back to tracking the fishing boat. Another crew member yanked open a locker in the stern and pulled out a stack of blankets. He opened one up and tossed it over Blazer's shoulders.

Blazer strained to see forward where the fishing boat had gone. "Do you still have them?"

"I got 'em," the pilot answered. His throttle was open, and he bore down on the slower fishing boat.

Blazer rose to his feet despite the wind-chill and tried to catch his balance as the boat started bouncing over three-foot swells. He wiped his eyes again and scanned the marina ahead of them. He spotted the fishing boat, fifty yards away and closing on the north entrance to the marina. Blazer glanced to their starboard at the breakwater, wishing they could jump the breakwater and try to cut them off.

He spotted movement on the rear deck of the fishing boat, then a winking light—a muzzle flash. A moment later, bullets began tearing up the patrol boat. The cops dove to the deck as chunks of glass and plastic bounced and flew around them. The pilot ducked but stayed in his seat. He wrenched the wheel hard to port.

Blazer looked up in time to see where they were headed. The boat had steered into the last inlet and was now aimed at the last pier. He tried to brace himself. The boat slammed sideways into the pier, crashing into the stern of a sailboat and sending rooster-tails of water everywhere. The cops tumbled together, landing in a heap on the deck.

Blazer managed to wriggle free of the tangle. He threw himself into the cockpit before the pilot or any other maritime cop could do so. He found the engine still running. He wrenched the throttle backward into reverse, and the engine roared. The boat slid easily backward. He glanced back and swung the wheel to position the boat. The sudden motion caused the maritime cops to lose their balance and fall again. He then pushed the throttle all the way forward. They tumbled again, but the boat shot forward, quickly picking up speed. They closed on the north entrance to the Marina, and Blazer searched for the fishing boat.

He found it in the distance, backlit by a wall of gray. The fog had grown thicker out here on the water. It was now swirling over the city and the bay. It was starting to brighten with the approaching dawn. The Bay Bridge provided a spectacular visual as it was slowly swallowed by the fog. It looked like it was painted on a gray-white canvas, with its lights glittering in sparkling detail, outlining the bridge against its backdrop.

Blazer stared intently as the boat seemed to enter the gray wall beneath the bridge and fade away.

The boat crew lapsed into a moment of silence. Then the pilot turned to Blazer. "You know, we could have just stopped and picked you up."

Steve began to shiver again. He just shrugged.

CHAPTER 2

Streetlights reflected off the canvas of fog, creating the optical illusion that the mist was there to brighten their day. One hour had dragged by since the shootout, and Steve had just returned from his outing on the patrol boat. They'd used radar to search for the boat, but it was already lost in the fog and the growing ship traffic.

"Two cops killed, Blazer," Cameron said as Steve found him. He'd had time since the bust to get himself worked up. "The guy must have come from the boat. We found wet footprints where he waded to shore and snuck up behind them."

Steve nodded. He wanted to say something comforting to the Lieutenant, but they had a crime scene to run. "You going to be OK, boss?"

Cameron took a shaky breath. "It's always a risk," he mumbled, so low Steve almost didn't hear him. "When you first put on that uniform, the thought of putting your life on the line is such a distant thrill, you almost don't even think about it. But it's always there, you know? Nobody jokes about it, so it almost goes away. Until someone else gets hurt or killed, or until someone questions how cops do their job."

Steve listened, feeling every emotional word.

"We all know the risks. And we all think it can't happen to us."

Steve stayed quiet, and the silence drew out for a moment.

Cameron suddenly looked up at him. "It was him."

"Your ghost?"

Cameron nodded. "He killed them; I know it. You saw how he came from out of nowhere. I still didn't get a good look at him, but I know it was him."

"We'll get him," Steve vowed. He looked up when he saw another car stop outside the yellow crime scene tape. He recognized the car and excused himself to go meet the occupant.

Captain John Stanson stepped out of his car looking a little disheveled. The hair surrounding his balding head was unkempt, and he was wearing simple jeans and a T-shirt, his badge and gun clipped to his belt. Despite the chilly foggy morning, he wore no coat. He spotted Steve and steered toward him.

"I've been getting updates since I heard," Stanson announced.

"Chester and Lange. They're both gone."

"Run it for me."

Steve knew the man well. His concern for his men knew no limits and often transcended the political correctness that plagued this city. The two of them shared far more than a few years on the Force together. Stanson had first recognized the talent of a much younger Steve Blazer in the military Special Forces community. In the ongoing war on terror, John Stanson had for many years been an occasional contract worker with the CIA. Blazer was part of an Army Special Forces team. The two of them crossed paths on several special missions together, and in the process formed a bond deeper than either expected. Stanson poured his knowledge into Blazer, giving

Steve a crash course in the art of spying. Years later, after their lives had taken diverging paths, they came together again in San Francisco. The Captain saw in him a man in transition, a crusader looking for a cause coupled with a warrior seeking a war. Stanson got Steve through the police academy and onto the force. Steve's drive and ideals got him where he was today. He built a reputation for himself, taking the same soldier's drive from the military and applying it to law enforcement.

Steve led the Captain toward the Lexus with the bullet holes. "Background: Vice rolled a player busted in a Potrero drug house connected to a gang from Little Saigon, and he turned us on to a shipment being met here tonight. These three were here to meet a fishing boat dropping off what we can only guess was Golden Triangle Opium, or maybe even refined heroin. They saw us and sounded the warning. The fishing boat made a run for it. I went out with Harbor Patrol to search for the boat. In this fog, they were long gone."

Stanson's face had gone dark at the words 'Little Saigon.' He kept listening as he took in the scene.

"The real problem is over there. Someone attacked Chester and Lange right in the middle of the shootout. We haven't been able to identify him, but he was not Asian. Only description we have is that he's white. He stole their unmarked and fled the scene, leaving two cops dead." His voice took on the proper inflection for this announcement. Stanson lowered his head, mouth twisting with quiet rage over the dead cops.

"Have Cameron check GPS for the vehicle."

"It's in the works."

"What can you tell me about this drug house?"

"I can fill you in on that," Cameron said as he joined them. "You know we've had an upsurge in heroin deaths down in the Mission and the Tenderloin, three in one week. We've been trying to figure out which gang is dealing this new stuff. You remember the shooting in Little Saigon about a week ago?"

"I remember there were no bodies," Stanson said.

"No bodies, no injuries, but a whole lot of brass up and down the street. I went to try and find out if they have anything to do with this new stuff. I talked to Inspector Dy from Asian Crimes and I found out this is not an isolated incident. There's been some gang wars over the past couple of months. That same day, some young Vietnamese pusher gets popped in a drive-by, and Dy finds this stash on the body. We had it tested, and it's the same smack we've been chasing all over the Mission. I convinced Dy to let me work the homicide with him so I can pursue this drug source, and we rolled an associate of the deceased. Seems this new heroin is coming in direct from the Golden Triangle. This associate couldn't tell us anything else, but my theory is, all this gang fighting is someone's attempt to control this new drug source."

"This is like the BTK gangs of the 90s." Stanson saw a look on Steve's face and explained. "In the late 70s, there was a wave of refugees coming here from Vietnam, Laos, Cambodia, Thailand. They were fleeing the war and its aftermath. Some of the young kids formed gangs and they became known as the "Born To Kill" gangs, because some of the GIs in 'Nam wore that phrase on their helmets. They were a brutal bunch. Most of their activity was in New York, but they started to branch out near the end. They had a faction in San Jose, but they never made it here. Most of the gang was rounded up and put in prison in the early 90s."

"What do you know about Little Saigon?"

"Back in the '70s," Stanson said, "San Francisco set up this city-funded housing area for Vietnamese refugees. Back in 2004, the city officially named it 'Little Saigon,' like the one in Orange County. For a while when they first set it up, there was a scare about Communists taking up residence there, but that all died down. Now the war is so long ago, the place has kind of faded into the background. The Asian Crimes Task Force has kept a close eye on the place, but there's always been resentment between us and them. In a lot of ways, going into Little Saigon is like going into Vietnam like it was during the war."

In his mind, Stanson was carried to another time and place.

Inspector Chandler, one of the remaining Vice cops, approached the group. "There's something you guys should see."

He led the group over to the bodies of the two dead cops. A CSI stood over them, having just finished photographing the bodies. Chandler lifted the sheet off of Chester and pointed out the corner of a card tucked under the dead man's riot vest.

Steve glanced at his Captain and saw his face go cold and hard as stone, like he'd seen a ghost.

Cameron snapped on a pair of latex gloves. He carefully drew the card out and held it up for a quick examination. He turned it over to show to Blazer. It was a playing card. "King of Hearts," Cameron said, "the Suicide King."

If it was possible, Stanson's face went even whiter. Blazer saw it. Stanson suddenly turned and marched toward his car.

"Is this some kind of serial killer?" Chandler asked.

"I don't think so," Steve said and took off after the Captain.

Stanson marched right up to the yellow tape, calmly ripped it in half and walked through without breaking stride. Steve laid a hand on his shoulder as he reached his car. "Sir, what is it? Do you know something I should?"

"Blazer, I may be out of the loop for a while," Stanson said, almost as a monotone. "Work the case. If someone's bringing in dope from the Golden Triangle, I want to know about it." He slammed the door shut and got the engine racing. Steve watched the middle-aged man whip his car around like a pro and speed off.

"What about the cop killer?" Steve asked the retreating car. He stood there until the car disappeared.

"Blazer!" Cameron called out. Steve turned and walked back to where Cameron stood over the bodies of his men. Employees of the Coroner's office had arrived and were standing by a few yards away to remove the bodies.

Cameron drew Steve aside. "The department has heard the news. We've got cops showing up from all over. Officers are starting their shift and coming straight here. Guys going off duty are staying on to come assist. I'm going to set up an honor guard convoy down to the Medical Examiner's office."

Steve glanced around, seeing more uniforms than had been there previously. They stood solemn, in small groups, talking quietly or simply offering a brother officer a shoulder of support. Blazer nodded. "I think we should lead the way."

Cameron motioned to the coroner's team, and they stepped up to begin preparing the bodies for transport. Cameron then walked up to a group of uniforms, who eagerly awaited instructions. Cameron began with, "Here's what I want to happen..."

Steve returned to their SUV. He had one key to the vehicle, and Cameron had the other. Blazer pulled the SUV out of the stadium and drove out to the street, parking just at the end of the driveway. In moments, other SFPD patrol cars began lining up behind him.

Only now was Steve finally able to breathe. He sat still for a moment, staring out the windshield, letting his emotions catch up to him. Two cops killed and he saw them murdered, too far away to stop it from happening. His breaths came deeper and faster, a single tear ran down his face and his body threatened to break down in sobs. He took deep breaths for a moment to try and bring himself under control. But for the longest moment, his passions raged, and control seemed to elude him. Seeing in his mirror police cars lining up behind him, their lights already pulsating, did little to help him control his grief and rage. He continued deep breaths, trying to pull himself together. They were not finished here, there was still a lot of work to be done.

In minutes, Cameron reached their vehicle. He climbed into the passenger seat and motioned them forward. He gave Blazer a quick glance and noted the labored breathing. He knew what it meant. He was close to losing it himself.

Steve got them underway, pulling out into the street with a train of police cars following, red and blue lights blazing. SFPD rolled southward, paying their own tribute to two fallen cops.

***

The trip, by design, took longer than it normally would have. Rather than take the freeway, the convoy proceeded straight down Third Street. Along the way, the convoy had been joined by several officers from the local California Highway Patrol office, and a squad of motorcycle officers had taken upon themselves the duty of being road guards. The motor officers would block off streets for the convoy while a pair of bikes took the lead up front. Steve kept their speed low to keep everyone together. They rode in silence. As that silence stretched out, Steve glanced over at the Lieutenant. Where Steve had had his moment to break down, Cameron now had his. He saw Cameron's eyes closed, and a single sob convulsed his body. Steve could offer no words of encouragement, he just kept driving.

Minutes into their journey, he noticed the crowds now gathering along the street. He figured many of the observers were simply there to see the spectacle of all the police activity, whether or not they knew what it meant. But then he saw something else, something very heartening. Some of those spectators held their hands over their hearts. Some even held up American flags. And then appeared the cops from other departments. The word of two murdered SFPD cops must have spread beyond the city. The route must have been leaked by some officer somewhere, not that anyone took issue with the reasons why. At some intersections they passed, they began to see patrol cars from departments outside SFPD, two and three at a time with uniformed officers standing at attention and saluting. Most notable, Steve recognized patrol cars from San Mateo PD, San Mateo County Sheriff's Department and the South San Francisco Police Department. Steve felt certain that as the last of the convoy passed these officers, they joined in behind everyone.

The growing convoy finally reached Newhall Street and the office of the San Francisco Medical Examiner. There, they encountered one more honor, the street lined with more uniforms, every one of them saluting. It was hard for Steve to keep his emotions in check, seeing this, but he led the convoy into the parking lot. Steve saw the SFPD honor guard standing ready at a rear entrance, where bodies were received by the M.E. staff. He pulled his vehicle to the side. As he stepped out, he saw that other patrol vehicles behind him had also pulled aside to let the Coroner's van through. That van slid up to the entrance, and one SFPD officer guided the driver to the doorway. Blazer and Cameron made sure they were on hand with the honor guard as the bodies were unloaded. The line of officers came to attention and saluted as the bodies were loaded onto gurneys and wheeled inside.

Cameron glanced over the sea of cops milling about the parking lot. "Can you see that the boys are checked in?" he asked Blazer. "I'm going to do a meet and greet in the lobby." Steve nodded and followed the gurneys inside.

It took only minutes for paperwork to be filled out and the bodies officially turned over for autopsy. Steve found his way back to the lobby, which he found filled with uniforms from several nearby Law Enforcement Agencies. He searched the crowded room for Lieutenant Cameron. He found the LT in a quiet corner on his phone. As Steve made his way toward his Commanding Officer, he watched Cameron's actions. As soon as he ended his phone call, he was greeted by a uniformed Sergeant, who offered a hand and a quiet word. Cameron shook the hand, nodding. He glanced around the room, and suddenly stepped up onto a bench. "Can I have your attention, please?" he shouted. All quiet talking in the lobby ceased. "I want to thank everyone for coming to support us. It means a lot to us, and I want every one of you to know, we would be there for you and your department if, God forbid, something like this ever happens again.

"We don't have any press here yet, do we?" he

suddenly asked. Everyone glanced around the room. There appeared to be no reporters. "Good, because I'm not releasing anything to the media yet. This is for cop ears only. My name is Lieutenant George Cameron, I'm commander of the SFPD Vice Squad. Early this morning, we had a drug bust go bad. Responding to the scene, Inspectors William Chester and Justin Lange were murdered. I'll be notifying the families shortly. Suspect remains at large."

This last statement drew murmurs from the gathered cops.

"We'll get him, LT," Steve said quietly.

This brought more muttering, as if the cops in the room collectively said, 'Damn right.'

Cameron stepped down, and he gestured for Blazer to follow him. The activity around them began to pick up again and some of them began to leave. Cameron led Blazer and the rest of his squad to a darkened spot just down a hallway.

"I'm going to have to notify the families," Cameron said. "Chester had a wife and son. He's only eight. Lange's parents live in LA, I'll have to call them, and maybe notify LAPD." He turned to Steve. "While I'm doing this, I want you to run with the investigation. I've invited Inspector Dy from Asian Crimes to join us. When I talked to him, he had already heard and was on his way here. Maybe he can shed some light on what we're dealing with in Little Saigon."

"I can make a call to the Gang unit," Steve added. "Maybe someone there can ID those guys in the Lexus."

"If not, maybe some of the business owners in Little Saigon might know them. It's a long shot, and we may have to go door to door..." Cameron trailed off as two men made their way from the crowded lobby into their hallway.

One was Asian, and Steve guessed he was Vietnamese. He figured this to be Cameron's Asian Crimes Task Force contact. He was tall for his race, at least five foot nine. His black hair was kind of long and haggard looking, and he had a growing pot belly. A gray sport coat covered the snub-nosed .38 caliber revolver mounted on his belt, and his badge was hung from a breast pocket. The second cop was younger, white, six feet tall with light brown hair. He wore a black polo shirt over jeans and also had his sidearm, a standard Glock, clipped to his belt, along with his badge.

Cameron rose to make the introductions. "Inspector Vinh Dy, Steve Blazer, he'll be running things for a bit."

"Call me Vinnie," Dy said. Dy didn't offer to shake hands with Steve, simply nodded to him. Or was it a curt bow, Steve wasn't sure. His first impression of the Vietnamese cop was that of a man trying to look, act, sound, *be* as American as possible. "This is my partner, Inspector Scot Black."

Black had stopped next to Steve, and Blazer stuck out his hand. Black shook it. "I've heard about you," Steve said. "Don't you do a lot of off the books hand to hand training for interested cops?"

Black nodded. "I've been known to donate my time."

Dy stepped up to Cameron and offered a solemn handshake. "I'm sorry about your guys, LT. Anything I can do, let me know."

"Thanks," Cameron said.

"I understand you guys took out Joey Nang," Dy asked them. Steve noticed his grammar was very good, but he still had an accent.

"Who?" Chandler asked.

"I stopped by your crime scene and talked to a few people. Joey Nang was one of the guys in the Lexus. Before you sent him to his ancestors, he ran a Vietnamese gang in Little Saigon. They call themselves the Specters. Kind of like the VC back in the old country, they just appear and disappear out of nowhere."

Steve considered this, remembering Stanson's comments about the BTK gangs.

"Last year, Joey Nang hooked up with Mr. Bao Lin. The Specters had themselves a little hush-hush gang war. They muscled out a few rag-tag groups that were pulling minor heists and trying to run protection rackets. Those that survived the war were absorbed into the Specters. With Bao Lin now backing him, his gang is the most powerful down there."

"Who is this Bao Lin?" Steve asked.

"Colonel Bao Lin, formerly of the Army of the Republic of Vietnam, now a prominent businessman in Little Saigon, philanthropist. You name it, he does it. Including smuggling heroin."

"How do you know that?" Cameron asked.

"I've been trying to build a case against him for over a year now. But I've never been able to prove anything. Now I think I might have a chance." He turned to Cameron. "You know that crack house you busted the other day? The operators are back in action."

* * *

He stood like a statue; eyes hidden behind mirrored sunglasses. Stanson had brought a blue windbreaker from home, and he was glad he had, now that a light breeze was blowing in from the ocean. The fog from earlier that morning had not burned off, but now blew in sheets across the beach. The lenses of his shades had accumulated a thin layer of moisture from the blowing mist of the fog and the waves, but he didn't care. He just leaned against the front of his car, pretending to watch the waves. Behind him, across the Great Highway, was the western tip of Golden Gate Park, which stretched eastward into the city. At this time of the morning, the park would be filling up with joggers, bicyclers, picnickers, and employees of the many museums.

They could all have their safe and happy lives. He worked to protect that for them. His own life had been permanently changed decades ago by a little skirmish history books called the Vietnam War.

John Stanson was still in Junior High School when the war was at its worst, in the late sixties. But he was still connected to the war, connected by blood. Because of that connection, he'd studied all he could about the war. He knew everything about it, the good, the bad, the ugly truths the government wanted to hide away at the time. It was a period that changed America. The Vietnam War was hated by many at home. He saw them on the news, at the colleges, and even in person at his own school, students demonstrating against the war. He saw how violent those demonstrations got. Even then, as a kid, he saw their actions as pointless misdirected rage. That rage got turned around and pointed at targets who were themselves caught in the maelstrom, victimized by the situation. America had treated veterans like a plague. He'd seen the mistrust and contempt the students back home had for the brave soldiers who fought in the war. He'd personally seen the abuse heaped upon them by the very people they served. He'd seen GIs called baby killers and spit upon by the public even as they returned to the country they loved.

It was a dark chapter in American History, one people were trying to forget—or deny, in the case of the U.S. Government. The existence of Prisoners of War had been a hot topic for many years. The US and Vietnamese Governments finally reached a point where they denied any further captives in Vietnam. But at that point, Stanson not only knew POWs existed, but knew the locations of several camps where they were being held.

As a young adult, he'd been involved with a CIA unit that for all too brief a period worked throughout Southeast Asia. He tried to leave the CIA behind in the early 1980s. He moved back to San Francisco and joined the police force. He met a beautiful woman and married her. He'd grown old with that woman, and he loved her just as much as he had when he married her. They'd had their ups and downs, like any marriage. As they grew closer over the years, he saw how loyal and supportive she really was. As he moved up through the ranks of SFPD, she was a truly supportive wife. She became active in events sponsored by the department, and more than this, she became an ear to listen to any officers that needed support. She'd grown to accept his violent life as a veteran and a cop. One of the "downs" of their marriage was finding out they would not be able to have kids. Maybe because of this, she had adopted what seemed like every single cop he worked with. He respected her deeply for this.

He'd made a conscious effort to put the CIA behind him, but it wasn't to be. They reached out and drew him back in. He made a special arrangement with his case officer from the Southeast Asia unit. They allowed him to stay in San Francisco and keep his job, as long as he would lend his expertise to occasional assignments. The arrangement worked out at first, though he had little faith it would last. It did. He kept his wife out of that part of his life. Through it all, he tried to put the ghosts of the war behind him.

Until now, he thought as a new Chevy Impala turned into the parking lot. Without turning his head, Stanson saw the car park a few spaces away from his own. The man that got out was a few years older than him, his white hair fading back along the top of his head. His grey suit clashed with the attire one expected at the beach, even in this cool fog. As he approached, he took off his glasses so they wouldn't get fogged up by the mist.

The sight of that face at once catapulted John back in time thirty years, if only for a moment...

* * *

JANUARY 1981

"I, Ronald Wilson Reagan, do solemnly swear..."

John Stanson watched the TV with rapt attention. He was witnessing history, and he knew it, was more aware of it than many of the people in his classroom. To so many in this history class, it was a way to pass the time. The professor had a reputation for being a lazy left-wing nut job. He'd heard some of the students talking when he'd started the class a week ago, how Professor Sayers was an easy A if you just spouted back to him what he wanted to hear. Stanson soon found what he wanted to hear was liberal dogma and how it would save the world from evil closed-minded conservative thought. Sayers was a holdover from the hippie days of the late 1960s. Now, instead of demonstrating against the war and establishment thought, he fought the battle by indoctrinating college youth.

Stanson was a product of that time as well but came from a very different point of view.

The swearing in of a new President represented a

shift in the mindset of the entire country and Stanson could definitely feel it. Ex-hippie professors be damned, even some of the kids in his college classes over the last semester had expressed frustration over what Jimmy Carter's administration had done.

Stanson could not help but smile as Ronald Reagan completed his oath of office and shook hands with the Chief Justice of the Supreme Court, now as President of the United States.

He looked over at Professor Sayers. The man sat with a stone look on his whiskered face. He showed no emotion one way or the other, but Stanson knew the man had to be seething inside. Had he nothing to say about a new president who held the promise of taking the country in a new direction? Could it be this giant of liberal ideology had admitted to himself that his hero Jimmy Carter...had failed?

The ceremony on the TV over, Sayers walked up and turned off the tube, before the new president stepped to the mike to offer an inaugural address. With nary a word about the inauguration, he announced, "I will now hand back your first papers of the semester. You'll soon see, I'm a little disappointed in some of you."

For the next few moments, he walked among them, dropping packets of paper, their essays, on their desks. Only days into the semester, he had already memorized the names of most of the students there.

Stanson's was one of the first papers handed out. John flipped it over and raised his eyebrows at the fat 'D' scribbled on the front. What the hell? He flipped through the pages to search for any explanation, but he found no comments written by the professor. John had worked hard on this paper, and he knew there were no technical or grammatical issues.

It's starting, John thought as he glanced up at Sayers, still handing out papers. Sayers met his eyes briefly, but hastily looked away. He's not up to a confrontation, Stanson realized. John had never shied away from healthy debate, and he always stood up for his own personal beliefs. He *was* ready for a face-off.

"Professor?" he called out before he really knew what he should say. When Sayers turned to seek out he who summoned him, John held up his paper. "What is this?"

"Mr. Stanson?" It was a question to confirm for the class who he was. "Yes, your paper was about a particular incident during the Vietnam war, written almost from a fictional standpoint, which you turned into a general defense of America's reasons for being there."

"Did you have issues with my writing style?" Stanson asked. "There couldn't possibly be a problem with the facts I presented. As I stated in the paper, general observations came from military men I know who were there. The facts of the incident itself came from first-hand—"

Sayers waved this off, giving him a dramatic scoff. "The incident read too much like fiction. I admit you were fair to the Vietnamese villagers in your 'story', they at least came off as a proud people. But you were too over-the-top with your military characters. Nobody who wears the uniform of this nation is that noble."

Stanson's voice was stone cold. "*I* wear that uniform. I'm in ROTC and I just spent the last year and a half completing Special Forces training."

"Wonderful, another baby killer in the making," Sayers retorted.

John kept his cool. "I think you know as well as I do that the 'baby-killer' moniker given by so many that opposed the war was completely unfair and unjustified. The NVA and VC enemy—of the people of Vietnam, I might add—killed more babies than any GI ever did. Since you read my paper, you'll remember that one of the soldiers I wrote about was wounded but used his body to shield a baby after his mother was killed in the firefight. 'Baby-killer' was a nickname unjustly thrust upon the poor GIs by certain cowards here at home who burned their draft cards and ran away to Canada, rather than really do something for their country. Were you one of those people, Professor? Did you spit on any soldier you saw? A lot of those soldiers never killed a baby in their life but wanted to get home to their own children. If you had gone over there, you might have a different perspective."

Stanson realized as he spoke that every bit of activity in the class had ceased. Rapt attention was focused on the two. "If you want a debate about the merits of the war, I will gladly challenge your beliefs in a respectful way. But only if it's a conversation. I can't speak if I'm just going to be shouted down or ridiculed."

Sayers was strangely silent. Stanson made one last statement. "I get the sense that I'm going to be your worst nightmare, Professor. A patriot who speaks his mind—and doesn't give a damn about his grade."

The silence stretched out for several seconds, as the rest of the class watched with bated breath for what would happen next. Stanson sat back, feeling uncharacteristically smug. The slamming of a door outside shattered the strange tension, and a rush of activity in the hallway signified that class was supposed to be over.

With a quick confirming glance at the clock above the professor's desk, Stanson grabbed his backpack and walked out with his head high. As he reached the hallway, he could hear the other students, their spell broken, now gathering their belongings to leave.

Stanson paused outside the building. The January air was cool. The fog that had rolled in off the bay earlier this morning had burned off, leaving a blue sky with a few rolling clouds. Stanson glanced around him at the UC Berkeley campus. Students strolled casually around, headed for class, couples holding hands, smiling, sitting under trees talking, reading, studying. This had once been a hot bed of political activism, most of it contrary to what he believed, and in many cases knew. But like any other college campus, the kids were here to learn. History was made today. But all around him, the world rolled on.

"Um… hi."

Stanson looked over at a young woman who had stopped next to him and was smiling at him. She was very pretty, but in a subtle way, slim build, big round eyes that he decided were her most striking feature, a strong jaw line, brown hair that fell to her shoulders. As he smiled back at her, he did a mental double take. He felt a sudden attraction to her, one that snuck up on him. "Hi."

"That was interesting, what you did in there," she said, "Standing up to him like that."

Stanson cocked his head as if to examine her, more for her motives than her look. "Interesting like, I'm crazy for sacrificing a grade, or interesting like I'm a fascist who doesn't care about the plight of the Vietnamese?"

She laughed quietly at this but stumbled a bit as she replied. "Interesting like, I feel the same way, but would be too chicken to speak up like you did."

His smile widened as he stuck out his hand. "John."

She shook his hand, awkwardly but enthusiastically. "I'm Mary."

"Mary, if you feel the same as I do, what are you doing at a college like this?"

"Just trying to get a four-year degree with an as-yet undeclared major. So, um, this paper that caused such a stir in there…what was it about?"

He smiled at her courage, talking to a strange guy, even if she was in his class. "Well, why don't I walk you to your next class, and I can tell you all about it?"

She nodded her direction up the path, and they started out.

They hadn't gotten but a few paces when Stanson observed a young man running up the path toward them. Stanson noted his uniform first, green slacks and a lighter green dress shirt, with sewn-on patches. He was a pimply-faced freshman with reddish hair cut to his scalp on the sides, the top hidden by a green garrison cap. Stanson recognized the kid. He saw Mary's curious look and said, "He's from my ROTC group."

The boy stopped at groups he came across, for only a second at a time, telling them something and moving on, receiving odd looks as he broke away. As he left one such group, he nearly slammed into Stanson.

John grabbed the kid to keep them both from crashing to the ground. The boy stopped, and suddenly recognized him. "Lieutenant! We just heard on the radio. The hostages—the hostages in Iran have been released."

Before Stanson could say a word to the boy, he took off running again.

Stanson looked at Mary. "I need to get to a radio; they'll have news." He thought for a second. "Nearest one is the ROTC class. Would you like to come with?"

She stuck out her hand. "Lead the way, Lieutenant."

***

Even as the administration of Jimmy Carter came

to an end with the economy in shambles, John Stanson was able to afford a car, an ugly yellow Oldsmobile Cutlass Ciera. He'd been able to schedule his classes to where they were only Monday through Thursday, leaving Fridays and Saturdays open. He studied on Sundays. He was going for a degree in Criminal Justice. Law Enforcement was something he loved and believed in, so the material came easy to him. He'd found a job that at least seemed parallel to his goal of a job on a police force. But the job was in San Francisco. So, every Friday and Saturday, he would drive across the Bay Bridge and into the Tenderloin District.

John had found work as a bouncer at a disco nightclub. He'd worked at this club the previous spring up until being shipped off to Fort Bragg for a summer of training to be a Green Beret. At that time, the club had been a happening place, people lining up around the block to go in and show their moves to the latest techno disco songs. In his absence, the club's status had deteriorated. This was his second weekend back to work, and when he and the other two bouncers opened the doors, the line outside was admitted within the first twenty minutes. An hour later, Stanson was posted outside the club with two bouncers he'd become friends with. They sat in the chilly, foggy, breezy San Francisco night, talking and joking to pass the time.

"Is it just me?" asked Matt 'Muddy' Bayliss. "Or is Disco dead?"

There was a chorus of agreement.

"What is it the kids are listening to these days?" Stanson asked.

"I don't know, but it's got to be better than listening to ABBA all night like we do," said the second bouncer, a tall black man named Deacon.

"Hey, come on," John chided him. "ABBA isn't bad.

I don't even think they should be considered disco. Yeah, they have a few songs of that style, 'Dancing Queen,' 'Summer Night City,' that sort of thing. Beyond those, they have a wide range of musical styles they work with."

"You really like that shit?" Deacon grinned. "Not me, man. Give me some James Brown any day."

Bayliss scoffed at that. "Does he actually sing anything? It sounds like just a bunch of random screams by a guy in a fancy bathrobe." He then launched into an impression of James Brown, complete with limited dance moves and muted screams of "Hey!" and "Oww!" and a very comical, "Got to, got to—Hey!"

His friends laughed at the impression, Stanson in mild amusement, and Deacon despite the defamation of his musical hero. They fell into silence for a moment, the three of them leaning on a railing near the sidewalk.

"I met a girl," John said.

Muddy turned serious. "That's great, bro. Where'd you meet her?"

"She's in my history class. It's kind of funny, I told off this whacko professor and she came outside after class to congratulate me."

"You asked her out, right?" Deacon asked.

"Of course. We've hung out at the student union every day this week. I'm working here tonight and tomorrow, so we're getting together Sunday." As he spoke, he spotted a man walking down the sidewalk toward them. Stanson quit talking about his new girlfriend to watch the man for a moment. Stanson, from a position of an Army Special Forces soldier and an aspiring cop working toward his criminal justice degree, sized the man up. As he got closer, he could see the man appeared grizzled, not quite homeless but certainly hard. He did not appear threatening but looked like he could turn that way. He wore a long brown trench coat, hanging open to the January chill and exposing a rumpled suit. He was probably in his thirties, and had a scraggly growth of beard, already sprinkled with gray. The man parked himself on the curb not ten feet from them.

Stanson exchanged looks with his fellow club bouncers. "I got this," he said, and approached the man. He circled around in front of him, staying clear in case he tried to lunge at him. In his position on the curb, he would telegraph that move, and Stanson could dodge and defend easily. "How you doing, sir?"

The man looked up at him for the first time. "Oh, good, it's you. Listen, you're not going to be just another jerk and shove me off into the night, are you?"

Stanson smiled through the man's gruff manner. "That depends. Are you headed into the club?"

"Nah, I hate disco. Give me some Janis Joplin, some Jefferson Airplane, some Doors any day." The man glanced up at him. "You're a nice enough kid. I been kicked out of two bars already tonight. You wouldn't do that to me, would you? I couldn't take any more abuse right now. I got plenty of that when I got back from 'Nam."

This statement struck Stanson, and his smile faded as his interest shot up. "You were in the 'Nam?"

The stranger looked like he was about to launch mindlessly into another tirade, but the bouncer's reference seemed to catch his attention. He looked up at the bouncer and examined him for a moment. "You're too young to have been there, kid. But you look like you know a thing or two about our little police action. Maybe you had family serve there." It was a probing statement.

Stanson looked up at his friends, who were stepping warily his way. "It's OK, guys, I'll look after him." Muddy and Deacon shrugged and backed away, returning to the door.

Stanson stuck out his hand. "I'd like to shake the hand of a real American hero."

"Thank you kindly, son," the man said as he shook. "But I ain't no hero. I was just a foot soldier. I just went where they told me, killed who they told me."

"Where were you in Vietnam?"

The man lowered his voice conspiratorially. "I was in the war that never was, kid. Laos, Cambodia. We weren't supposed to be there, but we were there in force."

"Charlie was reinforcing its troops through there on the Ho Chi Minh Trail," Stanson nodded.

The man was still looking up at him. "You know your history, kid. Not like those punks at the universities who didn't know why they were marching. Bunch of hypocrites. Their march was just as much in lockstep with their ideology as we were with ours. Getting spit on when I came home was just icing on the cake. You ever been called a baby killer?"

"I've seen too much of that," Stanson admitted. "I was young, and it made an impression."

"I ain't killed a baby in my life," the man growled. "But you know they used to send the women after us. We'd get into a fire fight and never knew who we were killing until the fight was over and we could police up the bodies. You want to hear something messed up? I used to hear this from the villagers all the time, at least when they had grown to trust us. The NVA would come into the villages, demand tribute, take all their food, rape their women, and laugh it all off. They call it the 'patriotic duty' of the village to contribute to their little worker's paradise."

Stanson had to smile at that. The very circumstance this stranger had described was a central part of the history paper he'd written.

The man stood, suddenly appearing very able. His drunken stupor was gone. He stared the bouncer squarely in the eye. "John, you're a good man. Do yourself a favor and be at your ROTC office tomorrow. Someone will be there to speak with you regarding something very important. It could change your life." With that, the stranger shuffled past him and hurried up the street, walking faster than he had before.

Stanson stood in shock for a moment, watching him retreat and too surprised to pursue him. The man left as quickly as he had come, leaving Stanson to stand there and simply ask, "How did you know my name?"

* * *

It was Saturday, and there were very few classes happening on the Berkeley campus. Out of curiosity more than anything, Stanson arrived at the campus's ROTC office early that morning. His reserve drill had occurred last weekend, so no one was supposed to be there anyway. The office was locked, and he had no key. He waited outside the door. He spent the time pacing the sidewalk, examining the terrain for a distance around him to be aware when someone approached. He'd spent the previous summer and part of the spring going through the phases of Special Forces school at Fort Bragg in North Carolina, and observation of everything around him was becoming second nature to him. Fifteen minutes turned into thirty. As the time passed, he finally sat on the curb and lost himself in his thoughts, getting up every few minutes to move around and work the chill out of his body. He'd just sat down again when a shadow fell over him.

"I'm glad to see I've piqued your interest," the shadow said.

Stanson looked up into the face of the man who'd come to his club last night. The trench coat was still there, but the hair was now neatly combed, the beard with the hint of gray now shaved off. The impression he'd made last night of a bitter drunk booted from a bar was gone. He was polite, but all business.

Stanson jumped to his feet. The man stepped back as if he was walking away, then turned back to him, not yet meeting his eye. "How do you spell that word, piqued?"

Hesitantly, Stanson spelled it for him.

"Good. It amazes me how many people don't know that word. Walk with me, let's talk." The mysterious man began to walk down a pathway through a tree lined area, and Stanson hurried to catch up to him.

"My name is Ross. I'll leave it to you to wonder if that's a first name or last name. I represent a government agency with initials that are very well known and not very popular. I'll leave you to figure out who, but I can present documentation to show I'm not running a scam. To put it bluntly, kid, I checked you out. I know you just recently graduated from all phases of Special Forces training and I know the language you chose to learn was Vietnamese. And I know why. I know from interviewing a few of your instructors that you had a particular knowledge and further curiosity about the Vietnam conflict. Hell, son, I even read the paper that earned you that D."

"I wouldn't say 'earned' is the right word," Stanson interjected.

"And I wouldn't disagree with you," the mystery man named Ross went on. "That's the other thing I've come to like about you." He stopped and looked the young man in the eye. "You're a patriot, son, and I respect the hell out of that. This country may not be perfect, and the government may do the wrong thing sometimes. But this country was founded on ideals and principles, and some of us still believe in them. Even in the Company."

"The Company." It wasn't a question. It confirmed what Stanson had already deduced was happening, and still couldn't believe: he was being recruited into the CIA.

"John, I'm putting together a special outfit, and I think you would be perfect for it. But I can't tell you what the job is yet. First, I have to know if you're interested. It will mean hard work, travel, and there will be violence involved." He let out a brief chuckle. "You've heard the saying, 'travel to exotic places, meet interesting people—and kill them'? That's what I'm putting together. From what I know about you, you must trust that you would be perfect for this outfit. Once you're in, don't worry, if you feel it's not right for you, I will allow you to back out gracefully. But I think you'll fit right in. I hate to spring it on you, but I need an answer now."

Stanson stopped walking and leaned on a sidewalk railing. "A complete stranger wants me to join... 'The Company'...based on my Special Forces training only." He made sure Ross could tell he was weighing his options. "He swears up and down I'm perfect for what he has in mind, but he won't tell me what it is. Wants me to leave everything I have here, albeit not much. Family and friends..." He thought briefly of Mary. "...for some unnamed opportunity in the Intelligence community, the promise of action based on my personal beliefs and principles."

"And the promise that with your principles, you will make a difference," Ross said.

Stanson couldn't believe the CIA was actually interested in him. Weighing everything, it was sheer curiosity that swayed his decision—he wanted to see what was in store. "I'm in."

Ross couldn't help a smile, and he extended a hand. They shook firmly. "Excellent. There is...one small catch."

Stanson's face suddenly clouded. He wondered if regret was going to pounce on him so soon after making his decision. "There's always a catch. What is it?"

"You'll need to go through the Company's training program. We call it 'The Farm'."

* * *

Ross's voice, thirty years aged and slightly more gravelly, yanked him back to the present.

"John," he said by way of a greeting. "Usually *I* call *you* for the favors. Typically, you hate when I deviate from our arrangement. What's up?"

"Smith is in town." Stanson's statement was simple and to the point. He was a little surprised by the newcomer's reaction. The man in the suit stood frozen for a moment, a little flustered, but he kept silent. "He's apparently caught up in some sort of Golden Triangle smuggling ring," Stanson went on. "But that doesn't surprise you, does it, Ross?"

When Ross spoke, the Captain barely heard him. "No, it doesn't."

"You were already in town when I called. That's why this meeting happened so quickly. Like maybe you're here because of Smith. You were just waiting for me to call." Only now did the Captain turn to face the man. Ross had been there with him, slogging through those jungles. And when the group broke up, instead of coming home to rebuild a life in the world, Ross began a climb into the upper echelons of the intelligence community. He'd kept in contact with Stanson since those days. Ross was the one who reached out to him, first for one favor, then one more, until an arrangement was established for him to return when needed. He'd become Stanson's unofficial case officer. John figured he had similar arrangements with others, current and former members of the intelligence community. That was his own business. Since their time in Vietnam, Ross had become one of the few men in the world he trusted, albeit begrudgingly.

Until now, he thought again.

"I really hoped he was dead," Stanson told him. "I watched him take one in the chest in 'Nam. Would you care to explain why someone is killing cops and leaving Suicide Kings on their bodies?"

"After we were disbanded, I led some missions off the books into Laos and Cambodia. You know as well as I do the Golden Triangle Drug Cartels were still operating and our own people were involved. I heard the occasional rumor about this wild young guy who ambushed shipments and disappeared with them. It wasn't until recently that I've been able to confirm his involvement..."

Stanson jumped into his lecture. "Why is that crazy son of a bitch alive?"

"You convinced yourself he was dead. We never found his body..."

"Well, he won't be alive for much longer," Stanson stated. "When I find him, I will kill him. I will not allow him to go around killing cops or anyone else like he did over there."

"It's not that simple," Ross said loudly. Almost too loudly. The reason Stanson had picked this place was because the noise of the waves made it impossible for anyone to listen in, electronically or otherwise. Ross consciously lowered his voice. "The reason I was able to confirm it was him is because he's hooked up with Colonel Bao Lin."

Stanson searched his memory. "The businessman?"

"Bao Lin has done a lot to benefit the people of San Francisco's Little Saigon. When the government left them to fend for themselves, he set up low income housing and medical care for refugees. If someone has relatives back in Vietnam, he gets them over here. He's become a hero to those people."

"More like a figurehead. He's been financing all that over the years by smuggling heroin. Why hasn't anyone tried to shut him down?"

"I told you, it's not that simple. CIA considers him a valuable asset."

"For what?" John demanded.

"He is the eyes and ears of that community. He keeps a careful watch on those that come into the community. If those people are Communist spies for the homeland, he brings it to our attention."

Stanson grimaced in disgust. "And you just turn away so he can smuggle his dope. And he rips off the people he's supposedly protecting. Why wasn't I told about all this before?"

"People have forgotten all about that whole mess of a war..." Ross knew that was the wrong thing to say.

Disgusted with the whole situation, Stanson started toward his car. He stopped a few yards up the beach. He turned but couldn't look Ross in the eye. "Is there any word on my brother?"

Ross didn't answer for a moment. "John, after all this time, why would you ask me that?"

Stanson shook his head and resumed walking through the sand. In seconds, he reached the stairway up to the parking lot and headed to his car.

Ross followed him up the stairs. "I know it's hard to accept, but Bao Lin is untouchable—"

"It's not acceptable," Stanson roared as he wrenched open the door. He sat down and started the engine. He'd left his window open and now regretted that, as Ross spoke through it.

"You can't just confront him, John," Ross said. "He's protected by powerful people."

Stanson wrenched his gear shift into reverse. "You know me. I can get to him. I can get to anyone." He backed out and drove off.

CHAPTER 3

By American standards, the house was only average in size and simple on the interior. It was suitably large and furnished lavishly enough for maybe a large upper middle-class family. But by Vietnamese standards, the house was a palace. Located just north of Geary Street near Little Saigon, Bao Lin's home was a two-story Victorian style house nestled within a block full of similar residences. The rows of houses wrapped around a small park in the center of the block.

It was approaching eight-thirty in the morning, and Bao Lin was ready for breakfast. He entered his kitchen, where his assistant, a Vietnamese man of about fifty with a stout thick build, was cleaning up from meal prep. Bao Lin himself was in his late sixties. His hair was graying, and he was starting to feel his age. The assistant helped seat the former ARVN Colonel at a dining table. A meal of fruit, bread, and cold rice was waiting for him. Bao said a silent insincere prayer, in case Buddha was watching, and picked up the fork next to his plate.

"You've been in this country too long, Colonel," a hard voice announced behind him, sending his backbone into ramrod stiffness.

The fat butler reached into his coat for a weapon, but the man in the doorway behind his boss let his arm pivot down into view. A shiny silver Colt .45 was already trained on both of them. "Lose it," the hard voice commanded, and the butler slowly took his hand out of his pocket, leaving his firearm there for the moment.

"I am disappointed, Mr. Smith," Bao said, and turned his chair to face his American partner. "Your attempt to resupply my people failed. You have broken more promises to me, and now three of my best people are dead."

"Your best people are a joke," Smith said. "The cops were waiting for them. You should be glad I spotted them first. If the cops had arrested Joey Nang, he would have betrayed you, I guarantee it. This kind of sloppy work will get your people and yourself shut down."

Bao smiled confidently in the face of the gun barrel. "That will not happen."

Someone knocked on the front door, and Smith's gun turned to point at it, just ten feet away. He crossed the hall to the door and glanced out a window next to it. Three Asian youths stood on the other side. He smiled at Bao. "Looks like someone else is unhappy as well." He opened the door, standing behind it until the three had pushed their way inside. Only then did they notice the white man with the gun and raise their hands.

"Whoa, hey, what's going on, Colonel?" one of them asked.

"You are Danny Dinh, correct?" Bao asked the leader of the group, immediately taking charge of the meeting, and seeming to ignore Smith and his gun.

"Yes, sir. I have assumed command of the Specters now that Joey is dead. Those cops, man..."

Bao sensed he wanted to begin a tirade of curses, so he jumped in before it got off the ground. "I assume you relocated the drug distribution operation to where I told Mr. Nang."

"Yes, sir. Uh..."

Bao interrupted again. "I realize the fires of hatred burn within you now, but I wish to make it clear that we have a common goal in mind. Profit not revenge. With that in mind, I expect to see some revenue this afternoon from our new location."

"That might be a problem," Dinh brought up. "See, I made this connection with a gang in San Jose, and I sold them a couple grand of pure heroin. I had to dip into the supply from the last shipment, and now that we got nothing from last night, we're a little short on product."

Bao's face eclipsed into darkness. "And when was I to receive my bounty from this sale?" he demanded.

Dinh's tan face went pale. "No, no, it's OK, Colonel, I got that right here. I got six hundred for you." He produced a wad of bills, which the butler confiscated.

"As for the shipment we missed last night," a much calmer Bao said, and looked expectantly at Smith.

"I'm leaving to meet the boat tonight. Cleopatra Point, up near Fort Bragg. I'll have a new shipment for you in twenty-four hours."

* * *

The neighborhood had been dubbed Little Saigon for years, but the name had officially been adopted in 2004. The neighborhood seemed to be hidden in an area of just a few square blocks on Larkin Street, between O'Farrell to the north and Eddy Street to the south. A convoy of three unmarked police vehicles drove north on Larkin Street, passing through posts constructed on the sidewalk to form a monument, a sort of 'gateway' to the community.

They drove along the crowded streets. At Steve's quiet request, Cameron asked that Dy ride with Blazer—Steve wanted to ply the Inspector for more information on Little Saigon and Bao Lin. That left Dy's partner, Inspector Scot Black, to ride with Cameron. Inspectors Chandler and Green drove a third unmarked unit.

Steve could feel the eyes of resentment on them, though the looks were furtive. Some of the crowd pointedly ignored them, which was almost more frightening than overt looks of disdain. Despite being in America, supposedly a land of opportunity, the old distrust and contempt for outsiders—especially cops—was still there.

"Welcome to Little Saigon," Scot Black's voice sounded sarcastically from the radio in all three cars.

"Kind of hard to hide for a stakeout if everyone knows who you are," Steve said to Dy.

"Someone may tip off our dealers," Dy said. He didn't seem fazed by the possibility that their cover might be blown.

Steve picked up the radio. "Chandler, I want to keep you in reserve a couple blocks away, so we don't seem to be bunching up on this fish factory."

"Ten-four," Chandler said over the radio, "we're posting at Larkin and Eddy."

"Pull in here," Dy instructed, and Steve steered his black SUV to the curb behind a beat-up old truck. Ahead of them, where Ellis Street crossed Larkin and bisected the neighborhood, was the small fish processing plant Dy had told them about. The face of the building sported a small kiosk where workers sold various types of fish from the day's catch directly to the public. The real action occurred behind that counter, hidden away from the public.

The way Dy had described the place, Bao controlled his own small fleet of fisherman, who brought in loads of fish to be packaged and shipped to several nearby markets and restaurants. At first, it was just in Little Saigon. Over the years, he'd branched out to Chinatown and was slowly conquering the rest of the city. In the meantime, the fishing boats made it easy to smuggle in heroin.

"A guy named Mr. Bok runs this plant," Dy explained to Blazer. "He supplies seafood to several nearby stores."

"So how do you know that they've started up the heroin operation here?" Steve asked.

Dy smiled. "This is my neighborhood. I take a tour through here just about every evening. Some of the perps that you guys busted at that stash house last week...I've seen them coming and going from this place. From what I've been able to put together, Bao's people bring the drugs in by boat, smuggle them to this plant, then distribute them to different sites. Since you guys are busting their stash houses, they simply consolidated and set up the processing lab here. They probably started the day after you guys busted the last stash house."

"What happened to Mr. Bok?" Steve wanted to know.

"He has no say in the matter. Colonel Bao Lin helped get him and his family out of 'Nam and settled here twenty years ago. The Colonel is calling the favor in."

"Blazer," Cameron said over the radio, "We're set up north of the target on O'Farrell."

Steve looked around at the crowds passing by. He saw numerous people looking at their vehicle. They were obviously cops, and stuck out to people suspicious of anyone not like them.

"This is not even close to being undercover,"

Steve said. "So, I guess we wait. Maybe someone will make an obvious buy." He took a moment to scan the streets, not really looking for anything in particular, just taking in his environment. "I did some research on this neighborhood," he said. "Considering the stranglehold this Colonel has on Little Saigon, I looked up crime stats. This place is a vacuum. I could not find any major crimes reported in this little area. It's been quiet like that for a long time. Seems kind of strange for an area plagued with gang activity."

"There are two reasons for that," Dy said. "First, most major crimes here go unreported. Second, these people try to police themselves. Colonel Bao has gone to great lengths to perpetuate the mistrust that the Vietnamese have of the white man. He always says we don't need white police in Little Saigon. It's a strange form of pride with him. Any crime committed—by someone not connected to his organization—is met with swift retribution. Any grievance the neighborhood has, they come to him, and he deals with it."

"It's like he's set up his own little Communist haven right in downtown San Francisco, USA," Steve said. "This is going to be like the Vietnam War, all over again."

Dy didn't respond to the comment. After a moment, he said, "You in the mood for Chinese food?" Steve glanced at him. He could not decide if this was a joke.

* * *

Two hours passed. Little Saigon seemed to have gone from warily spying on the intruders to ignoring them. Dy went on a food run to a Hunan food restaurant he knew around the corner and returned with a bag full of white containers. Steve opened one to find chunks of meat in a brown sauce that smelled sweet. Dy explained it was like Sweet and Sour Chicken, and Steve ate it, enjoying the taste.

As the afternoon dragged on, Steve noticed Dy looking in the mirror on his side of the SUV. Without being too obvious, Steve checked his own mirror, detected nothing unusual. But he was further intrigued when Dy casually glanced out each window, then back to the mirror, like a practiced routine. "What are you looking for?" he finally asked.

"Nothing," Dy said, too casually. The question caught him off guard. "Just checking the foot traffic."

But the routine continued, and Steve watched, without appearing to do so. He soon found himself following the same routine.

The radio came to life again. "We got a motorcycle coming out of a side door," Lieutenant Cameron broadcast to the group. "OK, he's turning east on Ellis."

Steve watched the bike, a brand new sleek green and black Kawasaki, with a rider dressed all in black, with a bulky helmet hiding his head. The bike accelerated across Larkin and disappeared from their area of operations. They let it go for the moment, until—

"Hey, that bike just turned up here at the south end," Inspector Green broke into the channel. "Looks like he went around the block. Wait, he's pulling up to a white Lexus."

Blazer adjusted his rear-view mirror, and found he was able to bring the motorcycle into view, a block behind them. Dy twisted in his seat to scope the area behind them.

"He's making a cash drop," Dy muttered. "That's gotta be Bao Lin in the Lexus. Let's take him."

Steve's hand paused over the ignition. "Do we

have cause?"

"We have two dead cops and witnesses we can interview."

"Good point," Steve said. He could work with that premise. He grabbed the radio mic as he shifted into drive. "Green, stay with them, we're moving to intercept." He hit the gas and swerved out into a U-turn.

The Lexus started to pull forward, and the bike lurched into a reckless U-turn.

Steve had one problem. When posting at Larkin and Ellis, it was for surveillance on the fish processing plant. With the bike and the Lexus nearly a block behind him, he couldn't readily get to them—Larkin was a north-bound one-way street. Steve didn't let that deter him. He glanced over the traffic and caught a break—the stoplight behind him was just turning green, and the cars stopped there were still some distance away. They started as he pulled out and made a U-turn, going against the oncoming traffic. As he sped head-on at them, several cars honked. One pulled into a lane at his left, and another stopped altogether. Steve managed to steer between them. Tires screeched as more cars swerved to avoid him.

Beyond the bike and the Lexus, the Vice Inspectors' car rolled out of the small parking lot out onto Larkin Street. Steve saw the bike turn north toward him, and he suddenly wrenched the wheel left, swerving across two lanes, and stopping. He and Dy were out in an instant. He had his Beretta out, leveled across the hood at the bike as it skidded to a sudden stop twenty-five feet away. "Police, off the bike!" he roared. Dy started circling to the right flank. Steve caught peripheral images of Green's car beyond the bike. It was sliding to a stop in front of the Lexus as that driver tried to make a run for it.

The biker gunned his motor and swerved to

his right. Steve followed with his gun as the cycle bounced up onto the curb in front of a building sporting a line of shops.

The bike stopped suddenly, partially hidden by a parked car. Steve could clearly see the man unzipping his jacket to pull a gun. "Don't do it!" he yelled.

A silver revolver cleared the jacket. Steve squeezed off a round as the gun leveled at him, and the rider toppled off the bike. The bike hit the sidewalk with a rattle and a crunch.

The single gunshot spurred the crowds into movement. Many there on the streets had stopped momentarily to watch the police action. But now that it had turned to gunplay, everyone ducked for cover or vacated the street altogether.

Steve rose from his crouch. Cameron's unit stopped nearby straddling the center line of Larkin—he'd followed Steve's lead and fought now minimal oncoming traffic to get to the scene. Cameron and Black stepped out with their weapons up and ready. Steve glanced over the rest of the scene. Dy was poised behind the passenger door of Steve's SUV. Chandler and Green were parked blocking east bound Eddy Street. Both of them had their guns drawn on the Lexus, stopped at the west side of the intersection. The Lexus sat quietly in the middle of everything.

Engine noise suddenly sounded over the area.

Everyone looked toward the fish plant.

By now the streets had cleared of other cars.

Two more Kawasaki Ninja bikes were coming toward them.

Steve saw muzzle flashes erupt from one of the riders. At the same time, a line of slugs kicked up sparks as they caromed off the pavement next to his SUV. Steve quickly ducked behind the front of his SUV, where the engine block provided good hard cover. When set, he turned his gun on the new threat.

He held his fire for the moment. He saw Scot Black still in the open. Black was ten feet from his car, and he turned and shoulder rolled back toward it.

The first biker steered around the back of the unmarked unit, rolling up along the driver's side. Everyone noticed the MAC-10 gripped in the rider's left hand. The biker skidded around the front corner of the unmarked. The MAC-10 turned on Blazer.

Scot rose up from out of nowhere, facing the biker. He lashed out with his left foot, which collided with the tinted visor of the biker's helmet. The biker was thrown off the back of the cycle and landed in a dazed sprawl on the pavement.

Scot, however, had misjudged his kick, if only by a little. As the rider was thrown, the bike kept going, and the handlebar knocked Scot in the rear, throwing him onto the hood of his car. The bike toppled and slid on its side toward Steve's SUV. Blazer jumped aside as the bike slid into his front left wheel. He noted immediately that the damage would be minimal.

Scot sprawled onto the hood and rolled off the front. He came up in a crouch in time to watch the second rider.

As the bikers approached, Cameron had stayed in a crouch at the rear of the unmarked, on the passenger side. He saw where the first biker went and tracked the commotion by sound. He glanced back and caught Scot's action but resumed his watch on the rest of the bikers.

Instead of firing right away, the second biker gunned his engine and swung wide to Cameron's left, hitting the opposite sidewalk. Riding behind the momentary safety of a line of parked cars, he pointed the MAC-10 over the tops of them and held back his trigger in one prolonged burst.

Cameron found himself caught in the open next

to his car, a situation he was becoming frustratingly familiar with. He ducked down as the line of slugs stitched into the unmarked unit just above him. He rolled onto his back on the street. His gun was still out in front of him and he put out round after round. He could feel nine-millimeter bullets hammering into his car above him and knew one of them was meant for him. He kept firing, watching his rounds shatter windows in the parked cars, and waiting for the bullets from the MAC-10 to find him.

Steve carefully watched the whole scene and joined in as Cameron and the last biker exchanged fire. His Beretta pumped out bullets faster than anyone could count, even as the MAC-10's hungry rounds sprayed the whole scene. But the rider sacrificed maneuverability for a steady aim as he left the curb through a gap between the parked cars. The MAC-10 seemed to drop, and the last three rounds sparked off the pavement behind Blazer's SUV.

Steve thought he saw one of his shots hit leather. The bike wobbled. The rider was traveling over thirty miles an hour still and couldn't stop himself. He plowed into the back of a parked Cadillac. The bike stopped, but the rider did not, instead flying over the handlebars and smashing helmet first through the back window.

The scene was momentarily calm. Blazer, Black and Cameron rose to their feet, stepping out into the open, their eyes moving around three hundred sixty degrees, searching for other potential dangers. Steve looked over at the unmarked Vice vehicle. Chandler and Green emerged from cover there. They'd stayed focused on the Lexus, but at least found cover from the gunfire. They now ventured out; guns once again pointed at the Lexus.

Scot bent over the man he'd kicked off the bike, pulling off the black helmet to feel for a pulse. He found one and rolled the guy over to cuff him.

Steve and Dy closed in on the Lexus, guns ready and eyes alert for any danger that might manifest itself. Steve glanced back at Cameron and motioned over to the biker sticking out the back of the parked car. "Check him."

The passenger door to the Lexus suddenly opened. "Out of the car," Chandler barked, tensing on his weapon. Steve had a good view from across the roof of the car as an elderly man rose into view. Chandler stepped forward and turned him around. He tried not to get too rough as he pushed the man against the hood of the car. Dy stepped forward with a pair of handcuffs, and he slapped them on as Chandler held the man in place.

Steve glanced over at Cameron as he hauled the biker out of the smashed car window. The Lieutenant glanced back at him and shook his head—the biker was dead.

Green and his partner pulled out the driver of the Lexus. They guided him to the front, where they cuffed him and checked him for weapons.

Dy reached into the back seat and pulled out the small backpack they'd seen delivered to the passenger. He opened it and pulled out a stack of ruffled twenty-dollar bills. "Look what I found," he smiled. "Let me guess, Bao. Mr. Bok is paying you for the privilege of letting you use his plant."

Bao Lin smiled at the Vietnamese Cop. "You are making a very foolish mistake, Inspector, and you know it."

Steve was getting the sense that something else was going on here, but before he could confront Dy, additional police cruisers arrived. Three units spilled onto the scene from the south. As uniformed officers emerged from their cars, Green went to brief them.

Dy dragged the handcuffed Bao Lin to a patrol car that had pulled up nearby. He handed his prisoner off to the uniform. "Keep an eye on him."

Steve was walking back to his truck, and Dy caught up to him there. "We should get this biker back to the station," he said quietly, "as soon as possible."

"Maybe we should get him checked out by EMS first," Steve said as Scot led forward the one he'd kicked.

"No, this one's fine," Black said, jerking his prisoner to a stop. "I didn't hit him that hard." He held up the helmet he'd removed. The tinted visor was cracked with spider-web lines extending from the impact point in the center. The young Asian man stared at them defiantly.

"That was a nice move, by the way," Steve said. "OK, get him into that unit." Scot turned and dragged his man toward a nearby squad car.

"Tell them to take off and we'll meet them at the Mission Station," Dy called after them as he backed away. "And to not let him out of their sight."

With uniforms now on site, locking down the scene, Lieutenant Cameron confronted Steve. "Let's get up to the fish plant before they destroy any evidence."

Steve nodded, and headed for his SUV. As he got in, he called out to the officer who now had custody of Bao Lin. "Bring him up there with us." He got them underway and swerved around, this time going the right way on one-way Larkin Street.

In thirty seconds, Blazer stopped his SUV in front of the fish plant, parked across several lanes of the road. Cameron parked next to him, and Dy and Black joined them in moving to the plant's entrance. As they moved in, Steve heard voices echoing in an alley off to the left, and he motioned that way.

At the alley entrance, with his weapon ready to

cover his entry, Steve glanced around the corner.

People were spilling out a side door of the plant and running away down the alley. Steve broke into the open and ran toward that door. He intended to try and catch at least one man running from the plant—

As he came abreast of the door, one last Asian male burst from the door, nearly running him down. Steve grabbed him and wrestled him against the wall. He roughly turned the young man around and held him for a moment to insure he had a solid grip. Steve holstered his gun and cuffed the man.

The rest of the team had gathered around the door in case anyone else tried to escape. Two uniformed officers appeared at the mouth of the alley, having seen the plainclothes cops head that way. Cameron motioned them in. Steve handed off his suspect to one of them.

"We're going in," Cameron announced. Everyone readied their weapons.

The door was left partially open by the evacuating Vietnamese workers. Steve positioned himself beside the door, and the others lined up for the entry. Blazer glanced around to confirm everyone was ready. Cameron gave him a nod. Steve held up three fingers, making sure everyone saw them, and counted down to one. Then he lunged through the door.

In the lead, Steve rushed into the plant, playing his Beretta over the scene. They found themselves in a wide-open area, much of it taken up by machinery. A lengthy conveyor belt system stretched almost the entire length of the warehouse space, with barrels and metal vats scattered around it. The smell hit them and they saw that many of the vats contained discarded fish guts. In one corner, a massive walk-in refrigerator stood with its door open.

The plant was now empty of people. The cops

spread out, and Cameron directed two uniforms to check out an office area he'd spotted. He motioned another uniform to a set of stairs and directed him to "Clear that area."

Steve came around the conveyor system and stopped face to face with exactly what he was looking for. Through a partially open door, he saw a pile of white powder on a small electronic scale. He pushed open the door, played his gun over the room and found no one left inside. He saw long counters full of paraphernalia. Piles of powder sat on the countertops, many with rumpled brown bags made of waxy paper piled nearby. Someone had stacked small plastic bags at the end of one long counter, next to another scale. A box on the floor was half filled with identical baggies full of the white powder. Steve looked over at the other counter, which was completely empty. Must have been used for fish, he thought.

Steve looked over the interior of the small plant. "Something's wrong," he said. "There's not enough dope here for the amount of money in that bag delivered to Bao. If this guy is such a big dealer, where's the rest of his stash?"

"Maybe that's what we almost got last night," Cameron brought up.

"Right," Dy added, "They use this place to manufacture and distribute, like the dope house you busted on Monday. Maybe Bao Lin now has dealers and other distributors come here to pick up their stashes, and they go and do what they want with it. Dilute it, sell it, whatever."

"Inspector," a uniformed officer called from the open side door, "We have a problem."

They hurried for the door. When the group reached the street, they saw two new cars among the police vehicles, both white Chevy Impalas. With a glance, Steve checked the license plates. Government issue. Steve noticed three suits surrounding Colonel Bao Lin, and one of them was removing the handcuffs. "Hey, hey," Steve called as he hurried over. "What do you think you're doing?"

"Are you in charge of this screw up?" a fourth suit demanded as he moved to intercept the big cop.

"That's my prisoner," Steve growled.

"Not anymore, sport." The agent, an average height man with close trimmed brown hair and glasses, produced an ID. "Kimmins, State Department. We have orders to take this man into our custody."

"Why is the State Department involved with this?" Cameron demanded.

"It's National Security, sir, we can't discuss it. Inspector Dy, you've done this dance before, you should know better."

"Hey, you can't just take him," Steve insisted. "There's a million-dollar drug operation going on in this building, which my prisoner has to answer for."

"Inspector, I think you'll find this building belongs to a Mr. Bok Tranh, a local businessman. I'd check with him." He turned a cold shoulder once again.

Steve clamped a hand on that icy shoulder, and forcibly turned the Fed around. "Look, pal, I've done this dance before, too. State would have no interest in this guy. But I bet the Company does."

Kimmins's glare turned colder than his shoulder. "Look, Inspector, even if I could discuss it, I wouldn't do it with you."

Steve glanced at Bao Lin, who was already being seated in one of the white cars with his driver. He could tell the Vietnamese Colonel was enjoying the exchange. Kimmins and his people returned to their cars, and as quickly as they'd come, the Feds were off.

"Green, Chandler," Cameron said, "Start taking down the lab." Behind them, the two Vice cops motioned to a pair of uniformed officers, and they led them back into the plant.

Cameron and Blazer remained frozen in place. They watched as the federal cars retreated down Larkin—it was still closed off, so they drove against the one way signs. Blazer seethed inside as he saw the Impalas stop next to the Lexus left at Eddy Street. Two of the Feds got out to run interference with the uniforms still posted there as Bao Lin and his driver were allowed to return to their car. The Lexus started up and disappeared up Eddy Street.

Blazer approached Dy. "Come here," he growled. He grabbed Dy by the coat and dragged him toward his SUV. He was aware of Scot following. "Why do I get the feeling I'm being dragged right along with your personal vendetta?"

"What are you talking about?" Dy said. He tried to come off innocent, but he sounded genuinely scared.

"You were watching for Bao Lin's vehicle," Steve burst out. "You probably knew there would be a payoff, but you also knew the Colonel would be rescued when we busted him. He probably called the damn feds himself as soon as we stopped him. Hell, for all we know, he's known we were here the moment we entered Little Saigon and planned all this just to draw us out and mess with us. I hate wasting my time, Inspector, and I hate not knowing what's really going on."

"It wasn't wasted," Dy shouted as he knocked Blazer's hands away. "What's going on is, we've got dope in that building, and that's dope that will never hit the streets. Yeah, I know a few things about Bao's operation. Like how he tries to keep his distance, so he has his errand boys deliver his take from the distribution. And yeah, I knew someone would come to his rescue. I've tried to bust him before and Kimmins showed up to bail him out. The man is protected by powers higher than us. I think it is the CIA, like you said. He does them favors, and they look the other way while he deals drugs. But I try to stay one step ahead of him, so I can take down his next drug lab. And now we have two prisoners at Mission Station that we can roll for information."

"What about that cop killer?" Cameron demanded from six feet away.

"We can ask about him too."

CHAPTER 4

Blazer and Cameron worked the crime scene for a short while, cataloguing evidence and drugs. With suspects to interrogate, much of the police entourage returned to the Mission District Police Station, leaving only Inspectors Chandler and Green from the Vice squad to wrap up the crime scene.

At the station, their two suspects were deposited into interview rooms and left to sweat the delay in their questioning. Blazer and Cameron were joined by Scot Black and Vinnie Dy for a quick strategizing session. Captain Stanson joined them in their requisitioned room. Blazer and Cameron briefed the Captain.

"Do we have a fingerprint ID on them yet?" Stanson asked.

"Don't need them," Dy said. "I know them. The cocky kid on the motorcycle is named Kenny Xuan, spelled with an X. He pronounces it 'Shuwan'." The guy we caught at the lab is Tuy Vo. I've seen both of them grow up and join the Specters."

Steve pointed to Dy. "Why don't you and Black work the interviews? I'll join you in a moment."

Hearing this, the group trooped down a short

hallway to a cluster of three doors. The first and third doors were interview rooms, each nearly bare except for a table and a few chairs. Between the two rooms, a third room was set up to be able to view both other rooms. It was not very spacious, but it was able to accommodate a handful of people to watch an interview. One-way glass was set in both walls so a suspect couldn't see if anyone was watching. However, with countless cop shows and movies, there wasn't a suspect who'd experienced that room who was not aware someone was watching from the other side of the mirror.

Cameron opened the door to the observation room. Blazer and Stanson approached as well, but Steve cornered the Captain outside the observation room. "Are you alright?"

"I'm fine, and I'm eager to hear what this kid has to say." Without another word, he pushed his way through the center door.

Steve entered the first door and stood menacingly in the corner, listening to Scot's interview.

"You're a lucky kid," Scot was saying. "Opening fire on police officers like that, you're lucky all you got was my foot in your face."

Xuan's arrogant smirk creased into a condescending smile. "Yeah. That was a pretty good kick you did there."

"Thanks. Care to tell me about the drugs we found in the fish plant?"

"Oh, those weren't mine." He gave the cops a condescending smirk.

"And the cash?"

"I found that," Xuan said. "It was a lot of money, so I took it to Bao Lin so he could track down the real owners and return it."

"That's very civic minded of you," Steve muttered in the background.

"I bet the Colonel would be proud of you for coming up with that story on the spot like that," Scot continued. "And how long do you think his good graces will last when we tell him about the discrepancy we found?"

The smile faded. "What discrepancy?"

"There was probably ten grand in that little knapsack," Scot explained, gauging the prisoner's reaction. He didn't flinch, so his guess was close. "But what would happen if Bao Lin heard rumors that maybe there was a few bucks missing? Maybe you gave him ten grand, but maybe he was supposed to get fourteen."

"He'd never believe it," Xuan tried to spout, but they could see his walls of resistance tumbling down.

"I think I could sell it. But then, he might have already taken his revenge on you. See, Colonel Bao Lin is not in jail. Colonel Bao Lin had people take him away from us before he ever left Little Saigon. And those people have tried to tell us that the Colonel is not the one bringing in drugs, but some of his people are. Correct me if I'm wrong, but you are some of his people."

"No way, man, you're not going to con me. He needs me..." He trailed off, realizing he'd said too much.

Scot leaned forward in his chair. "What would he need a piece of alley trash like you for?"

But, in the background, Steve knew the kid had said his last words to the cops.

* * *

Tuy would be a little easier to get information from. Steve knew this the second he and Scot walked into the room. Tuy, who couldn't have been more than eighteen, was looking up at them with a blank stare, but Steve saw the hint of fear in his eyes. Once again, he let Black and Dy take the lead in the interviews. Thus far, he was impressed with the younger Inspector's techniques.

"Stand him up," Black commanded as soon as they entered, rattling his handcuffs. "You're finished, kid. Your buddy Xuan gave you up. The Colonel's CIA buddies told us to arrest *you* for all that dope in the fish plant. No lawyers, no trials, you go to jail."

"You can't do this," Tuy was begging. "The drugs not mine."

"They all say that," Steve said as Black cinched the cuffs tight.

Tuy suddenly went into a tirade in a foreign tongue, and everyone froze. The kid kept talking, and he seemed to be repeating the same phrase over and over. Steve hesitated, wondering what was going on and how he could use the situation. He saw the look of interest in Scot's eye and realized that Black could speak Vietnamese.

Scot turned the boy, planting him back in the chair, and leaned in toward him. He stared calmly into the eyes for a second, seeming to regain his composure, then said gently, "How did the Colonel betray you?"

"My sister," Tuy said without hesitation. "He promise to bring her out of Vietnam for a year now. But he wouldn't do it until I repaid him for bringing *me* here." He seemed to break down, and a tear slipped from his eye. "He lie to me. I do everything for him. I work in his plants, I deliver his drugs, I even join his stupid gang. But still, he no bring her here."

Scot sat down opposite him. "I'm sorry about your sister. But can you tell us about the drugs?"

"He'll kill me. He already mad because Dinh sold

half the supply and they ran out at the fish plant."

"They have to get resupplied," Scot prodded, "Where and when?"

"You bring my sister here?"

Scot let his head drop. "I'm sorry," he said. "Bao Lin probably brings refugees in illegally, so we have no way of knowing what his plans are for your sister. What I can do is protect you from him." He hit upon an idea. "I can also reach out to Immigration and give them my name and number. If your sister comes through legally, they can get in touch with me, and we can put the two of you together."

"Her name is Kim," Tuy mumbled. "She only nine years old. I bought a pink bunny doll to give to her…"

"I hope you get the chance." Then in Vietnamese, Scot said, "Can you help me?"

Tuy looked up from where he was staring at the table. "The American. The big soldier. I heard him tell the Colonel this morning. He going up north to meet the boat again. A place called Cleopatra Point, sometime tonight. He say near Fort Bragg."

In Vietnamese, Scot said, "Thank you."

Steve slipped out the door. He stepped over to the observation booth and opened the door to enter. He needed to talk to Stanson, plan out how they were going to sting this "big American soldier" Tuy had mentioned.

George Cameron was alone in the booth.

"Where's the Captain?"

"He just left. Hey, that American he was talking about—" Cameron cut off as Steve suddenly ran from the door.

Steve stormed out into the lobby of the police station and scanned for the Captain. He found no sign of him in the lobby and headed for the main entrance.

When Steve reached the parking lot, he was two steps behind the Captain's car as it pulled away from the curb and took off up Valencia. He stared after the retreating car.

Steve went back inside. He found Cameron, Black and Dy gathering outside the interview room.

"Where is this Cleopatra Point, anyway?" Dy asked.

"He said it's near Fort Bragg, up north," Scot said. "I'll map it online."

"Let's jump on the phones," Steve announced. "Call the Coast Guard, have them patrol up and down the shore in that area. I want that boat. And I want DEA and the local Sheriff's Department involved in the search for this 'American soldier'." He started to back out the door.

"Where are you going?" Cameron asked.

"Something's up with the Captain, I'm going to try and find out what."

* * *

Steve made it from Mission to Cow Hollow in just under ten minutes. When he pulled up outside Stanson's house, he checked for vehicles in the driveway. The one he'd seen leaving the station was not there. He hurried up the steps and pounded on the door.

The door was wrenched open, even as a frantic voice called out from inside. "John?" Mary, John Stanson's wife of thirty years, greeted him with a sigh. "Oh, Steve. I thought John had forgotten something."

"He's not here?" Steve asked, already knowing the answer. He noticed the worry lines and fresh tears that marked her face. "Mary, what happened?"

She turned and started walking back inside, and Steve followed to listen. "He stormed in here maybe ten minutes ago, grabbed a couple things and took off. Didn't say where he was going, didn't say a word, didn't even look at me. He scares me when he gets like that. I'm always afraid I'm not going to see him again."

"Did you see what he took?" Steve asked. He feared he already knew the answer to this question, too.

She waved a hand around as she racked her brain for the right words. "He took a... backpack. It looked like it was full. And he took a couple of his guns."

Steve nodded. He had an idea what was inside that pack, since he had a similar 'bug out bag' at home. He wondered if he could still catch the Captain heading north if he went home to get it first. "Thanks," he said over his shoulder, and hurried toward the front door.

"Wait. Steve!" Mrs. Stanson yelled after him. She was right on his tail as they made the door. "What happened to him? What's going on?"

"I'm not entirely sure myself, Mary," Steve said. He turned to look at her as he walked backward down the steps. He saw fear in her eyes and said with compassion, "But I'll bring him back to you."

As he left, she felt better but not by much.

For years, her husband had come home from policing the city and told her of the incredible adventures of Inspector Steve Blazer. Hearing Blazer himself offer his reassurances did bring her a small sliver of relief.

John didn't talk much about his CIA connections, but he'd let it slip out in conversation one night, when Steve had become more than just a friend but part of their lives... he'd told her that he knew Steve from his days in Intelligence. She knew her husband thought of this young super-cop as the son he never had. As she'd gotten to know him over the last few years, she'd grown to feel the same way.

She knew Steve was a man of action, like her man. If he made a promise like this, he would make it happen.

But she couldn't help but be carried back thirty years, to when she was a newlywed. John had an obsession with the Vietnam War. There was a family connection that he didn't talk much about, but John studied every aspect of that war, the significant events like the Tet offensive, the military's use of Agent Orange, the way the vets were treated when they came home, and particularly, the soldiers who were classified as "Missing in Action." John knew so much about the whole war, it was like he'd actually been there. For all she knew, maybe he somehow *had* been there.

She always hated the sudden goodbyes when he had to leave on a lengthy case, or on the mysterious trips he frequently took. She knew those were for the government. This time was so sudden, it hadn't felt like one of those.

Something was wrong. But she knew Steve would bring him back to her.

* * *

The November sun set early, and an approaching storm system dropped a dark blanket of clouds over the city. After his ordeal at the fish plant, Bao Lin decided to have an early dinner and sit in front of his fire for the evening. He had just sat down to a plate of roast duck when a familiar voice called out behind him. "You impress me, getting the United States Government to do your dirty work for you."

The American was back, in his home once again. Having already gone through this today, Bao Lin didn't react as severely. Sitting nearby as if part of the background, his fat butler didn't reach for his weapon, but glanced nervously between his boss and the American named Smith.

"You have been trained too well by my people."

Bao Lin smiled, even though Smith couldn't see it with his back turned. "You sneak up on people like a true Vietnamese. You would have made a good freedom fighter."

Smith let that one go. "Colonel, regardless of what resources you have up your sleeve to keep you out of jail, I think it's careless of you to continue your drug operation here. There's a couple of cops here that seem to want to blow through any obstacle you or I put in their way. They're not going to let a simple thing like the CIA stand in their way of nailing a big-time drug smuggler."

"If you are referring to Inspector Dy," Bao Lin said, "he is of no concern. Many times he has tried to put me in his jail, and many times have I thwarted his efforts. I rather enjoy watching him fail like that."

The Colonel wasn't taking him seriously, but Smith held his temper for the moment. "May I propose to you that we take this next shipment out of town? I have connections in Portland and Seattle. We can sell it there for just as much money."

Bao Lin was losing his good humor. "My obligations are here. I will sell it here."

"That's what I figured you'd say," Smith said, resigned to what he was about to do. "So, I expect you won't like me much when I tell you I'm taking this shipment off your hands. Your irresponsibility just cost you a cool two million."

The fat butler finally pulled the gun, now that his boss was being threatened. But from out of nowhere, a loud shot exploded across the room. A .45 caliber bullet pierced the butler's heart. The force of the shot drove him back, but he desperately tried to keep his feet underneath him. It didn't work. He simply toppled back, glanced off the corner of the table and plunged to the floor, knocking over a chair on the way down.

Bao turned suddenly in his chair at the gunshot. He watched his man fall, then sat frozen for a long moment. There was no compassion at the loss of his manservant, and only a twinge of fear at the possibility of losing his own life. Mostly what he felt was anger at the betrayal from this American. "You are the lowest life form in this world. My associates from the Golden Triangle will surely kill you slowly when they learn of this betrayal."

Smith stepped forward, and a long object swung down from behind his back, until the end rested on the table next to Bao Lin. The Colonel involuntarily looked down at it. It was a bamboo pole, one that usually sat mounted on the wall of the office here in his home. He told people it was a martial arts weapon he'd acquired from a great master many years ago in Thailand. He'd actually acquired it in the early 1970s when he briefly ran a prison camp in North Vietnam. Many American soldiers had been beaten with this pole.

Now it was used to suddenly knock his plate of food aside. Rice and duck were scattered all over the table. "This look familiar, Bao? It was mounted in your office. This is what you used to torture my countrymen."

The Colonel hadn't moved. "If you cared so much for your countrymen..."

"You're right, Bao, I don't care," Smith growled, a hateful sound that at the same time conveyed the fact that Smith was starting to enjoy himself. "I do hate my country, and I do hate the people in it. But guess what. I hate you more, and your whole pitiful and heartless commie excuse for a government."

All at once he brought the pole down on Bao's wrist with a tremendous force. Both felt bone give way. Bao cried out, unable to stifle his outburst.

Bao lunged from his chair to his left, away from

the six-foot bamboo pole. He growled through the pain. "You accuse me of being heartless," he roared as he held his injured wrist. He faced Smith for the first time.

"Yeah," the big American chuckled. "Ain't that a kick in the ass?" He lashed out with a jab. He nailed the unprepared Vietnamese Colonel in the chest. Bao stumbled back but caught his balance. Sharp pain there told him he might have a fractured rib.

Smith lashed out again. But Bao recovered from the shock and pain of his injuries. He sidestepped to avoid the flying bamboo pole. He followed through with a kick toward Smith's torso.

Again, the American soldier had anticipated this. Being older and weaker than he was thirty years ago, Bao didn't have the kind of force behind his kick that he wanted. Smith was easily able to deflect the blow off his shoulder. At the same time, his own foot kicked inside Bao's stance, shattering his former employer's supporting knee. Bao crumpled to the floor, giving a roar as the pain surged up his body. Without waiting, Smith brought the pole down again on the Colonel's other knee, shattering bone there as well. Bao screamed again.

With his victim helpless on the floor, Smith knelt next to him. "Cops should be here any minute now, if anyone heard that shot. Then again, we're close enough to Little Saigon, maybe no one will report anything suspicious. I can't stick around; I got a boat to meet."

Bao looked up with wide eyes as Smith produced a knife out of nowhere. The silver blade flashed as it caught the brightness of a streetlight outside. Smith smiled at Colonel Bao Lin's wide eyes as he plunged the knife down.

* * *

Lieutenant Cameron sat at his desk going over a catalogue of the evidence that Chandler and Green had brought him from the fish lab drug bust. Blazer was out—"Tracking leads" was the official story, but he knew Steve sometimes pursued his own leads. He worried when Blazer went out on his own, whether he was in over his head or breaking the rules to catch his bad guys. But thus far, his solo work had not landed the unit or the department in hot water.

He glanced over at where Scot Black was working on a laptop. He was typing a letter for Tuy. He'd heard what Black said to Tuy in the interview and deduced how he would go about reaching out to Immigration. Two letters would go to San Francisco's Immigration office, which he knew saw a massive influx of refugees trying to enter this country. Most of them were Chinese or Vietnamese, just like Los Angeles had mostly illegal aliens from Mexico. Tuy would keep the other letters so he could keep in touch as he hid from Colonel Bao and his minions.

He looked up as a familiar but unwelcome face appeared in the doorway of their Tenderloin Station office. "What do you want, Agent Kimmins?" he announced the Fed's presence to the rest of the cops in the room.

"I was hoping to talk to the Inspector I spoke with earlier." Kimmins appeared nervous but was trying to appear superior. He gave away his nervousness by running his hand through his hair.

"Inspector Blazer is unavailable at the moment," Cameron said. "But I'm his boss if you'd like to talk to me." He instantly regretted saying that, because now Kimmins would do just that.

"I just want to reiterate that Colonel Bao Lin is not your problem. I don't know why local cops were messing with him in the first place."

"Gee, we were just trying to get drugs off the streets. What were we thinking?"

"Look, Bao Lin is in a sensitive position. Not only is he a hero to the people of his community, but he helps us in ways you don't even know."

"I can take a stab, though," Scot said, jumping into the conversation. "Vietnam has been kind of a bitter and violent country since the war. Maybe some higher ups want to stop their puppet people from leaving the country, so they send some Commie spies over here to stir up trouble. But Colonel Bao, he watches out for things like that, and he tells you about it."

"OK, so you have a general picture of what his position is," Kimmins relented. "He's also valuable in the trade market. Vietnam is becoming a valuable trade partner to the US and Bao Lin has contacts and associates in that world."

"Yeah, his Import/Export line is vital to national security." Cameron shook his head. "Do you really give a damn about trade?"

"OK, maybe some people in the Colonel's employ run some drugs from the mainland. Sure, he hates that, but he has to tolerate it because of the position he's in."

"What are you trying to tell me, Kimmins?"

"I'm telling you we're aware of the problem and we will deal with it in due time. Colonel Bao is in a position now to help us nail some major international players. We need his organization intact, and we need the support of his community to do that."

Scot shook his head. "You need to keep him happy by letting him suck his community dry."

The phone on Cameron's desk rang and he picked it up, eager to exit this conversation. "Lieutenant Cameron." Kimmins looked on as he listened for several seconds. He was perturbed at being cut off like that, especially since he seemed to be making no progress, and his attitude didn't change when he saw Cameron's face go slack. "Man, that's almost poetic. OK, Vinnie, we'll be right over." He hung up and stood up, putting a jacket on over his shoulder holster. "Listen up," he announced to the rest of the present cops, "We got a big one. We have to go."

"We're not done here," Kimmins pronounced.

"Oh, man," Cameron shook his head as he laughed. "I'd hate to be in your shoes right now. You know, for the sake of your investigation. The people's hero, the man who's supposed to be helping you nab "international players" on the side while he smuggles his own drugs, Mr. Import/Export himself. Your Colonel Bao Lin just got himself murdered in his own home."

* * *

Dy waited. Every few seconds, in between conferring with other officers as they sealed off the neighborhood, he'd glance at his watch. He noticed crowds of Vietnamese people gathering on the south side of the street. In the dark he couldn't gauge their reactions. He wasn't sure if they'd be happy to be out from under Bao Lin's oppression, or sad and angry that they'd lost a major philanthropist. They didn't have to fear him anymore. They didn't have to pretend to respect him anymore. They didn't have to think about him at all anymore.

He glanced again at his watch. A vehicle appeared at the nearby intersection and approached the crime scene. It was another Crime Scene Investigations vehicle. Two more investigators filed up the steps into the dead man's home, where they would take pictures and check carefully for prints, blood, hair, fibers. Dy glanced at his watch one more time.

He watched every individual police vehicle that arrived, searching for ones he would recognize as belonging to Vice Squad. He felt a wave of relief and excitement when those two unmarked SUVs made the turn from Geary Street together and parked along the curb nearby. Dy ducked under the tape to go meet them.

"Thanks for calling," Lieutenant Cameron said as he met with Dy. "You said it was pretty gruesome inside, how bad is it?"

Dy glanced over the group entering the crime scene, Cameron, Chandler and Green. He also saw Scot Black and nodded to his partner. "Somebody took their time and had fun doing it."

Dy led them into the Colonel's home. Scot in particular examined the home leading up to the crime scene. Being familiar with Vietnamese culture, he took in the décor, the artwork, the photographs from Bao's younger days in Vietnam, even some ancient weapons displayed. The place looked orderly enough until they reached a living room. In an adjacent dining room, Scot took passing notice of the plate of food scattered across the table. The body of the butler/bodyguard lay in a nearby doorway. A CSI was standing over him, snapping pictures.

They found Bao's body in the living room, just feet from the entrance to his dining room. He was sprawled there with blood sprayed in places around him. His torso was a disgusting mound of blood and meat. They could see obvious bruises on parts of the corpse. The Medical Examiner, a black woman in her late forties, was stooped over the body, checking his wounds. She glanced up at the new plainclothes cops, then continued her examination.

"He obviously knew the guy, since we found no sign of forced entry," Dy explained. "The butler got it first, one round straight through the heart. But the killer took his time with the Colonel."

"What can you tell us, Doc?" Cameron asked.

"I'm still cataloguing visible injuries," the woman said. "So far, I've got one broken wrist, and both knees shattered by a heavy blow." She stood to walk them through the next part. "Once he was down, the killer decided to have some fun. He sliced open the stomach, ripped out the intestines and started feeding it to him. I'm guessing the Colonel was alive for a while after he was sliced open."

Those that heard these details winced at the mental images it conjured up. "Like the Vietcong used to do to uncooperative villagers," Dy said.

"Someone wanted him to suffer," Scot observed. "Do we have a murder weapon?"

"No, but we know what did some of the damage," Dy said, pointing to the floor nearby. A six-foot bamboo staff lay there, snapped in half. "Recognize that, partner?"

"A Bokken." Scot knew the weapon.

"We're testing it for blood and tissue."

Scot turned to the M.E. "I need to know what you can tell me about the blade cut. Maybe we can get a make on the kind of knife used."

"Who's in charge here?" a voice boomed from outside.

Cameron winced when he recognized the pseudo-superiority of Agent Kimmins' voice. He wanted to avoid the fed, but when he turned, Kimmins spotted him through the crowd of police officers that was trying to keep him out of the crime scene. "Lieutenant, you have some explaining to do. That's a hi-level operative you just allowed to be murdered. I want a list of suspects, and I want to add a few names to it."

"Like who?" an angry George Cameron demanded as he approached the front door.

Kimmins sensed he had the upper hand and took it. "For starters, where's your man Blazer?"

***

Just up the street, in a Lexus similar to the one Joey Nang had died in, Danny Dinh watched the sea of flashing red and blue lights. He'd been in the crowd outside Bao Lin's home for a few minutes and had been able to hear snatches of conversation between cops. He'd learned about the murders. He pulled out his cell phone and punched in a number.

"Mr. Jiang, it's Danny Dinh. Yes, I'm glad you're satisfied with the product. Listen, I would like to ask for a favor." He might be young, but Dinh knew how to respect his elders, especially those of other cultures, no matter what the relationship between their nationalities was. "I would like to assemble a hit team. Yes, I know who we're going to kill. And I know where. This has to happen soon, tonight."

Danny Dinh's final words to Colonel Bao Lin had been a lie. The gang he'd sold the heroin to was not in San Jose, but actually a Triad gang in Chinatown. If the Colonel knew, Dinh would have been killed—doing so might expose their operation to the Chinese and invite a turf war.

But it seemed Smith had turned the tables on Bao. It was time someone taught him how the men of the Golden Triangle really operate. Dinh did not feel particularly obligated by any kind of blood oath to Bao, but their business was becoming chaotic. He made an oath to himself to bring it under control. His control. For that to happen, he needed to bring down Smith. The old man was too wild of a card to be left alone. Dinh did not want to wait until Smith decided *he* wasn't needed anymore. That bloodthirsty son of a bitch would be taken care of tonight. *But* he wasn't dumb enough to take him on alone. Smith may be old, but he made his bones in a jungle hell thousands of miles away, in the aftermath of a war that seemed thousands of years ago. Dinh had never been to the country of his parents, who were long dead, but he knew enough about the war and his culture. With the help of his Triad friends, he would take down Smith once and for all. Tonight.

CHAPTER 5

Stanson had a lot of time to think on the road north to Fort Bragg. He'd consulted a GPS map of the area while he drove, and located Cleopatra Point, just over a mile north of Fort Bragg. As his car traversed the winding wooded sections of Highway One along the coast, he thought out plans and strategies. He'd left just before dusk on the four-hour drive, so he would have a few hours to recon around the drop off point before Smith showed his murderous face.

Then something else occurred to him, and he slipped on his Bluetooth to make a phone call. Dividing his attention between the road and the phone, he tapped the screen, checking the internet for a particular phone number. He tapped it, and the call went through.

"Mendocino County Sheriff's Department," a female operator answered.

"This is Captain John Stanson, San Francisco Police Department." He gave his badge number. "I understand one of our inspectors called you to ask for assistance in a BOLO?"

"Yes, sir, I have the sheet right here. We got a call from a Lieutenant Cameron. We're to be on the lookout in the coastal areas for an unidentified suspect, height six foot two, weight approximately two-thirty, dark hair. He is supposed to be meeting a boat either on a beach or in any isolated coastal area."

"Good. We got some additional information and a couple of tips. He's been sighted down near Point Arena and may be on his way to Ukiah. I want to move the search down there."

"Alright, sir, I'll put that bulletin out."

"Thank you so much," Stanson said and ended the call. His satisfaction was grim. He hated having to misdirect local cops, but it would keep them out of his area of operation. He didn't want to have to worry about a uniform stumbling onto his fight with Smith. They would insist on bringing everyone in and letting a judge sort the affair out. That line of action risked Smith finding an opening and killing another cop. Stanson needed Smith alone. This was personal. He quickly looked up a second number and put through a call to the *Coast Guard*.

* * *

Steve Blazer's mind was equally occupied. He intended to bring the Captain back from what he now believed was some kind of mysterious personal vendetta. He wanted to drag him back from doing the kind of stupid things that the rest of the department thought he himself probably got caught up in too often. But in the back of his mind, he toyed with the idea of joining the Captain on his crusade, whatever it was. He was angry at Stanson for keeping him out of the loop like this. But deep down, he knew this mission had to be a righteous one.

His phone rang. He glanced at the screen, hoping it was Stanson, but it was not. "Blazer."

"It's Cameron. Where are you?"

"About two hours north of the city." He'd detected a sense of urgency in his boss's voice. "What's wrong?"

"Bao Lin was murdered an hour ago."

Steve was silent for a few seconds. "I don't know whether to be happy we got another drug dealer off the streets, or angry that half our case just went up in smoke."

"Well, you better be worried. Kimmins wants to put you on the suspect list."

Steve let out a silent sigh. "Thanks for the warning. I guess you'll just have to keep him off my back for a while. I'll deal with him when I get back."

"Which will be when?" Steve knew Cameron had already figured he was going after the drug shipment. The Lieutenant had to be wondering why he was going alone.

"Don't know yet."

Cameron sighed over the phone. "I'm going to assume you're on a mission to intercept those drugs with the DEA, Coast Guard and Mendocino Sheriff's Department. Any further inquiries from Kimmins will reflect that."

"That's a safe bet. Thanks, LT." Steve killed the call.

* * *

Steve drove on. Ahead, Highway One twisted away into the darkness. But by now, he was starting to feel the effect of being up for nearly twenty-four hours and surviving with only three hours sleep the night before. He yawned, and his eyes closed on him involuntarily. He forced them open and jerked his wheel to avoid running into the side of the mountain.

"Come on, Blazer, you're almost there," he said aloud to himself, thinking maybe it would wake him up. But a minute later, he felt another yawn coming on. He shook his head in frustration and hit the power button on his radio. The San Francisco rock station he usually tuned in was out of range, so he hit the search button. The first station he found was classical. "Yawn," he muttered, letting the button change the setting automatically. Talk radio came up next. "Not in the mood." Next was country. "Not even." An Oldies station was next, and he listened to the classic song they were playing for five seconds while the radio waited for him to tell it to stop or go. He didn't touch it and the radio moved on. The next station, near the bottom of the dial was what he was looking for, rock. It was a classic rock station. Steve smiled a thin contented smile as he recognized the song. It was 'White Rabbit,' by Jefferson Airplane. This was one of his favorite songs from the late sixties.

As he drove on into the night, he realized that the song was from the Vietnam era, appropriate considering their current case. The song came out at a time when America was engaged in a war against Communism in a jungle eight thousand miles away. At the same time, the very ideas behind Communism were taking root in America's youth at home. Anyone who knew the concept behind the song knew it was about doing drugs and in the late sixties, the drug culture really became prevalent in the States. America's youth were getting high on free drugs and free love. They bought into the myth that these substances that "The Man" had banned really expanded your mind. Drugs were everywhere, the man couldn't eradicate them. The drug culture even found its way to the GIs in Vietnam, and Marijuana and LSD became a big problem there. When many came home from the hells of war, their drug habits came with them, and many GIs remained addicts and even died from their habit.

Efforts to decriminalize, or even legalize, at least some narcotics had developed over the years, and now were ramping up. Steve kept up with those efforts, because he opposed them. He'd seen the dark side of drugs, wasted shells of human beings who cared for nothing but their next high. He'd seen this sort of thing much of his life, even before becoming a cop, even before his days in the military. It had become a personal vow that he would do everything he could to remove drugs from the world.

He set the radio station and listened to the song, even joined in singing on the chorus. It seemed to wake him. The next song grabbed his interest as well, 'Paint it Black' by the Rolling Stones. This was another favorite of his from the era of the Vietnam War. He settled into his drive, letting the music take him to another time and place.

The SUV continued through the Jackson State Forest, tall redwoods laughing to themselves as this apparent crazy man drove among them, singing at the top of his lungs to keep himself awake.

* * *

The forest ahead of him thinned visibly. Steve noticed a sign on the road ahead, Fort Bragg, three miles. "All right," he said to himself. He wasn't a coffee drinker, so he'd already resigned himself to purchasing stay-awake pills at the next minimart.

Not to be confused with the North Carolina Army Base Steve knew from his younger military years, Fort Bragg was a sleepy northern California town of about five thousand. It was a popular tourist attraction for its beaches, souvenir shopping and scenic forests. It was also one home of the "Skunk

Trains," a modern take on a classic steam engine train. In the old logging days of the northern California coast, those trains carried timber cut from the forests to the lumber mills on the coast. Now they took tourists on sight-seeing trips through miles of beautiful redwoods.

Steve crossed a bridge and glanced at what he could see of the lights of the marina below. The main drag of Fort Bragg was Highway One, which was fronted by tourist shops and other establishments on either side. Beyond them to the west, the ocean was visible, the coast dotted intermittently with rocky shoreline and small peaceful beaches. Steve scanned the town as he drove through. Fort Bragg seemed to be closed down for the night. It wasn't until the north side of town that he spotted what he was looking for, a twenty-four-hour minimart. According to the street sign, Highway One was also known as Main Street and West Elm intersected it, leading down toward a nearby beach and bike path. He pulled in and parked to the side of the store.

An irritating buzzer sounded loudly as he walked inside. He started walking the aisles, looking for caffeine pills.

He almost didn't look up when the buzzer sounded again. But when he noticed the Asian man in the leather jacket looking over a rack of junk food near the front of the store, he was instantly suspicious. Was it a coincidence? He was in the middle of a case involving Vietnamese gangs and dope from the Golden Triangle. He was on his way to intercept a shipment of that dope. He'd just found out a major player in that case was murdered. And now, here, a young Asian dressed like a thug walks into the same convenience store he did. Steve didn't believe in that kind of coincidence. He replaced the small package of pills back on the rack and edged toward the front of the store.

A second man came in behind his friend. "Excuse me, can you tell me where Cleopatra Point is?" he asked the clerk.

Now this kid is asking about Cleopatra Point? It was obvious they were from the city, most likely connected with the late Bao Lin. What was their angle? Were they here to collect his latest shipment of Golden Triangle Heroin? That was the most likely scenario. Steve took a casual peek around the corner, and with some interest, checked their clothing. Pop culture these days dictated that gangbangers wear bulgy clothing several sizes too big. It was a ridiculous fashion trend picked up by all walks of life, but for serious gang members it served a practical purpose, to hide weapons. These guys wore ill-fitting jeans, shirts, and jackets, and could easily be concealing firearms.

Another theory occurred to him. Maybe these guys were here for revenge on the death of Colonel Bao Lin. If this was the case, who exactly was their target? The mysterious cop killer? Clues to his place in Bao Lin's organization began to solidify in his mind, and Stanson's mission to this area added new certainty—and new confusion—to the mix.

Another question nagged at him. Where was the law enforcement? Lieutenant Cameron would have notified local cops of their search for a suspicious boat and a cop killer. Coast Guard boats would be patrolling heavily off the coast. Fort Bragg should be crawling with sheriff's deputies. Why hadn't he encountered any patrol cars?

One thing was certain. Letting these guys go on was not a great idea. He needed to at least investigate them.

He stepped into the open, staring intently at the two.

One of the young men looked up at him and whispered something to his companion.

Danny Dinh glanced up at the big stranger his Chinese buddy had pointed out. "What do you want?" he nervously asked as Steve approached. Blazer glimpsed his hand twitching, drifting away from his body as if moving into position—he was preparing to go for his gun.

Steve stopped eight feet away. "I'm a police officer, guys. I'm curious why the two of you want to know about Cleopatra Point."

"What's it to you, pig?" Dinh asked.

Steve smiled at the pathetic insult. "See there's a lot of rumors floating around about that place, none of them good..."

Before Steve could finish his sentence, both men turned at almost the same time and bolted through the door. The store clerk looked on in sudden panic as Steve rushed past to pursue them.

Several things happened in the next second. As Steve made the glass door, he heard one of the young Asian men shout something. The language sounded like Chinese, though he didn't know the difference between Chinese and, say, Vietnamese...

Steve stopped just outside the door, and his eyes went to the only significant thing in the parking lot. Two late model Lexus sedans were lined up several yards away. The Asians ran toward the cars. Blazer saw the back doors on one vehicle suddenly pop open. Another young Asian scrambled out with a weapon. In his half-second view of the gun, Steve recognized it as an MPK.

With safety in numbers, the two from the store turned and drew their own guns.

Steve turned on his heel and rushed back through the door. The sights of three guns weighed heavy on his back. Any millisecond, their first round would crash through his chest and he'd be dead…

"Get down!" he shouted to the frightened clerk as he raced past.

Gunfire exploded behind him.

* * *

Stanson had arrived in Fort Bragg just after nine o'clock, and he drove slowly along Highway One for several miles, getting a feel for the terrain, and specifically the coastline, even in the darkness. He located the turnoff for the Point, but kept going, scoping out roads that connected to the Highway for another two miles, as he'd done for everything south of the target area. There were roads that shot off the Highway and traveled for miles inland. These roads had once led to lumber camps all over the surrounding forests, but now gave access to homes and farms.

Finally, he turned around and headed back south. He'd picked out a spot an eighth of a mile south of the Point to leave his car, a small parking lot for a beach. That way, he thought, if he didn't get a chance to kill the man before the delivery, he could hurry back to his car and still be able catch up to him on the trip back to San Francisco.

Stanson left his car in the parking lot of a scenic overlook that offered a view of ocean surf crashing on treacherous rocks. He'd parked close to the edge of the lot, right next to the tall grass and brush that blocked a view from the road. He loaded himself with essential things from his ruck sack: a canteen full of water, binoculars, a windbreaker that would keep the wind chill to a minimum, navy blue to help him blend in with the darkness. He checked over extra ammunition for both his spare guns. One was a powerful .357 Colt Python Revolver, which he'd brought as a kind of sniping weapon, and the other was a Colt Government model from his Vietnam days. It was an old weapon, chambered in .45 caliber, but he'd taken care of it ever since his days in the jungle. It was also black, to blend in with the night, with a wooden hand grip. It was an elegant weapon, and very sufficient for this job.

Loaded down for the mission he'd taken upon himself, he withdrew a small stick of dark green camo-paint from a pouch on the ruck. He also pulled out a small tube of suntan lotion. He squeezed out a bit and smeared it over his face and hands, any exposed skin. He then did the same with the camo-paint, making his face and hands dark like the night. Applying the sunscreen was an old trick that made it easier to clean the camo-paint off later. He pulled on a camouflage military soft cap, then slipped into the vegetation and disappeared from the world.

In an instant, he was carried back decades, to the jungles and grasslands of Vietnam. Sure, the land and vegetation were different, but the feeling was the same. He still wondered, like he did back then, if this would be his last foray into the field, never to walk out of the jungle alive.

But this mission was different.

Stanson quickly brought himself back to the present day and forged ahead, scoping out the land. He soon found himself in an area of bushes across a small break in the cliffs from the Vista Point. He paused there and brought his binoculars into play, scanning the area around him. Below him, a tiny beach was carved into the shore, and it was far too rocky for anyone to enjoy recreating there. He noticed the trail that crept up the cliff, exiting at the top near the observation deck. It seemed an obvious route from the beach to the road, and he resolved to make this his observation point.

He checked his watch and found he had over two hours until the meet was supposed to happen. With plenty of time to burn, he made his way out into the open and around the break in the cliff. He passed the trail head and reached open pavement at the Vista Point. He knelt behind the ornate rock wall and scanned the terrain below and to the north with the binoculars. Directly below, the ocean crashed against the rocky shore. But to the north, maybe a hundred feet away, another small beach stretched along the shore for at least a hundred yards. Scenes like this dotted the shore, where cliffs became rolling hills, and trails led down from vista points to rock-strewn beaches.

A cloud bank had settled over the area, and a growing breeze was starting to stir the bushes around him. He swept the binoculars out over the ocean, but a light fog was swirling off the coast, so he couldn't see any boats.

The wind almost covered the sound of an engine approaching from the highway, but Stanson finally jerked his eyes from the binoculars to the road behind him. He distinguished the new sound, and then noticed the light illuminating the trees across the highway. He surged back to his feet and ran in a slight crouch back the way he'd come. He started cursing himself as he heard the vehicle slowing down. It shouldn't be Smith this early, but he didn't want to be seen by *anyone* in this area, so he wouldn't be remembered when the body was found.

If the body was found.

Whoever it was, they *were* stopping at this vista point. This was an odd hour for an outing on the beach, he thought. Whoever it was, they would see him in the open unless he made this last thirty feet. He heard the crunch of tires on gravel as the vehicle turned off the road to enter the vista point. He surged past the trail head, and finally dove into the tall grass an instant before headlights swept over the area.

Stanson lay absolutely still and listened as the vehicle circled through the small parking lot, sweeping north to south and finally stopping to face the highway. The headlights were extinguished, and he slowly sat up. Keeping below the tops of the grass, Stanson peered between the stalks at the vehicle.

It *was* Smith, and he was early. Stanson recognized him by his dim profile, a dark human form against an even darker background. He must have moved the delivery up for some reason, John thought, and touched the revolver on his hip for reassurance. Not yet, he told himself. No matter how much he wanted to kill this son of a bitch, he needed to wait until the drugs arrived.

From the looks of things, that wouldn't take long.

Smith had gone to stand by the wall, gazing like a statue out over the ocean. Stanson watched him closely until something else caught his eye. A dim flash of light appeared out on the water, then repeated. He glanced at Smith and saw the powerful flashlight now in his hands. It flicked on, then off, then on and off again.

He was guiding someone in.

Smith then hurried around to the trail and started to make his way down.

He stopped suddenly. Stanson froze, watching the silhouette carefully. Smith started surveying the area, his eyes sweeping over John's hiding place and moving on. He knows I'm here, Stanson told himself, and he tensed, ready to bring up his .45 and start blasting.

Smith started down the trail once again.

As quiet as he could, Stanson slid like a serpent

to the edge of the grass, where the cliff fell away to the rocky beach. He watched for several minutes as Smith continued flashing his light out into the ocean, and the incoming boat drew closer. At long last, voices drifted up the incline as Smith helped his rendezvous guide a twenty-foot boat resembling a rubber raft past rocks and up onto the shore. One of the voices rose in a high-pitched warning, and though he could not hear what was said, Stanson detected an accent. The boat pilot was Asian, probably Vietnamese.

With Smith down by the water, away from the truck, Stanson took a chance. He bolted from the grass and crept up to the truck, keeping the vehicle between him and where he believed Smith was. Maybe the truck would provide him some information.

He paused at the driver door, grasping the handle. One sudden fear hit him—would the interior light turn on if he opened the door? Then again, Smith himself was trying to remain clandestine, and flipping a switch to keep the interior light off was a simple task to help that pursuit. He quietly pulled the handle. The truck door opened. The light stayed off. Stanson smiled grimly as he looked inside.

He pulled out a small flashlight, with a red lens that dimmed the brightness. He played the light low over the interior. A burst of static suddenly alerted him, sending a wave of adrenaline through him. He tensed, ready to retreat from the truck, until the light paused over an object mounted under the dashboard near the center console. A police scanner. OK, Stanson thought, he's keeping up with local police traffic. He filed that information away for later.

The light played over a couple of normal items, a gym bag sitting on the passenger side floor, the remnants of a package of bottled water, some food wrappers. The light rested again on an item on the passenger seat. It was a book about the history of logging in the Fort Bragg area, likely purchased at a nearby tourist gift shop. He leaned in to examine this further. The first page showed a semi-detailed image of the local area. One thing immediately stood out; a small X drawn on a spot somewhere inland. A simple X on a map, he noted. More memories of his history with Smith flooded his brain, and he shook his head to bring himself back to the present. He studied the area surrounding that mark, including a road that seemed to lead to the area—

A voice from the water reached him and looked up suddenly, placing the flashlight beam against his chest to render it invisible. They must be returning. Stanson backed away from the truck and closed the door softly, then leaned in and pushed with his hip to close it all the way. That accomplished, he turned and padded quickly back to the tall grass, where he once again dropped into its depths.

In seconds, Smith reached the trailhead to enter the parking lot, two other men in tow, each of them carrying bags. As they passed by his thicket of tall grass, Stanson saw the gym bags close up. He also saw the ancient submachine guns carried by each party. If he took Smith out now, he'd have to deal with those weapons, and he would lose. Better to wait till they were out of the picture before he made his move.

With occasional grunts from the exertion, Smith led two smaller Vietnamese men up the trail to his truck. The two Asians stopped several feet from the truck. "You show us money," one of them demanded loudly as they dropped their bags.

Smith seemed to detect a hostile and distrusting quality to their voices. "OK, OK," he said. He opened the driver door of his truck and pulled out the bag Stanson had seen. He handed it to one of them, who unzipped it while his partner watched the American carefully.

Hoping to preserve the relationship he'd built with these distributors, Smith said, "Zhang, you know me. We have a trust between us."

Stanson smirked in the darkness. He knew that tone. In his short time working with Smith in the 'Nam, he'd grown to mistrust that tone of voice.

As if fate agreed with that thought, far to the south, a fast volley of gunshots sounded. It must have been a mile or two away, but the sound carried through the quiet darkness, even over the distant sound of the waves. Zhang and his companion seemed suddenly eager to be gone. Zhang said something in Vietnamese to his partner and they backed toward the trail, leaving their bags, and taking their payment. At the trailhead, they turned tail and ran down the sharp slope. Stanson heard one of them slip and fall with a skidding sound, and his partner shouted something. He glanced over the edge and found them racing for the boat.

Stanson turned his attention to Smith. He was hurrying around the front of the truck, where he grabbed the bags and ran them to the back.

Stanson had drawn his .45 and slowly thumbed back the hammer, but at that point he knew he wouldn't get a good enough shot, even at this close range. The truck was in his way. Smith hurried around the driver's side and tossed the bags into the cab. He jumped in and had the engine running in a second. With tires spinning out, the truck spun around and roared toward the entrance.

Stanson was on his feet in an instant, sticking to the grass as he ran back toward the highway. He burst out onto the hardtop as the truck accelerated northward.

What's wrong with this picture the Captain

asked himself. Why isn't he going south toward San Francisco?

The truck disappeared around a bend in the road. With his own car back to the south, Stanson knew he'd never catch him. Smith had just slipped through his fingers.

Maybe.

He took out his phone and brought up his maps app. He searched for the road he'd seen. He found it a few miles north of Cleopatra Point. Stanson had requested that Coast Guard and Law Enforcement move their search farther north, and with his police scanner, Smith may have heard this. The shooting they'd heard just now to the south may have spooked him further. If he wanted to remain anonymous, he couldn't really travel north or south just yet. In the night, he would be too obvious moving through the area, better to try escaping the area hidden in plain sight among all the other normal traffic. He was likely going to hide for the night, but where? The most likely place was…the X on the map.

Stanson made sure the map was saved on his phone. He hurried back into the brush and back toward his car.

To the south, the gunshots continued.

A gun battle this severe in this neck of the woods, with the circumstances he himself was enmeshed in, it could only mean one thing.

Blazer was on his trail.

* * *

Steve bent low as bullets punctured the windows behind him, shattering the glass and letting the shards fall where they may. The bullets seemed to follow him as he made his way around a rack of generic pastries and packages of cookies. Several of the packages exploded as bullets picked them off.

Steve found himself in an aisle bordered by beverage coolers and bread racks. With Beretta in hand, he popped his head up for a quick look. He found a decent view through the windows of the parking lot outside. He dropped down the second he spotted the line of gunmen outside. A fresh volley of lead peppered his post, and glass from the coolers to his right was smashed into pieces. To avoid the falling glass, he crept quickly along the back aisle of the store toward the door at the back marked "Employees Only." He dove through the door, even as nine-millimeter slugs tore chunks of wood out of the top half.

Steve rolled and found himself wedged against a wall. A foul smell reached his nose, and he attributed it to the bucket of water with the mop stuck in it, sitting four feet away. But beyond that bucket, a door at the end of the hallway beckoned him. He sprang to his feet and reached it in two seconds. He grabbed the handle and pushed through.

The cold darkness wrapped her arms around him. He frantically checked his surroundings. He was at the side of the store, his SUV parked just a few feet away. He had spare weapons in the back, but did he have time and opportunity to go after them? Two quick bursts of gunfire ripped the night again, helping him decide.

"Check around the back," one of the Asians shouted. A second later, he heard an engine race and tires screech as one of the Asians got his vehicle under way.

Steve moved as soon as he heard that. For now, they had him outgunned, and with no law enforcement apparent anywhere in town, he decided to escape and evade.

They may try to flank me, he realized. It would

take precious seconds to open his car and fish around in his gun locker. He turned and headed around the back of the store. The light was more sparse here. He found himself in an alley and raced across toward a six-foot chain-link fence. Headlights stabbed him in the dark as the first Lexus reached the alley to the south, searching for him. He jumped and scaled the fence.

He found himself in front of a building, a large lumber and warehouse store. The yard was covered by powerful floodlights on the building, exposing him in the open. Shouts from the Asians reached his ears, and he raced toward the building, seeking any kind of shadow. He glanced back to see one of them trying to climb the fence. He saw the man bringing up his MPK. A burst from the weapon echoed across the night. Bullets sparked off the pavement to his right as he reached the cover of the building.

Steve raced to the west end of the building. Farther away, he saw stacks of lumber, different sizes of boards, just sitting in the middle of the yard. It was a large open storage area, with a forklift parked on one side. It almost looks like a maze, Steve thought, and raced toward the stacks. It was a good fifty yards away, and the distance looked greater the closer he got.

Behind him, the main gate suddenly burst apart. Pieces of chain link and plastic slat were instantly mangled and scattered as the Lexus smashed through. Steve turned as he ran and fired several shots at the car as it steered his direction and charged.

There was more shouting behind him. He couldn't hear what they were saying, but he could figure out the gist. Both sides of this skirmish had figured out who the other one was. They wanted, needed, to kill him. His efforts to put a stop to their mission had failed, and now he needed to survive.

Steve reached the stacks of lumber. He plunged into the maze, just ahead of a line of bullets that shredded wood next to his passing head.

Steve heard the voices again, and one seemed to echo very close to him. He instantly dodged to his right, ducking in between two stacks. He found that most of the passages between the lumber stacks were big enough at least for the forklift to drive through. He paused to listen again and try to interpret what he was hearing. The echoes in this yard may be a little deceiving, he decided, and that would be factored into his actions. But then distinct voices reached him from the north. They're trying to box me in, he realized, and started looking around. His eyes rested on the top of the stack next to him. Having the high ground could pay off, he decided, and sought out a way to the top. He found a foothold and started up.

Like a spider, he crawled onto the top. He stayed flat, to avoid being silhouetted against the cloudy sky. Condensation moisture had accumulated on the boards, and he ignored it soaking into his pants. He tilted his head to scan the ground on first the south, then the north side of the wood. He spotted moving shadows to the south, and then a distinct figure creeping up the north side of the stack. In just moments, this guy would be directly below.

As quietly as he could, Steve slid his body over to the south end of the stack and froze to carefully watch the young Asian man below. He slid his Beretta back into its leather sanctuary, lifted himself quietly into a crouch and launched himself out into space.

The man with the gun didn't know what hit him. Steve dropped the eight feet in a practically horizontal position and landed perfectly, tensed arms and hands clamping down on his shoulders as the full weight of his body collapsed his victim to the ground. He landed on top of the falling body, letting it cushion his landing. To make sure the man didn't get up, Steve grabbed the back of his head and slammed it face first into the hard ground.

But the cry of pain when they first landed was inevitable.

"Tang Xi?" a soft voice called out from beyond the stack, and Steve sought out the voice. A shadow rustled around the corner from the north end of his stack. Before he was seen standing over his victim, Steve quickly crossed the passageway to the next row in the maze. He crept along that stack, coming up behind the voice, until he was at the corner, within striking distance. The Asian turned to continue his search and Steve struck. He kicked his left leg out, knocking the MPK away. It clattered to the ground. Steve brought his right knee up and into the Asian man's kidney. He doubled over to the side, letting a cry escape his lips as he went to his knees.

Steve pushed past and snatched up the MPK. The Asian suddenly looked up with wide eyes as Steve brought the MPK down on his head in a solid butt stroke. The Asian killer went to the ground in a twist. Ordinarily, he would cuff the man and attempt an arrest, but now was the not the time. Not without cover officers watching his back, not with two more killers stalking him. Not when he was out in the cold as he was.

Steve detected movement off to his right as two more men sprinted around another stack of boards, attracted by the noise. Steve let off a burst from the MPK as he danced backwards. He dodged in between two more stacks, trying to once again lose himself in the maze. Bullets tore into the wood, throwing shavings everywhere.

Steve zigzagged through the maze, away from

the gunfire. He suddenly found himself stepping into the open at the edge of the lumber stacks. He stopped to orient himself. Just to his north was the perimeter fence of the lumber yard, and it turned and blocked the west side off as well. Beyond the western fence, he could hear the crash of the surf. He decided that would be his best way out of here. In that direction, he spotted an old rusty shed with a flatbed truck parked next to it. He broke from the cover of the lumber and sprinted in that direction. Seconds later, a fresh burst of automatic fire erupted behind him, spurring him along.

At the back of the truck, he leapt, and rolled onto the flat bed. He kept going, scrambling onto the roof of the truck, and then onto the corrugated steel roof of the shed. A line of slugs tried to follow him, punching holes into the back of the truck and shattering the dirty windshield.

Steve sighted on the muzzle flash and let go a long burst from the captured MPK. His assailant ducked back into the stacks of wood. The MPK came up empty in his hands, so he dropped it to the ground. He slid down the back side of the roof and dropped several feet to the ground, now outside the yard.

Steve found himself in darkness, away from the sparse light of the lumber yard. His eyes adjusted quickly, and he looked around at the wide open space around him. Throughout the grassy terrain, he saw no cover, nothing to conceal himself. He was able to read a nearby sign that identified the area as "Noyo Headlands Park." The coast beyond was steeped in the shadow of the rock formations. Maybe he could find a place there to hide, if he could make it that far. He took off running. He heard the shout behind him, which spurred his desire to find cover. The ocean was getting closer, the crash of the waves louder. He veered northward, soon seeing the coastline, and he searched for any kind of sanctuary from his pursuers. In the darkness, it seemed none of the Asians had picked up his trail yet.

He reached the edge of a short cliff, with waves crashing and frothing onto dark algae-covered rocks just twenty feet below. Further along, he spotted a ledge just a few feet down, cut into the coastline by centuries of random sporadic surf. He jumped down to it. He paused there, looking out across the wide open terrain between him and the lumber yard. He thought he saw shadows moving, but it might have been the darkness playing tricks on him. He no longer heard their voices over the surf pounding in his ear from below. He crept along the ledge, watching the lumber yard and looking for his opportunity to put some more distance between it and himself.

Just as he rose once more to scope the area, something suddenly barreled into him. They found me, he suddenly realized, feeling a body knock him backward. He fell back onto the ledge and threw an arm out to keep from rolling off the edge into the wet rocks below.

Instinct took over before he realized. He saw motion that swung down toward him, and he threw up his left hand. He caught a wrist inches from his body and put an iron grip on it. He then saw that wrist was molded around a shiny knife blade that looked awfully big. He struggled but found himself locked in this position underneath the man with the knife. He looked past the blade to the face that was only inches from his own.

The attack and the struggle suddenly stopped.

Captain Stanson.

He wore a green Army soft cap, and his face was streaked with dark camouflage paint. Stanson bared his teeth in a smile, and even in the darkness, Steve saw that smile fall short of his eyes. "Welcome to *my* world, son."

A screech of tires reached their ears. Stanson let his protégé up and they glanced over the side of the ledge. A quarter mile away, they saw the Lexus burst out of the gate that it had shattered. The vehicle fishtailed loudly onto the road and headed away from them, toward the highway. In moments, they saw the headlights of both cars moving fast, indicating that the Asians had left in a hurry.

"I was a mile north of here when I heard the shots," Stanson hissed. "What are you doing here, son?"

"I'm after the drugs," Steve said. "Same as you, right?" It was a pointed question.

"The drugs are here," Stanson said. "I found Cleopatra Point. I saw them get picked up."

"My guess is they were picked up by our mysterious cop killer," Steve said. "I'm also guessing, you know him. Don't you?"

Stanson did not answer right away.

Frustrated, Steve once again scanned the coastline toward the lumber yard, using all his senses to search the night and the environment around them. "There's still no cops around," he muttered. The darkness covered the flash of guilt on the Captain's face.

Steve surged up and crept out from their rock ledge. The Asians had most likely fled the area completely, but he continuously watched for any signs of them. At the same time, he figured that, if the store clerk was OK, he would have called for help by now.

Steve started toward the fence, and Stanson followed him. Steve then broke into a jog, and the Captain joined him, managing to keep up. He led them further to the south toward the lumber yard fence. His intent was to get to the other side and circle toward the convenience store. He paused at the southwest corner and scanned the terrain ahead, finding no threats. They jogged the fence line to the next corner, by the alley that ran between the lumber yard and the convenience store, and once again checked the area.

Steve noted the sirens in the distance—finally, police were on the way. He scanned the parking lot where the Asians' cars had been and confirmed the vehicles were gone. That meant the clerk was probably OK, but he meant to check and make sure.

Steve ignored the shards of glass splashed across the sidewalk and trampled over them to the door. "Hello?" he shouted. He checked the front counter area and saw the scared clerk pop up from behind. He was holding a baseball bat. "It's OK," Steve said, seeing the bat. He opened his jacket to expose his badge. "Police, remember?"

"I called the Sheriff," the clerk stammered.

"Good. The shooters should be gone—" he cut off as Stanson appeared at the door.

"We don't have much time." The Captain glanced at the clerk, nodded to him. "How you doin'?" The clerk's jaw had dropped at the sight of his camo-painted face. Stanson nodded furtively for Blazer to follow him back outside.

"Just tell the cops I was here," Steve said, and they bolted out the door.

"Who are you?" the clerk shouted as they departed.

Steve didn't stop to answer.

"I'm not sticking around to talk to the Sheriff," the Captain said. "I suggest you come with me." They reached the SUV and jumped inside. Steve had the vehicle careening from the parking lot in seconds.

Moments later, they were traveling north on Highway One. Steve saw the flicker and reflection of red and blue lights before Sheriff's cruisers rounded a bend in front of them. He pulled to the right but did not stop the truck. Three patrol cars passed him, headed for the convenience store.

"My car's just over the bridge," Stanson told him.

"Now we're running from the cops?" Steve said.

"Moment of truth, Captain. I'm after that drug shipment. Are you with me or not?"

Stanson took a deep breath. After a moment in deep thought, he finally spoke. "Alright, son. It's time you knew what's really going on."

CHAPTER 6

The black SUV sped northward, across an old trestle and out of the city of Fort Bragg.

"Where's your car?" Steve asked.

Stanson pointed to a vista point parking lot ahead and Steve pulled up beside the vehicle. Stanson jumped out, and in seconds was back, throwing his ruck sack in the rear hatch. He returned to the passenger seat and Steve got them under way again.

Stanson pulled out his phone and brought up his mapping app. "I have a pretty good idea where he's going. There should be a road up here..."

Steve found it and made the right turn. They found themselves winding into the coastal hills. He turned on his high beams, but still couldn't get a good feel for the terrain outside.

"From what I could tell off this map, this is mostly farmland," Stanson said. "But near the end of this road there appears to be the beginning of an old logging road. My guess is, he found some old logging camp to hide in for the night, and tomorrow, he'll just slip away among all the normal traffic."

The miles, and the silence, seemed to stretch on. Steve tried in vain to discern the terrain outside but could only see the occasional light from a farmhouse or other residence. Stanson busied himself searching for any sign of what could be a logging road. Finally, with a glance at the phone screen, he said, "The road ahead curves to the right and ends, so..."

The curve appeared, and at the apex of that turn, Stanson spotted what he was looking for, a driveway that was grown over with bushes and ferns. A large rusted gate, which retained some traces of green paint, sat across the driveway.

"Keep going," Stanson directed him, now scanning the road revealed by the headlights. He spotted a cul de sac, and directed Steve to, "Turn around here."

Blazer parked his SUV, facing back the way they'd come and killed his headlights.

"We go on foot from here," Stanson said, eagerly climbing out.

Steve joined him at the rear hatch and placed his ruck sack next to Stanson's. They geared up and checked over their weapons. As Blazer finished checking the load on one of his pistols, he saw the Captain approaching the gate. He used his red-lensed flashlight to examine the gate. "There," he said as Steve approached. "The lock has been pried open, but he positioned it so it looked like it was still secured." He looked up into the dark forest. "He's in there, somewhere."

"Who is he, Cap?" Steve said patiently.

Stanson glanced at him, and Steve could see the look of pain and resolve even through the camo paint on his face. As he'd said before, it was time Blazer knew.

But first Stanson tugged at the gate, pushing it open just enough for them to walk through. It was difficult to see the logging road, which was completely overgrown with brush and ferns. Then Stanson led them off the road into the forest. He intended to use this as cover, but keep the road in sight nearby

"His name is Eli Smith," Stanson finally said. "He was part of a group I was involved with after the Vietnam War."

"Since when were you in the Vietnam War?" Steve asked.

"I wasn't. Jeez, kid, how old do you think I am? I was a teenager when the really heavy shit was happening over there. But I followed the news on the war very closely." Stanson stopped for a moment, and Steve knew it wasn't to catch his breath. He'd heard the break in his mentor's voice—the Captain was fighting his emotions. He took a breath. "I wasn't there. But my brother was."

Steve's steps faltered. "I've known you all these years, I never knew you had a brother."

"I don't talk about him much. My big brother Jed was ten years older than me and I idolized him. When I entered Middle School, he was already a Sergeant in the Green Berets. He went missing in his second tour in 'Nam. All through High School, I soaked up every bit of news about the war. While all my classmates were marching and protesting, I was looking into the heart of the beast. That's what got me into the CIA. All through my years at Berkeley, while everyone was rallying against the country and protesting everything America stood for, I was writing papers that supported the Anti-Communist reasons behind the war, and especially how Communism treated that region after the war. I also did ROTC and got very active in the military. I got my degree in three years instead of four, and I spent two years training with Special Forces. While at Berkeley, I was visited by a guy just a few years older than me, named Ross. That's it, just Ross."

"Déjà vu," Steve muttered. This was close to how

Stanson had drawn him into the world of special operations during his military days.

A light rain began to fall, the water finding its way easily through the tree branches overhead. For now, the two were protected sufficiently from the weather, wearing sturdy coats, and Steve had a camouflage poncho stashed in his ruck sack that he would bring out later. Stanson led the way through the darkness, and Steve kept just a few feet behind him, trying to listen to the story.

"Ross recruited me into the Company, and I ended up on a field ops team in Thailand working with him." Stanson once again paused to collect himself. "Our mission became near and dear to my heart. We went into Vietnam, Cambodia and Laos after MIAs and POWs."

Steve was stunned to hear this. He suddenly felt like he was hearing a piece of history.

***

1982

In less than a year, John Stanson was landing at Nakhon Phanom Royal Thai Navy Base. The plane was a charter arranged by the CIA. Stanson had heard all the stories about "Air America," secret air mobile missions in and out of Vietnam, Cambodia, Laos. He suspected that this plane was related to it, left over from it, or a continuation of it. Back at the Farm, he'd met with Ross, where his mentor had confirmed that John was still interested in his Special Ops outfit. When he told his protégé where he was going—but still wouldn't divulge what their mission was—Stanson's imagination was already speculating on what was really going on.

On this flight, he was the only passenger. The

lone plane slid to a halt in the middle of the tarmac, far from any terminal and any other plane. The strange move set Stanson's nerves on edge for a moment, and he bounced from one side of the plane to the other, checking portals for any activity. He didn't have any weapons to defend himself if anything should go down. He remembered the tradecraft that had been drilled into his head for the last year and started searching the plane for anything he could use as a weapon. Then, through one portal, he saw a vehicle approaching.

A white SUV pulled up to the plane. He recognized Ross getting out of the passenger seat. The driver, a black man with close-cropped hair, was looking the plane up and down. Ross made his way to the starboard entry hatch. Relaxing just a little, Stanson made his way to the entrance, and was ready when the door was opened from the outside.

The door dropped down to become a short staircase. Stanson ducked outside and bounded his way down.

"John, welcome to Thailand." Ross met him at the bottom and shook his hand. "This is Nakhon Phanom Royal Thai Navy Base, or just NKP. We have a small warehouse space in an isolated neighborhood a mile from here, but we'll be staging here out of NKP. We've spent the last few months looking over intel reports and setting up weapons assets."

Conversation for the moment dropped off. Ross was all business, as if he wanted to get Stanson out of there and to that isolated neighborhood as soon as possible. Stanson let himself be swept along. He went back to the plane and yanked open the underbelly door. He retrieved his only bag and threw it into the back seat of the SUV, then piled in with it. Ross returned to his position in the passenger seat.

"John, meet Harry," Ross said, indicating the

driver. "He matriculated from the Farm in the class before yours." To Harry, he said, "Let's go." Harry got them underway. He offered no greeting to the new guy, and Stanson took that cue, offering none in return. He was noticing a pattern, where last names were not used frequently, if at all.

The trip to their isolated neighborhood took just minutes. Like an enthusiastic tourist, John's eyes darted everywhere, taking in the sites outside the airbase. But he silently begged Ross to finally explain to him the mission they were here for. When they pulled into an alley behind a warehouse, Ross still had not spoken. As they clambered out of the SUV, Stanson finally asked.

"Ross, I've been training at the Farm for a while, and I've only seen you a few minutes at a time very infrequently since I started. I'm here, right where you want me. Don't you think it's about time you told me what the mission is?"

Ross smiled. "Come on in, son. You can meet the guys, and I'll tell you all about what we're here for."

He wrenched open a door to the warehouse, and John and Harry crowded in after him. He found himself in a dark corner of a wide-open bay, and gradually his eyes got used to the gloom. Ross kept walking across the warehouse, and the other two followed. They approached the opposite corner, and as he got closer, Stanson examined the setting.

It was set up like any company area or ready room for any of the military units he'd been attached to. At the right was a small lounge area. Two padded and garishly colored benches that looked tacky and uncomfortable were positioned at right angles. The benches faced a TV with rabbit ears. The TV was on and showing a Thai kids' show, but only one man was on the bench, and he appeared to be asleep. Farther to the right, in a darkened area,

Stanson could see several cots with mattresses, a sleeping area. Each area was partitioned off, giving at least some sense of privacy. On the other side of the lounge area, Stanson could see a table set up, and two men were poring over a map there. A fourth man stepped out of a room built into the corner, and Stanson could see it was a kind of armory. That man closed a door, which was really more of a cage, and latched a padlock to secure it.

Seeing the boss, the group stopped what they were doing and gathered near the table as Ross addressed them. "Everyone, this is John. We'll get to further introductions later. Right now, John wants to know what it is we do."

After over a year of preparation and suspense, Ross finally began to describe their mission. "Look around you, son. We're in Thailand. This is the neighborhood of the Golden Triangle. And just to our east is a little piece of real estate called Vietnam. Our country fought for that land, to try and keep it from falling under the rule of a form of government that kills the human spirit. That fight damn near tore our country apart, and a lot of good men lost their lives in that fight. Many of them did not know what they were fighting for, didn't realize how crucial the fight was. But you and I know. Some sacrificed their lives, and some simply lost their freedom."

Stanson had long suspected what the mission here might be. He'd known from the beginning that Ross was interested in his political viewpoint, but just as important, his knowledge of the Vietnam War. He felt like Ross's buildup was confirmation of what he believed all along.

As if reading his mind, Ross said, "When America pulled out of Vietnam, we left some 2500 MIAs behind. We're setting up a unit to go in and look for them."

Stanson was nodding even before the words registered. He was silently basking in triumph, not just that he'd simply guessed right. He was suddenly incredibly excited at the prospect of being a part of this mission. He wanted to get started right now, right this second.

Harry met his eyes and finally spoke. "I take it you approve of what you've been dragged into."

"Absolutely," John said enthusiastically. He couldn't tell by Harry's demeanor whether *he* approved. His fervor mellowed a bit. "How do the politics of this whole thing work?" he asked of Ross. "I've been following the news for a long time, and Vietnam has denied for years that anyone was left."

"And you believe them?" Harry asked.

The question was enough to satisfy him initially, but Ross went on. "The war ended in 1975 when North Vietnam broke the peace treaty and invaded the south. Saigon fell and the American embassy was evacuated."

Stanson remembered his research on the end of the war. The Paris Peace Accords, a treaty signed in Paris by representatives of the US and North and South Vietnam, took effect in January of 1973. America pulled most of her troops out of the country that year. However, North Vietnam violated the treaty on several occasions, and over the next year quietly moved troops into positions near major cities. The US military and Intelligence knew about this, but per the treaty, military forces had left the country, leaving a small contingent in the US Embassy in the city of Saigon. Just two years later, in April of 1975, North Vietnamese forces moved into Saigon. At that point, to Stanson's disgust, the US congress refused to offer any further aid to their South Vietnamese allies. The city fell to the Communists. The American Embassy was evacuated and abandoned. He was always blown away by the footage of choppers landing on the Embassy roof every couple of minutes to pick up passengers, and then taking off, only to have another one standing by to land.

"In 1973 when the treaty was signed, North Vietnam made a token gesture of returning a bunch of prisoners they'd been holding. But we at the Company knew of several prison camps that were still active. Gradually, other people at the Company have kind of backed off on the issue and forgotten, but not me. I've been personally monitoring those locations, and I mean to go in and check them."

Stanson looked over at his new boss with a new admiration. The man was a dedicated patriot. He felt the same debt to those who fought that war that John himself felt. If anyone was still here, Ross was determined to bring them home. "They seem to be keeping the flame of hope alive at home," Stanson commented.

"Yeah, we've gotten wind of a couple of missions to try a search. Some of them have been publicity stunts, and some have been ultimatums to try and force Vietnam into giving up information about any POWs they might still hold. A lot of families of service members want full investigations, and they're willing to do anything for information about their soldiers. I've got to warn you, John, what we do here may be unpopular with the US government. Vietnam has stated for the record that they have no more prisoners of war held captive. I know it's bullshit. But in the interest of diplomatic relations, the US has accepted it. And Vietnam has played that diplomacy for all it was worth. Any time there has been an inquiry, they ask for more and more aid, concessions, whatever they need at the time, in exchange for information that may not be verifiable.

The Communists have played dirty from the start, so now it's our turn."

Stanson's excitement level was still high. His mind had wrapped around the new mission. He was busting with patriotism and a call to duty, anxious to get to work. He did, however, have some nagging doubts. Ross's devotion to this mission seemed to mirror his own, but he suddenly wondered if the mission was official, or if they were there as part of someone's guilt trip. Either way, he vowed to give his heart to the job.

"Let's get you settled in, John. We're already planning our first trip into the jungle."

* * *

1983

He was used to the chopper rides by now. For nearly a year, every couple of months, they would board a helicopter, the familiar Bell UH-1 "Huey" chartered from the mysterious 'Air America' group that had ferried Stanson into Thailand in the first place. That chopper would fly them out into the jungle of some backwater pieces of real estate in what had once been North Vietnam. Ross had promised in the beginning that he had a list of past and present prison camps, and those camps were checked. To Stanson, their continuing mission was so noble in its purpose that it actually felt like a fantasy the first time they went in. And yet, they were successful. The first camp they had raided actually yielded a group of four American servicemen. The camp was destroyed, guard towers and huts blown up or burned down. Over a dozen Vietnamese soldiers were killed during the raid. As they pulled out on foot back to their landing zone, Stanson knew none of it would ever be publicized. The US would never admit to continuing operations in Southeast Asia, and the Vietnamese would not make claims of military incursions into their sovereign territory, or they would have to admit they still held Americans captive. The group flew back to Thailand, where the freed prisoners were nursed back to health over several days, debriefed by Ross, and then provided a means to quietly slip back into the US with a plausible cover story. Two months later, Ross and his team would do it all again.

Stanson glanced around the chopper. There were six men total, the same six he'd met when he first arrived. They'd treated him like any new guy for a while, somewhere between hazing, mistrust, or simply ignoring him for the time being. Except Harry. Despite his initial cold reception, he and Harry had become good friends. And despite a deliberate avoiding of using last names, Harry had disclosed his name as Harold Wayne. Their eyes met across the chopper, and Wayne nodded and smiled.

The chopper flew over the Cambodian border into Northern Vietnam, flying nape of the earth to avoid any radar. They were *really* low, Stanson felt like he could reach out and pick leaves from the trees. Before he knew it, they were descending into an open clearing. Following his training, Stanson tensed at the door, waiting for the skids to hit. He could see the grass below flattened by the wind from the rotors. When they touched down, he leapt to the ground, ran out about thirty feet, then dropped his light ruck sack and went prone behind it, using it as cover in case there were any ambushers waiting in the tree line. Around him, the others did the same, forming a 360-degree perimeter around the chopper. Behind him, the helicopter lifted away and steered back the way they came. It would return to NKP, and return twenty-four hours later, following a different route to this same landing zone.

One by one, the team stood and donned their equipment. They did a quick weapons check. Harry Wayne carried an extra surprise, an M-79 "blooper" grenade launcher, and he dropped open the breach to make sure it was loaded, then flipped it closed again.

The men gathered around Ross. He did a simple nod to the trees, and they started out on a march to find the next location on his target list of possible prison camps. His information had been good so far.

Today, they were walking through the jungles of North Vietnam, near the border with Cambodia. They operated much the same as Infantry patrols had during the war, though it was now more than seven years after the war ended. This was still a hostile part of the world, and Cambodia was in the midst of its own civil war. The Khmer Rouge worked these hills and jungles, and they made frequent cross-border excursions and even raids of villages. The jungle trails were filled with mines and booby traps, and the team needed to be on their toes to stay alive.

Pol Pot still ruled Cambodia, and his Khmer Rouge fighters were now engaged in fighting Vietnamese forces. Just a couple years ago, Khmer Rouge forces had invaded Vietnam, and pillaged numerous villes on or near the border. Those raiders were driven back by Vietnamese forces. Vietnam then in turn invaded Cambodia, and Vietnamese soldiers still held areas in the eastern portion of the country, near their own borders. Ross's intel said a group of Americans was being held in a camp along the border and used as laborers. Those Americans had been moved from location to location every few months, as the needs of the invading forces evolved. If the tide of the fighting shifted, those Americans could easily be killed on the spot and lost forever.

The morning wore on, and the team walked silently through the jungle. Stanson had memorized the topographical maps, and he noted land features as they passed them. They soon came to a ridge that would provide their observation point. The camp lay just beyond.

The team moved quietly and carefully up the ridge and found a small clearing from which to stage their raid. Ross and Stanson took up positions to watch the camp beyond, and Ross ordered a two-man team to scout off to the east.

The camp appeared empty. Stanson noted the features, similar to every camp they had raided in the last ten months. There was a small cluster of huts along the east side. The structure was typical, a frame with flimsy walls that in some cases only extended partway up to the ceiling. Other walls had window frames but no glass in them. The roofs were made of straw, thick enough to let the frequent rainwater slide off the edges. The floors were three feet off the ground, to guard against any possible flooding. Many jungle dwellings in this part of the world were built like this. The poor structure was further proof that this was designed to be a temporary location. The whole camp was surrounded by a loosely assembled, and therefore easily breached, bamboo fence.

As he noted each detail, Stanson grew more and more apprehensive. The camp did not look occupied. He had to wonder if they had come all this way for nothing.

As if in answer to his prayers, a lone man stepped out of one of the huts. He stretched as if just waking up. Then he looked up at some of the foliage surrounding him. He looked *up*, Stanson noticed, and filed that information away in case it led somewhere.

Something else hit him. One feature typical of most camps they'd raided was missing—guard towers. "Where's their over-watch?" he wondered out loud.

"There," Ross said, "the tree at that far corner. I see a two-man position up there. They're using the natural camouflage, but they've added to it."

Stanson trained his binoculars on the tree in question. It took a moment, but he finally saw the movement, a man ducking between branches to check the surrounding areas. The treetop perch offered a decent view of the surrounding areas, though it was limited by some terrain features. One of those features was the ridge they now hid behind. Stanson took the moment to scan other trees in the area, but so far could not find another "guard tower."

The two-man team returned, led by a CIA paramilitary named Dryden—despite everyone's avoidance of last names, this was what he insisted on being called. The group stayed low below the ridge.

Ross motioned them lower. As Dryden reached him, Ross said, "Stay down, we found spotters in a tree down there."

"I know," Dryden said, "We spotted them too. We found the dirt road that passes nearby. Still no sign of our boys yet."

Stanson continued to scan the area and confirm terrain features. The road to the east was on the map they'd studied. To the west, a narrow river scooped southward briefly to touch the jungle just a quarter mile from their location.

The camp was occupied. But was this a prison camp, or simply a military outpost? Were there any captive Americans?

They had to wait a couple hours for the answer. The sun was falling to the west when activity at the camp began to pick up. Two more men came from the hut, and they began building a fire, presumably for cooking dinner. Several minutes later, an entire group came from the hut, and they massed toward the east side, where the road passed nearby.

Moments later, a large group of Vietnamese entered the camp from that direction, and they herded a small group of four other figures. Those figures wore tattered black pajama-like outfits—like the Viet Cong used to wear, Stanson surmised. The men were taller than the Vietnamese. Through his binoculars, he could see they were white. They were very thin, almost emaciated, and walked slightly stooped, as if the world had beaten them down. Two of them walked with a limp.

Stanson was getting more and more excited. "We found them."

As they watched, one of the men stumbled and fell to his knees. Two of the Vietnamese swooped in and began swinging long sticks, beating the man about the back and torso. There was a flurry of shouting, curses in Vietnamese. A second man threw up his arms to avoid the blows from the sticks as he waded into the flurry. His shouts were audible from the ridge. "Stop it! You're killing him."

Harry adjusted his grip on his assault rifle, a CAR-15. With a glance, Stanson could see his whole body was tense, ready to explode into action.

"Easy, buddy," Stanson urged him. "They'll get theirs."

The scene was representative of how they knew many POWs were treated—and reaffirmed to each of them of their mission here.

One Vietnamese began barking orders at the men beating the prisoners. The prisoners were picked up and their weakened bodies were wrestled over toward one of the huts. For the first time, the team noticed a series of posts driven into the ground. There were ropes dangling from those posts. As they watched, the man who had fallen was strung up. The Vietnamese soldiers wrapped the ropes around his wrists. Another soldier went behind him near the huts. He picked up another rope, which they now saw was part of a pulley system. He pulled the two ropes, and the man tied up was raised first to his feet, then off the ground. He let out a brief cry, but then went silent.

Stanson was watching the man's anguish through his binoculars. He saw the movement of his body. He couldn't hear the sound his body made but could imagine it. "Son of a bitch. His shoulder just dislocated. Looks like he passed out from the pain."

The other three men were lined up in front of their strung-up comrade. The soldiers lined up behind them, AK-47s at the ready. The one who'd gone to his friend's aid was still shouting, and now crying, "You're killing him."

The man giving the orders barked another one, and a moment later, someone brought him a bucket of water. He threw that water in the face of his prisoner. The shock of the water woke him, and he suddenly started screaming again.

The commander wanted his prisoner conscious for his pain.

The soldiers looked on, some with blank looks and some with sadistic sneers. The commander stepped up behind the screaming strung-up prisoner. He twirled a bamboo stick, flailing it like a sword. He started shouting in Vietnamese, then swung at the prisoner's back. He cried out again, this time the bleat choked off in his throat. The commander swung again.

Through the binoculars, Stanson could see blood on that bamboo branch.

"Dryden," Ross said. "Head off to the east and get ready to move. Take out that tree spotter first. Weapons free when you hear my shot. Harry, ready on the blooper, I need the fence breached, and I want those buildings to burn. That commander is mine."

They all knew what this meant. They were jumping the gun by a great deal. Their plan was to observe through the night, get into place, and hit just before dawn when the senses of the guards were at their lowest. They were now still an hour from dusk, and their chopper would be almost back to NKP by now.

For all they knew, this public torture session would lead to an execution. Each of these CIA men was like Stanson, a cauldron of anger that their nation's heroes were now on the verge of a death no one would know of. No way they would let something like this happen while they could stop it. No way. They would follow their original plan and kill 'em all.

With a smile on his face, Dryden picked up and moved off, with one other man. Next to John, Harry dropped open the breach of his M-79 grenade launcher, made sure a high explosive round was ready to fly down range. He closed it back up, quietly so it would not be heard down in the camp.

"Ross, we have some good cover off to the left there," Stanson nodded to a patch of trees down toward the river. "Harry will have a good angle on the huts when the shooting starts."

"Go," Ross said. "I'll join you after I take this son of a bitch out."

John and Harry rose and trotted off, keeping just below the ridge. When they reached a plateau twisted with exposed tree roots, they dropped to the ground and crawled rapidly across them. One tree had been downed nearby, and they slithered up to it. Stanson glanced over at Harry, and knew he was gauging the distance to the row of huts across the way. Stanson picked his targets, the soldiers holding rifles on the remaining prisoners. The bad guy on the ropes would be Dryden's target. Dryden would be across the camp, but not in a position that would create a dangerous crossfire.

Stanson raised his CAR-15 over the downed tree and sighted in on one soldier to the left.

Ross's shot split the afternoon. The camp commander suddenly stiffened as blood erupted from his chest. He fell backward and landed spread eagle.

From two different positions, Stanson and Dryden fired simultaneously. The soldier holding the ropes was next to go. He fell, and the tied-up soldier fell with him. Stanson hit his target from behind. In this situation, he had no issues with shooting a bad guy in the back.

Harry's grenade launcher popped. Just yards away, a section of the fence was splintered by the explosion. A second canister arced across the camp and pierced the thin wooden wall of a hut. An instant later, an explosion gutted the building. They could actually see the walls bow outward as windows and doors belched fire. Fire caught and began to consume the hut. Harry had already reloaded and launched his third grenade.

Men suddenly spilled out of the second hut. Six more Vietnamese soldiers joined the ones on the field. Those six were the last to leave the hut alive. Two more were caught in the door when Harry's grenade entered through a nearby window and exploded. They were bathed in fire and shrapnel that found an outlet through the same door. Only pieces of their bodies reached the outside air.

Automatic fire could now be heard over the echoing explosions. Stanson checked the Americans. Satisfied, he saw that their military training had returned. As soon as the gunfire started, they dropped to the ground.

He suddenly picked out muzzle flashes in the tree-line across the camp. Dryden had switched to automatic and was hosing down the enemy soldiers. There were now six Vietnamese in the camp, and they seemed to orient their fire in Dryden's direction. Stanson used that, taking the time to pick out his targets and snipe them. One shot could easily be lost in the confusion, and Stanson took out two more men before the Vietnamese figured out the game plan.

The Vietnamese briefly turned their rifles in Stanson's direction. They first sent random bursts of lead into the trees. Stanson ducked for the moment, thinking maybe they hadn't yet discovered their cover. That thought was soon dashed. A row of slugs tore into the top of the dried tree trunk, showering them with wood chips.

Stanson caught sight of Ross coming around the end of the ridge. His boss ducked behind a tree, stopping to inspect activity in the camp. The surviving Vietnamese appeared to be scattering, running for shelter, but throwing out random bursts to cover their retreat.

A loud yell suddenly rang out across the camp. All three on the west side checked the source, and knew it was not good.

Dryden had broken cover and was screaming like a crazy man. He fired off a burst from his CAR-15, and his rounds chased one Vietnamese soldier running for the tree-line. Dryden continued to fire. He stopped on a very small rise just to the south of the first burning hut, but he was completely exposed, and acting like he did not care.

His magazine ran dry.

At that very instant, a single crack split the camp. As he reached for a spare mag, Dryden spun and fell to the ground.

Surveying the action from behind his tree, Ross had seen where that shot had come from. Stanson followed his line of sight to the treetop observation post—Dryden had apparently been unsuccessful in his attempts to take him out.

"Son of a bitch," Ross muttered. He quickly sighted on movement he saw there and pumped off two single shots. The treetop rustled, and a Vietnamese soldier plunged through the leafy branches. He landed in a heap in the center of the camp.

As soon as the dead man landed, Stanson jumped from cover. He regretted for a moment leaving cover so quickly, fearing a second gunner might be in the tree. Behind him, Ross took care of that by hosing the tree house with lead. No one else appeared. Stanson had seen at least one gunner escape toward the north, and he kept his rifle oriented that way. Ross and Harry left cover behind him, scanning the area three hundred sixty degrees for any further threats.

"Harry, cover the north, and kill that last hut on our way out," Ross ordered. Harry slung the empty 'blooper' grenade launcher and grabbed his CAR-15. Ross diverted away to check on Dryden, where one of their teammates was already kneeling over him. Approaching the downed Americans, Stanson saw what happened when Ross reached them. Dryden's partner looked up at the boss and shook his head.

Stanson reached the first American, the one crying for his tortured friend. As he reached him, Stanson got a better look at the man's condition. He was dirty and smelled like he was long overdue for a shower. His body was emaciated and scarred. He saw no blood. Stanson grabbed the man's wrist and felt for a pulse, and he found it strong. Nearby, the other two Americans were rising to their knees to see what was going on. "Listen up," Stanson announced, "We're American soldiers. We're here to take you home."

All four men's eyes went wide. The first man surged to his feet and scrambled over to his friend to check him. The other two looked at each other, and one whispered, "Home?"

Stanson followed the first man. His friend had sprawled on the ground, his wrists still tied though the ropes were limp. Stanson crouched and whipped a knife from his boot. He sawed at the ropes and took a moment to triage the man. His back was bruised, and one blow had split the skin. Stanson eyed the dislocated shoulder.

The man was still conscious, breathing steadily, though his breaths were broken. "Did you hear, Sarge?" his buddy whispered to him. "We're going home!"

"Take these ropes and form a sling for that arm," Stanson directed him. As he did so, Stanson finally took the opportunity to ask the question that came up with each rescue he made. "I'm looking for someone, he's also MIA. His name is Jed Stanson. Do you know him?"

At first, he got no response, and he leaned in, catching the man's attention. He repeated his question. He got only a shrug in response.

Nearby, Stanson caught Harry's gaze. John knew the look, and he knew that Harry had read his expression as well. Wayne knew the situation with his MIA brother, and could tell that his friend had come up with another disappointment.

Ross joined their group, and the last two men on their team were carrying a crudely fashioned stretcher, made with two straight bamboo logs and a poncho folded around them. Dryden's body lay on that stretcher, covered by another poncho. Stanson felt the dejection of the entire team, losing one of their own. But he looked at the four Americans in their tattered clothes, bearing the scars of the war that burned in them long after their country willfully forgot them. Somehow, they stood just a little taller. Even the injured man had been helped to his feet.

Ross surveyed the entire plateau, the smoking and burning huts, and the bodies of the Vietnamese soldiers. The smoke and noise might attract patrols of the Khmer Rouge if they happened to be nearby. "I just called the chopper," he announced, "they've already refueled and are returning. Let's move out. Harry, if you'll do the honors."

Harry nodded. He stayed as the others filed toward the ridge where they'd hidden. As the prisoners and their rescuers left the camp, he backed toward the trail after them. He leveled his M-79 grenade launcher and loosed one last 40mm cartridge. His aim was true, and the last hut belched fire through its windows and doors, gutted by shrapnel and flame. It joined the other huts as they burned to the ground.

In just over an hour, the group had returned to their landing zone. They spread out among the jungle growth near the edge of the clearing, lest a group of Khmer Rouge come along and take an interest.

Stanson maintained his battle alertness, constantly scanning the jungle around them with his eyes and ears. He felt thrilled, happy that they had found four more Americans to bring home. At the same time, there was an underlying disappointment. Jed was still out there, maybe dead—or maybe waiting to come home.

"Thank you," a voice croaked beside him. It was the American who'd cried over his buddy being tortured. "I'm Sergeant Willoughby, US Army. I was on an Infantry patrol back in 1969. We were ambushed and I was captured. I don't know how long I've been with this same group of NVA. We just came to that camp maybe a month ago. They move us around a lot. It's getting to be springtime, so they planted a little farm just up the road from that camp location. My buddy, Sergeant Harlowe, he's just had really bad luck. He's survived two bouts of malaria in the last two years. In one of them, he was working too slow, so the guards beat him. Got him so bad they broke his knee. They braced it, but still made him work, and the leg didn't heal right. He ain't walked right since then. I was afraid it was going to happen again when he fell today."

Stanson felt his heart doing a mile a minute, listening to a slice of this man's life for the last fourteen years. "How did you get through the day, going through shit like that?"

Willoughby didn't seem to know how to answer that question. "It's like…it's all we know. The war seems so long ago. What year is it?"

"It's 1983. April."

Willoughby was shocked to hear this. "So many years." He seemed to drift off for a moment. "It will be nice to get back to Mississippi, though." He got lost in a daze again, as if dreaming of his home. "I'm sorry about your buddy dying."

It was the only lucid thought he could express for the moment. It was just as well. Stanson had detected the sound of helicopter rotors, and their chopper was soon a speck that began to grow on the southern horizon. For Sergeant Willoughby, Sergeant Harlowe, and their two friends, the tragedy that was their Vietnam experience would soon be over. In minutes they would leave this hell behind.

* * *

The helicopter deposited them at NKP and took off for parts unknown. The Land Rover they had driven to the airfield in was still parked against a nearby hangar. It was a bit of a walk, and difficult for the liberated Americans, but they moved with eagerness now. Dryden's body, now sealed in a body bag, was loaded into the back. With four extra people, it was a tight fit to get everyone in. Harry got them underway, headed back to their warehouse headquarters.

Ever observant, Stanson picked up on something wrong as they reached the warehouse. It wasn't just the fifteen-year-old Mercedes parked in the alley where typically only their Land Rover was parked. It was Ross's reaction to that vehicle. His brow furrowed; eyes narrowed. John could see the man's mind now racing.

"Harry," Ross said, "take our new friends into town and get them some real food. Take your time, come back in an hour. John, help me take Dryden's body inside."

Now everyone was curious about the issue. Ross slipped from the vehicle, and Stanson followed him to the back. They hoisted the body bag out, and Ross quietly closed the back door. The truck immediately shoved off and disappeared behind the neighboring warehouse. When it was gone, Ross and Stanson carried the body to the door and inside.

Whoever their visitors were, they didn't seem to care about the element of surprise. When they entered the warehouse, Ross strode boldly across the wide-open space, not knowing what to expect but acting like he did.

Standing in their common area, Stanson saw three men waiting for them. All three wore casual wear, khaki pants and heavy white cotton button down shirts. One was taller than the other two with a slightly receded hairline, and he wore a green bush vest over his shirt. A nine-millimeter was stuffed in the front of his pants.

One man stepped forward from the group. He was older, and his gray hair was mussed. He looked rumpled, like the heat and bustle of Thailand was not his scene. "Ross," he greeted them. "I take it your latest foray into the bush was not the success you wanted."

Ross lowered the body bag to the floor. "It went fine."

The older man smirked at the ironic reply. "Can we talk in private?"

Ross replied a little too loudly. "We're all friends here, Agent Johnson. Speak your mind."

Stanson watched closely the man Ross had called Agent Johnson—the name was most likely an alias. Johnson turned away, eyes glancing around the spartan setting inside the warehouse. It seemed to be a body language thing, a way to distract the agent.

"Agent Ross, I want you to know that your team has done an outstanding job this past year, bringing our people home from Vietnam. Even in the times when you checked a location and found no captive Americans, your service to your country and her people has been exemplary. But for the moment, your team is going into stand-down pending reassignment."

"Johnson, you can't do this," Ross shouted. "We freed four of our guys today. I've got more sites to check—"

"Damn it, Ross you were ordered to stand down yesterday!" Johnson exploded. "You went behind my back and bribed that Air America pilot. You've put all our asses in the spotlight. This has become a diplomatic and political nightmare, and the Company wants it stopped."

Stanson couldn't believe he was hearing this. He

believed in this mission; he was doing a great service to his country. Not only were they cutting that off, they were taking away his opportunity to find his brother. "Bullshit!" he shouted. "Our guys are still out there. We just proved that. Do you really give a damn what the diplomats say? North Vietnam has been playing them since the treaty. We're here to set this shit right, and I intend to do that!"

Stanson took a breath. His blood was boiling, he felt his self-control slipping away. When his blazing eyes examined Johnson, the patronizing smile there was almost too much.

Johnson turned to leave. His entourage started with him, and they picked up the body bag with Dryden's remains. They started for the door. Johnson stopped next to Ross and put an ironically father-like hand on the Agent's shoulder. "We'll meet again in three days. In the meantime, see that your charges get sent home through your usual channels."

Stanson glared at their backs until they were out the door. He then turned his ire on Ross. "What the hell did he mean, you were told to stand down?"

Guilt showed on the older man's face. "I met with them before we left. I had to report that in the last camp we checked, we found only one skeleton half-buried. I gave him the dog tags we found. The fact that we found no one fit their agenda." He huffed an angry sigh. "They gave me the song and dance about the political bullshit. US Diplomats are trying to reconstruct relations with the Communist government. The Viets know this, so for the last couple years they would dangle the potential release of POWs in exchange for political favors. The diplomats negotiate and grant them those favors, but the POW release never happens. They've recently started denying that they hold any more prisoners. Diplomats are now accepting that story. Now this team finding POWs is becoming an embarrassment to those negotiations."

"It's not embarrassing the Americans," Stanson sneered. "It's embarrassing the Vietnamese. The US wants to help them save face to keep those two-faced commies at the negotiating table, and they're sacrificing all the MIAs to do it."

"They're about to sacrifice *us*," Ross exploded. "They want to reassign us and they already threatened to shut us down and send us back to the States. The next step is to wind up hunted down and terminated by some contract wet-work specialist. I'd rather stay alive and find a new way to contribute to our great nation."

"Our great nation?" Stanson shook his head. "How can you say that after what they just did?"

Ross's voice dropped to a low rumble. "America didn't do that, son, just a few cowards buried in the bureaucracy. You still have your beliefs, John. You love this country as much as I do. That's why I brought you on board. Hold on to that."

Stanson calmed down for a moment, letting those words sink in. "No," he suddenly said. "No, the hell with that, and the hell with them. My brother is still out there somewhere, even if he's been reduced to just a dog tag. I came here to find him, and any others. I'll go rogue if I have to."

"No, John. I need you. I need you with me to make this right."

At that moment, the door opened, and Harry and the others led the rescued prisoners in through the door Johnson had just left. The prisoners spread out to look around the warehouse space, and the team members started to show them around. Harry edged up to John and Ross. "I was going to take them to get some food, but I decided we should hang in the background for a few. We saw them leave." With a glance at his friend John, he added for Ross, "Everything all right?"

Without answering the question, Ross called out, "Everyone gather around."

The team guided their new friends over. Ross gave them a speech he'd given several times since they'd been in Thailand. "Men, you're on the first leg of your journey home. No matter what you feel, or what you've heard goes on back home, your country is proud of you. Never forget that, and never doubt it. That being said, I hope you're not expecting a parade or a hero's welcome when you get home. Soldiers coming home from Vietnam a decade ago were not made to feel welcome generally."

Stanson knew that firsthand. When his brother Jed came home from his first tour, young Johnny and his parents had been waiting at the airport. Two random passersby, a couple, actually took a moment out of their day to assault him. The woman called him a sadistic murderer, and her boyfriend spit in his face. They continued on their way. Jed wiped it off and went on to meet the family like it had not affected him. But young Johnny could see that it had.

Ross went on. "We've put together a briefing for you to go over that will show you how the end of the war came about and how things have changed back in the states. I want to get you guys back home in the next couple days, but we won't be able to do it the traditional way. You're going to have to reappear in your lives with a cover story regarding where you've been the last few years. Typically, we'll have you say you came back quietly after the war and retreated from life for a while to get your head on straight, so you went to work odd jobs in a neighboring state the last few years. Beyond that, you just can't talk about where you've been or what you've done. The longer you stick with that cover story, the better.

"In the meantime, let's feed these guys and clean them up. Harry, will you do the honors and order us some takeout. Use the big menus. I have a feeling our new friends will be hungry." The big smiles on the ex-POWs told him he was right.

* * *

Three days passed. Stanson was continuously on edge, knowing what was coming for their team. No matter how much Ross pleaded with him, Stanson didn't know if he could accept the loss of their primary mission. What Ross had said had merit. Stanson was a patriot to his core. That made it more difficult to turn his back on POWs he knew were still out there. Stanson kept himself busy by preparing for a next mission he knew may never come.

Before their last flight to Cambodia, Ross had shared with him another location of a POW camp site. Stanson took several opportunities to study maps of that location and the surrounding terrain. He'd told Ross at the time he'd go in alone if he had to. He didn't know if he could or would, but maybe this would show the team how serious he was—and not the least, show himself.

Except for the tension in their warehouse, it was a typical afternoon. While Stanson busied himself at the table with the maps, Harry and the others relaxed in the lounge area watching Thai television with half an eye or reading or sleeping in the bunk area. Because of the tension and the uncertainty, when Ross entered the warehouse, everyone rose to gather in their briefing area.

Ross was not alone. Trailing behind him was a large man, over six feet tall, muscular, with thinning blond hair and a certain darkness to his face. Stanson recognized him as one of the enforcer-types who'd come in with Agent Johnson before.

Ross glanced around the circle at each of his men. His eyes seemed to linger on John Stanson. "Guys, there's no way around it. We've been reassigned. Because we're here and in place, ready to go at a moment's notice, the Company has a task they'd like us to take on."

"Son of a bitch," Stanson muttered. He was about to turn on his heel, grab a rifle, walk out the door and disappear into the countryside of Thailand.

"John, bear with me. You'll want to hear this. There's rumors of a drug ring working out of the Golden Triangle. They'd like us to investigate."

Harry spoke up. "There's been rumors about drug rings from these parts since the war. A lot of GIs got strung out in country and most of them got supplied by the natives."

"A lot of them continued their habits when they got home," Stanson growled. "Heroin was just as prevalent back in the States. The hippies buying the shit really were doing their patriotic duty. Some of those rumors say that the CIA itself was running those drugs to pay for the war."

"That's never been proven," the newcomer stated.

"Guys, allow me to introduce Eli Smith, formerly with the United States Marine Corps," said Ross. "He was with Security forces at the US Embassy in Saigon when they were overrun in '75."

"Just a green Marine, all of eighteen," Smith grinned.

Stanson eyed the newcomer. If he was an eighteen-year-old Marine at the Embassy during the fall of Saigon, that made Smith just a couple years older than himself.

"Smith has been looking into drug activity here in Thailand, so he's going to be our point man on this job."

"As I was saying," Smith began again, "A lot has been made of allegations that the Company smuggled opium and heroin out of the Golden Triangle. The press has played up the myth. They're even making movies about it. There have been numerous internal inquiries, but nothing has ever come of it."

"Is this someone's way of proving once and for all that we're the good guys and we don't do that shit?" Stanson asked. "To show you we're not drug smugglers, we're going after the real drug smugglers?"

Smith smiled, and it gave him a look that Stanson instantly disliked. "There may be something to that." He paused a moment. "I've been looking into cartels in this area, and I've made some connections between some people, including shipments being sent out to the States and who picks up those shipments. I've found a couple of sites that I suspect are being used, up in the northern part of Thailand, near Burma. I'm not sure which ones yet. We're headed down to Bangkok. I've got some people I can ask."

"Ask?" Harry brought up.

Smith grinned again, and Stanson decided on the best adjective for the image—sadistic.

"They may have to be persuaded."

Stanson could tell where Harry was going with his one-word question, and he could tell that Harry was as incredulous as he was. This sounded less and less like a mission and more like their team being used as someone's personal strike team.

For now, he could only stick around and see how it played out.

* * *

They rode the streets of Bangkok in a rented panel truck. Smith ran point on the mission, and he remained tight-lipped about what his plan was. When asked about shelter away from prying eyes of curious citizens and Bangkok Police, Smith mentioned a safe house but gave away no clue as to a location. Smith procured the truck, and Smith did the driving. Smith had elected to keep the team to a minimum, taking only the three of them and leaving the other three at NKP. Once their transportation was obtained, Stanson and Wayne were relegated to riding in darkness in the back, while Smith and Ross rode in the cab.

At first their conversation was limited. "I don't like this," Stanson mumbled.

"You and me both, brother," Harry responded.

In ten minutes, the truck ground to a stop. Stanson tracked by sound the cab doors opening, Smith and Ross approaching to open the back. Stanson shielded his eyes briefly from the sunlight when the doors opened to a limited view of the city.

"Time for a recon, boys," Smith said.

They hopped down to the pavement, and Stanson saw that the truck had been pulled into an alley behind a decaying two story building. Smith led them to the mouth of the alley. Their alley was cut off from the nearby streets by a small lot behind two buildings, and it offered them a buffer zone of safety. They got a better look at life on the streets of Bangkok. They observed men and women walking back and forth, riding bikes, carrying baskets of fruit and other foods, as well as cages with live animals like chickens and pigs, to a nearby marketplace.

"We have two targets. They rent that warehouse across the street. It's supposed to be used for importing and exporting a lot of foods from the market down the street. That's the legitimate front. After hours, they use the place as a way station for shipping opium."

The story was so thin they could see through it. John glanced from Harry to Ross. Wayne scowled, still not liking the situation, and Ross would not meet his gaze.

"Ross and I will make contact, posing as Russian shippers. We're going to lure them to the back of the truck. When we open the doors, you be there, weapons ready. We'll get them inside real quick-like and be gone."

Hearing the plan, Stanson took an extra moment to examine their destination. He found another alley next to the warehouse, where Smith would likely put the truck. He checked areas above and concluded there would be reasonable cover. He still didn't like the situation, and he believed nothing good could come of their actions here. But he was committed for the moment. At Smith's bidding, he and Harry boarded the truck again, and Smith got them under way.

The trip to their destination only took a couple minutes. As they waited in darkness, Stanson again tracked the sounds heard outside the truck. The doors slammed as Smith and Ross left the vehicle. Minutes passed in silence, while they were inside the warehouse. Smith was running a game on the occupants, a ruse to get them outside. They finally heard voices and another door closing. For a moment, Stanson could not tell what was being said, or whether the voices were in English, Russian, Thai...

The locks on the door were noisily thrown open, and the doors yawned open. Sunlight flooded in. Despite his eyesight being momentarily compromised by the sudden light, Stanson was ready with his sidearm aimed down at the two Asians standing there, shocked at their sudden turn of fate.

"Into the truck, now!" Smith ordered them.

Even as he punctuated that sentence, one of

them turned to run. Smith was on him immediately. The Asian tried to run past him, but Smith grabbed him with powerful arms. He threw the man back toward the truck. The Asian landed awkwardly against the bumper. He involuntarily stepped forward. Smith landed a devastating fist into the man's gut, then an uppercut to his face. The punch was powerful enough to overcome gravity, and the Asian flew up and back into the truck bay. He landed with his legs draping over the side. Harry leaned down and dragged the man inside. Smith grabbed the second one and bodily flung him into the truck. He swung the doors closed, and before anyone was ready, the CIA men and their prisoners were caught in darkness.

Harry was ready with a flashlight, and he searched frantically for a moment for their prisoners, lest they take advantage of the darkness and mount a quick attack. He found them huddled at the opposite wheel well, the unhurt man cradling his stunned and bleeding partner. Their terrified eyes stared back at the Americans.

"Keep them pinned," Stanson said, raising his weapon, "I've got them covered."

They rode on in silence.

* * *

Even with all his experience keeping track of movement of a vehicle while in a darkened space, Stanson was not as familiar with the streets of Bangkok as he could be, and there was no way to keep track of where they were. The trip took fifteen minutes, and the truck finally stopped. Stanson remained with his gun tirelessly covering the two Asians. Once again, when the rumble of the engine stopped, he was able to trace Ross's and Smith's movements as they walked down either side of the truck. In moments, the back doors were swinging open again.

"Stand up," Stanson commanded. He did not motion with the gun, and there was a reason behind this. A moment later, the two rose to their feet confirming his theory—they did speak English, they understood him. Outside, Smith motioned for the two to make their way down to the ground.

The one who Smith tangled with approached first. Stanson noticed a difference in the way he moved. He must have recovered somewhat during the trip. He suddenly took two running steps and launched himself out the back of the truck. With a scream, he lunged at Smith, going for the throat.

In the short time that Stanson knew Smith, he'd seen he was not someone easily surprised. As the agile Asian flew at him, Smith simply bent his legs, dropping down a couple inches. A powerful arm went up, perfectly aimed and catching the flying Asian in the gut. Smith turned, using the man's momentum to throw him. The Asian tumbled to the pavement and rolled, sprawling against a row of metal trash cans.

As the man came to rest, Ross stepped up to him, gun pointed down at him. "Get up," he said simply.

As the man got shakily to his feet, Smith directed the whole group, "Up the steps."

Stanson hopped out of the truck and was finally able to see where they were. They'd pulled into an alley not unlike the one these two were snatched from. The steps Smith indicated led up to the second floor of what appeared to be an apartment building. This must be the safe house Smith told them about.

Being the one familiar with the setting, Smith led the way upstairs. In through the door and down a short hallway, he let the group into a small two-room flat. Ross closed the door behind the group.

Smith didn't waste any time. As soon as the door closed, he grabbed the uninjured prisoner and maneuvered him roughly into a wooden chair poised in the center of the room. Stanson found from the beginning that he needed to be able to react to what someone unpredictable like Smith did, both to keep up with the action and to survive any situation. As the first Asian was secured to the chair, he grabbed the second one to hold him fast from rushing to his partner's aid.

Smith had grabbed a roll of duct tape from a countertop nearby and was wrapping tape around his prisoner's wrists, taping them to the arms of the chair. "Put him there," he said, pointing to a second chair nearby.

When both Asians were taped to the chairs, Smith stood before them, examining them. They looked back up, both with defiant stares. But Stanson was more intent on Smith's expression. There was a wave of something dawning over the big American's face. He smiled down at their prisoners, but there was no cheer. He smiled with menace. Whatever happened next, Smith was going to enjoy. Stanson feared he knew what was on the man's mind.

"Here's the thing, guys," he began. "You don't know me. I know you. I know about your involvement in the opium smuggling. I know that up north in the Triangle, some bad guys are putting together a shipment to bring to your warehouse, which you will then distribute to several other buyers."

Smith suddenly pulled out a knife, a large Army-issue bayonet. The razor-sharp blade glinted from the light overhead. Stanson now had a better idea what might be coming, and he wanted so badly to step forward and put a stop to the impending torture. But he stayed riveted where he stood.

Smith kept talking, and waving the blade in the air almost casually, like it wasn't even there. "You guys are going to tell me who's bringing the shipment to you, and you're going to tell me who your buyers are. If you don't tell me, things will be very unpleasant."

He turned to the one who had already attacked him twice. It was more like he zeroed in on him. That man had a blood trail running down his lip. Smith leaned in close, leaning on one of the man's wrists, fastened to the chair arm. The Asian was not gagged, and he flinched ever so slightly, even as he tried not to react at all. "How about it, slick? Any names rolling around that brain of yours? Who's bringing you the opium?" As he spoke, as he kept his eyes locked into those of the Asian, he slowly brought the knife into position. It suddenly ripped upward, tearing open the bottom half of the man's button-down Hawaiian shirt. The Asian let out a soft gasp—that really had taken him by surprise. Smith seemed to feed on that. His smile widened ever so slightly.

"Go to hell, Yankee Devil!" the Asian shouted. "You all die!" He then let out a string of phrases in another language, and Stanson recognized them. The man was speaking Vietnamese. How about that, he thought, someone from Vietnam working the dope trade all the way over in Thailand.

Smith still stood over the man, looking down at him with a probing expression of curiosity. He suddenly lashed out, and the fist holding the knife smashed flat against the man's mouth. Blood sprayed across the Vietnamese's face, and he toppled backwards, chair and all landing on its back.

Stanson stayed where he was.

On the floor, the Vietnamese man leaned his head aside, spat out blood and at least one piece of a tooth.

Smith dropped to a knee next to him. "I'm sorry," he said, laughing the apology. "I guess I get carried away." He hoisted the Vietnamese back to his sitting position. "You know what? I like you. You've got balls. I was going to let you sit for a few minutes and go talk to your buddy over here, but I'm having fun with you. You're going to be harder to break, but we are going to have some fun."

He leaned in close, and all good humor dropped from his voice. "You know what I want to do? I want to see you from the inside out. I want you to see your own blood flowing." While his eyes held those of the Vietnamese, distracting him, the knife had moved into position. Smith suddenly wrenched the knife, slicing upward. Another button popped off. The man's shirt opened a little further. The sudden movement drew a soft cry of fear from the prisoner, which drew another sadistic smile from the American. Smith stood up and ripped the shirt all the way open, exposing the man's wiry torso. He rested the knife blade on his chest and traced it lightly over his skin, first up to his shoulder, then menacingly across his throat. "I want to slice you open and dissect you, and I want you to watch. I want to take out your liver and feed it to you." He leaned down from behind the man, now growling. "I want to cut off little pieces of your liver, pull open your bloody jaw and shove them down your throat. Then I'll slice open your stomach, reach in and take out the pieces, and I'll feed them to you again."

Smith had walked a complete circle around the prisoner. The knife blade once again rested on his torso, and Stanson saw a line of red appear in the moving blade's wake. The tip was carving a shallow groove in the man's skin, drawing grunts from the minor pain.

Stanson started to step forward to put a stop to

this insanity.

Next to him, Ross gripped his arm, holding him back.

But Smith saw the move. His smile only broadened. "You see, boys, it's like this. These Vietnamese people, they're very superstitious. They believe that if their bodies are maimed or mutilated, if they do not pass into the next life with their bodies whole, they will wander in darkness forever and will never reach the afterlife to be with their ancestors. The NVA and the Viet Cong used it on their own villagers all the time to scare them out of cooperating with our soldiers. I say, turnabout is fair play." He turned his attention back to the Vietnamese. "What do you say, pal? Anything to say to me? Any information you want to pass on? How bad you want to see the afterlife?"

"You American!" the man exclaimed. "I say nothing. You can't—"

"Say goodbye to your ancestors," Smith said. He waved the knife in front of the man's eyes for effect and quickly brought it down to the man's abdomen.

The Asian suddenly began shouting in Vietnamese. The voice stayed Smith's hand, and he listened as the man finally spilled his guts—only figuratively, for which Stanson was grateful. Even being the one without the knife, he was glad he would not have that stain on his soul.

Fifteen minutes later, with both prisoners sweating in fear but still alive, Smith stepped away from them. "I've got some names and some places we can check out. You guys meet me out by the truck, and we'll get out of here."

Stanson was only too glad to leave, though in the back of his mind something else, beyond what he had just witnessed, now bothered him. He couldn't quite put his finger on it…

He milled about the truck for five more minutes, with the others. He continued to share glances with Ross, conveying his emotions about what had happened. But he could not give voice to them, not yet. Now wasn't the time. Smith emerged from the flat and trotted down the steps. "Into the truck," he ordered, "we're outta here."

"What about those turkeys you carved up?" Stanson asked with a hint of sarcasm.

"Don't worry about them," Smith said. "Let's go."

Stanson stared Smith down for a moment, wondering what he should do. What *had* Smith done to the Vietnamese upstairs? Did he kill them? Did he maybe leave them the ability to free themselves? Considering the torture he'd witnessed, and yes, the line of work these guys were in, that wasn't likely. Stanson resigned himself to that thought. They're just drug dealing scum, you don't care about their fate. Behind him, Harry opened the rollup door, and he and Stanson hopped in. In moments, the truck was under way again.

The darkness and the noise of the engine outside gave him a strange solitude to think about the turn this mission had taken. He'd signed onto the CIA specifically for the mission Ross laid out for him. He agreed with Ross's and Smith's reasoning that the drug lords of this part of the world were getting too rich and powerful off misery in the States and elsewhere. Even if he wasn't searching for his brother and freeing other Americans, this mission was important.

A new sound introduced itself. Sirens drifted through the metal sides of the truck, and an emergency vehicle sped past them outside. This was quickly followed by a second, then a third. Stanson's heart sank as he realized... he suspected he knew where those vehicles were going.

What had Smith done now as his coup de grace?

* * *

For the next few days, Stanson watched Smith very closely. The big Marine was busy planning their next mission. He and Ross had frequently spoken in hushed tones in quick and hasty meetings. Stanson had tried several times to drift by and listen and had only caught bits and pieces of the conversation. Yesterday, Stanson watched from the lounge area, where the team was watching TV, while Smith spent an entire afternoon going over maps on the table. Finally, Smith had stepped away from the table and walked outside, presumably for a breath of fresh air. As soon as he was outside, Stanson jumped up and headed for that table.

The map, he soon saw, was a regional map including northern Vietnam and Cambodia. One area was circled in red, and a couple other areas were marked, though he couldn't make out what those marks might mean. He noticed another area, some twelve miles away to the south west, marked with a simple small X. Stanson found names printed near both marks, and he memorized those names.

He stepped away from the map for the moment, deep in thought. Something about those names was familiar to him, and he struggled to find the connection.

Minutes later, Smith came back in with Ross in tow. "Everybody up," he called. "Gather round. I have a mission prep briefing."

The team gathered around, and once again, Stanson stared at the map as he listened to Smith.

"We're inserting by helicopter here, a place we're calling LZ ten." As Stanson watched, Smith traced his finger in a direct line across the map, from the area where NKP was, across the small X to an area near the other markings. "From LZ ten, we hike four miles to a target we're calling Site Alpha-six. Note the open plateau here on the topo map. This is a Poppy field. They have peasants and villagers here harvesting the poppies, gathering the sap to haul out and refine into opium. We're going to shut down that operation.

"Note that this site is inside Cambodia," Smith continued. "Rumor has it the Khmer Rouge leave this site alone because they get a cut of the profits. But since it is territory more hostile than what you have usually encountered, we'll have to watch out."

Something clicked in Stanson's mind. He now recognized the name of the village near the poppy field. When Smith had 'interrogated' the two Vietnamese in Bangkok, one of them had given that name. He glanced at Ross as he realized why it sounded familiar. He then leaned in and touched the small X. "What's this here?"

"That's nothing."

Stanson allowed surprise to show on his face, though he did not expect Smith to answer his question. "Nothing? It's marked on the map; it must be something."

Smith stared him down, but his face soon became the condescending smiling mask that Stanson had come to hate. "This is an old map, and that is an old site. It used to be a storage site for opium harvested in another field nearby. I was with a team that shut the site down the week before I joined you here. That site is now inactive."

Stanson let it go at that point, but he continued to share looks with Ross. The team leader was blank for the most part, but he did seem to understand what Stanson was trying to convey to him. After the briefing, Smith took others from the team to ready some of their equipment. Stanson grabbed Ross by the arm and held him back.

"I know what you're going to say," Ross said quietly. "Site Alpha-six is right near one of the sites we were going to check for POWs."

"I suppose this was why you wanted me to stick with this dope mission."

"Among other reasons, yes."

"Do you think we'll find anybody?"

"I don't know." Ross lowered his voice even further. "But what do you think Smith would do if we did? Watch him closely, John. Don't turn your back on him for a second."

Stanson nodded, knowing exactly what he meant. He kept his other suspicions to himself for the moment.

* * *

Twenty-four hours later, their helicopter lifted off from the airfield at NKP. As the pilot picked his direction and reached a cruising speed, Stanson checked his watch. He then pulled a small olive-drab green Army-made compass and took a quick reading. The hatch to the Blackhawk helicopter was open, so he was able to see outside and monitor the terrain as they passed by. With some satisfaction, he noted their direction of travel. He once again consulted his watch and settled back to wait the amount of time he'd computed and monitor the ground features slipping away beneath him.

He felt eyes on him and glanced over at Smith. The big Marine was staring him down. His expression was blank, but his eyes were not. They pierced him, probing his mind. Stanson could see that

Smith had noticed his actions. Whether he knew what those actions meant wasn't yet clear. For the moment, Stanson didn't care if Smith had figured out what he was doing.

He was searching for a spot on that map, marked by the mysterious X. When checking the map, Stanson had noted the direction they would, or should, travel to get to Site Alpha-six. Was it coincidence that they would travel over the place where that mysterious X was? Once they were airborne, he confirmed that direction of travel. They were headed true to the site he sought. Also, on the map, he'd memorized some terrain features leading up to and surrounding that X. He'd computed the time it would take the chopper to travel that far. Now, like an eager traveler, he needed only to settle back and see the sights.

Even trying to settle to wait out the travel time was anxiety-producing. Several minutes into the trip, watching the minutes count down, he found himself checking his watch over and over. It became a series of accomplishments—the chopper made a certain landmark, he'd scan ahead for the next noticeable terrain feature, and check his watch when they passed it. One dread suddenly hit him. What if Smith suddenly decided to convince the pilot to alter their flight path—for security reasons, of course. If that idea occurred to him, Stanson's efforts would be in vain.

Smith continued to stare at him from the other side of the chopper. Stanson read the suspicious look in the Marine's gaze, and he knew he'd probably been figured out. But did Smith think he was a simple soldier, someone to follow orders and not ask questions? He was a highly trained Intelligence operative. At the very least, he'd be able to gather bits of information to read between the lines of any Op and maybe even run an angle of his own. Stanson had been more than vocal about his concerns about this team's current mission. Had Smith figured out what he was really up to right now?

Stanson settled down, but he kept watching his watch, now more discreetly.

The miles melted away beneath them. The chopper flew nape of the earth over the jungles of eastern Cambodia, staying low to avoid radars in the area. With growing excitement, still kept under wraps, he noted the time, and compared the terrain features that he saw outside the hatch. If his calculations were correct, they would be flying somewhere in the vicinity of the mysterious site that Smith claimed was shut down.

Stanson began frantically scanning the ground below, now not caring whether Smith saw him and figured him out. He hit upon a small snag in his plan. The jungle canopy below was intermittent, but he was suddenly afraid it would work against him and block his view of any activity below—

Off to the portside, through a break in the trees, he saw a flicker of movement. He focused on it. The movement was people. In fact, as the chopper passed by, they appeared to be running for cover. He saw a shape that appeared to be an off-road vehicle sitting half under a tree.

The chopper continued on, leaving the activity behind.

Stanson settled back into his seat. He had confirmation of something, but he did not know what. For a site that Smith claimed was shut down, it was certainly active. But those people could be anybody. He filed the information away.

In just minutes, the chopper was settling into the LZ.

* * *

The sun was setting behind them. The team had climbed a ridge that looked down over a sweeping wide-open plateau. That plateau was covered in green and dotted with poppies in bloom. A harvest was in full swing. Through binoculars, the team could see men walking among the plants, cutting them to scrape the sap from the bulbs there. Those men wore torn and ragged clothes, like variations of the military battle dress uniform. Around them and among them were Asian men in khaki type military uniforms and carrying rifles.

"Ross, check it out," Stanson whispered. "Those are Americans."

Next to him, Ross had his own binoculars and had already confirmed this.

"You think they're more POWs?" Harry asked on his other side.

"That would be my guess."

"Focus on the mission," Smith growled nearby. "These guys could be anybody. We're here to—"

"Shut up, Smith," Stanson growled. "We will take care of the real purpose of our mission. But if those guys are prisoners here against their will, they *will* extract with us. You were a Marine, you of all people should understand not leaving a buddy behind. They're coming out with us. Or so help me, I'll kill you myself."

Smith bristled when first told to shut up. But he seemed to listen to Stanson, and he relented. "OK. I agree to those terms. Now let's go kill these sons of bitches. Here's what I want..."

In minutes, Stanson was crawling through the grass toward the harvesting operation. Smith's plan was actually workable and made the most of their element of surprise. From their position at the tree line overlooking the plateau, they found a place where they could enter the grassy poppy field and not be seen by the Vietnamese. Stanson, Wayne and Smith did this, leaving Ross at the tree line with a rifle and scope, to watch over the operation.

They set off in different directions, and Stanson found himself alone as he moved quickly but quietly through the grass. The group was a good two hundred yards away, and he did not have much time to gain that ground. He slithered through in a high crawl, and every couple of minutes, he would slowly rise up just enough to gauge his distance and adjust direction.

He was nearly taken by surprise when a rustle in the grass sounded just feet to his right. He stopped and rolled onto his left side, facing that direction with his silenced pistol raised, his flattened form covered by the grass.

The face that found him was American. The man stopped suddenly; curious eyes locked onto the man in the grass holding the gun on him. Stanson waited, gauging his reaction. If the man panicked and called the guard over, that might work in his favor. But the man just stood there, frozen.

"How you doing?" he smiled at the man. "Can you do me a favor and call the guard over here?"

The man seemed to catch on to what might be going on—Stanson thought he saw a glimmer of hope wash across the man's face. He turned around and waved for the nearest Vietnamese soldier. For the moment, he stood there silent, waiting.

The man seemed to realize that his silence would help the situation. Stanson was able to listen to the guard's footsteps approaching, the grass rustling. When he was nearly on top of the intruder, the guard barked out an order in Vietnamese. Then in English, he shouted, "Why you no work?"

Entirely too facetiously for his situation, the

American prisoner said, "Someone would like a word with you."

The Vietnamese took one more step. Stanson still lay on his side, his gun sights pointed at the blue sky. As soon as the soldier's head appeared, he shifted his aim and fired a single silenced bullet.

The round found the soldier's nose and entered just to the side of his nostril. The bullet cored his brain, sending blood spattering out the back of his skull. He flopped onto his back in the grass among the poppies.

The shot was quiet, but the soldier going down was bound to be seen. Sure enough, Stanson heard shouting nearby. He rose to his knee, still below the level of the grass and grabbed the American, pulling him down to a kneel. He rose just above the level of the grass and checked the area.

Two soldiers were running in his direction, their AK-47 rifles up. Before he could line them up in his sights, automatic fire came his direction. He felt the first round zip by to his right, shaving shards from the grass until it kicked up dust behind him. The stream of lead began to shower him with shredded poppy blossoms.

Stanson dove to his left and into a roll, knocking the American aside and out of the line of fire. He came back to his knee, prepared to rise and fire on the run.

Even as he tracked his gun around toward the shooters, Smith popped out of the grass thirty feet away. With two unsilenced handguns, he pumped out a wall of lead. With their attention on Stanson, the soldiers were caught by surprise, and were cut down. Their bodies jerked and twirled for a second, then collapsed in the grass.

Stanson checked for other targets. A rustle in the grass practically behind him grabbed his attention, and he turned to see a Vietnamese almost upon him.

Stanson brought up his silenced pistol, but it was too late. The Asian kicked with his right leg, knocking the gun from the American's hand.

Stanson did not skip a beat. He swung with his left, and his fist smashed the side of the Asian's head. The Asian stepped back, shaking his head to regain shocked senses. He charged again, swinging and punching with both hands. It became a free for all, as the Vietnamese realized he would die if he did not win a fight with this man quickly.

Stanson stepped into the punches, making it easier to block them. His arms locked with the Asian's and they grappled. Stanson reached across his opponent's grip, trying to reach for the throat. The man slapped his hand away, and once again gripped his arm, seeking an opening somewhere.

Stanson grabbed the man's uniform and pulled him even closer, then brought up his knee. He connected with the solar plexus. The blow was not severe, but it was enough to throw the Asian off balance and break his concentration. Stanson then kicked down at a knee, and the man toppled to the side.

He took the American to the ground with him.

They rolled in the grass. For a moment, the Asian was on top of him, and Stanson felt desperate hands grip his throat. Faster than he thought possible, the lack of air affected his lungs, his vision, his strength. He started to see stars as he felt the fist grip his throat tighter.

His leg was free and he brought it up, and was able to hook the back of his knee around the Asian's neck. He pushed with his leg, prying the man off him. He flexed his leg again, trying to throw the man to the ground. It seemed to work, and the man fell back for a moment. It was enough for Stanson to regain his vision and his senses. He rolled to his knees and sprang into a crouch, ready for more.

The Asian quickly found his feet and leaped at the American.

He stopped suddenly, arched his back, then fell backward and collapsed into the grass. Stanson looked beyond the dead man and saw Smith standing just yards away, his pistol smoking.

Smith approached, and looked down at the body, no emotion on his face. He fished something from his pocket, and tossed it down onto the body, where it stuck to the blood splattered from the chest wound. Stanson saw what it was, a card from a poker deck—the suicide king. He glanced at the big Marine dispassionately. One of the many facts he remembered about the war was that Spec-ops soldiers often put such cards on their kills, as a way to intimidate the enemy.

Stanson didn't take the time to convey thanks to Smith. He felt like it would have been pointless anyway. Instead, he turned and sought out the group of Americans they'd found. "Everybody over there, to the tree-line."

For a moment, the group of three was confused. But the one Stanson had greeted motioned, and they hurried after him. Stanson, Smith and Wayne herded them away, all the while watching the area around them for any stray Vietnamese.

They reached the tree-line, where Ross popped up from behind cover. He beckoned them over, and the group gathered around him. "We're American CIA," he greeted them. "Do you understand?"

"Yes, sir," Stanson's friend said eagerly. The others nodded, just as excited.

"We're here to get you out." This brought smiles.

"Listen up," Smith said. "You guys were harvesting the poppies for someone. Do you know any names?"

Once again, Stanson's friend seemed to be the alert and forthcoming one. "We've been in a camp a few miles north of here. It's run by an NVA Colonel named Minh Van Vo. We only see him for a few weeks every once in a while, but he's a sadistic son of a bitch."

Smith smiled. "That's just the name I was looking for. Ross, get them going. I'll get the wind direction and get this field burning."

As he broke from the group, Stanson confronted the prisoner. "What's your name, soldier?"

"Hollister, Second Lieutenant, USMC."

"Are there any other prisoners at the camp you've been at?"

"Not anymore. We've been at this camp a couple months, we've been moved around a lot the last few years. There used to be eight of us. Colonel Minh has gradually killed us off."

"I'm looking for another POW," Stanson pressed him. "His name is Jed Stanson. He's Special Forces."

Hollister thought the name over for a moment. "Doesn't ring a bell. But I know that Minh has other camps that he runs."

Stanson was suddenly flooded with several emotions. He felt a moment of hope that his brother might be at one of those other camps. After a dozen years of him possibly being held captive, was he that much closer to finding him? Then doubt clouded his thoughts. With Smith on board their unit, would he ever get the chance?

Something else surfaced in his mind, another problem that struggled to make sense, but that he couldn't quite figure out. The image of the map popped into his brain. This site, as well as other sites that Smith had marked down, was one of several that appeared scattered over Northern Vietnam. Could those be other sites run by Colonel Minh? And what about other sites south of there, in particular the small meaningless X that Smith had marked there?

The inactive site with all the activity?

Ross started their group on a march back toward their LZ. Stanson lagged behind a moment, watching Smith in the distance. He'd gone back toward the field, where the bodies of the Vietnamese soldiers still lay. Smith had a couple of incendiary grenades. Stanson saw the marine toss those grenades into the poppy fields. He ran back toward the group. Behind him, twin explosions rocked the countryside. Stanson had a front row seat for the two fire balls that blossomed into the fields. Even from a hundred yards away, he felt the pressure of the explosions try to suck the air from his lungs. Flames spread and smoke billowed to the sky. By the time Smith reached him, the field was ablaze. His approach was backlit by a panorama of smoke and flame.

Smith's eyes blazed just as bright as the fire behind him. It was obvious to Stanson that he felt the mission had not gone as he'd wanted. "Let's go," he said.

* * *

When they arrived back at NKP, Ross briefed Hollister and the others on how they would get back to the States, the same way the men previously rescued would go. He sent Harry Wayne to escort them off to make those arrangements. Smith also made an excuse and broke off from the group. Stanson suspected he was going to make contact with Agent Johnson.

It worked out for him, he found himself alone with Ross. They ended up in the small kitchen area of their warehouse. Stanson leaned against a counter, fixing his gaze on his CO. Ross couldn't look him in the eye.

"Do you know anything about this Minh Van Vo?"

Ross still couldn't meet his eyes, but he was forthcoming. "He's a Colonel in the Vietnamese Army. He was a leading NVA officer during the Easter Offensive in "72 and led troops into Saigon in '75. According to what I've heard from Johnson and Smith, he inherited responsibility of several prison camps after the fall of Saigon. They've heard rumors he's using people from those camps to harvest poppies."

"Seems we have confirmation of that," Stanson said sarcastically.

Ross nodded. "They've talked about Minh being a major player in the opium trade, but never in more detail than that."

"Have they ever mentioned any other names of major players in the opium trade?"

Ross shook his head.

Stanson hesitated before voicing his own suspicions. What he was thinking could cost him his career—at the very least. "Is it possible that some of these Company players could have their own smuggling ring going on?"

Ross gave him a very dark look.

"I've heard a lot of rumors," Stanson went on, "even before I joined the Company, that the Vietnam War was financed by drug sales. In all my research, I've never been able to confirm this. Now that could be because it didn't happen, or it could be that the Company *really* doesn't want that information to be public." He beckoned Ross to the map, still stretched across the table. "What's this X here? The one Smith wanted me to ignore so badly. He says it's a site that has already been shut down. We flew over it on our way to Alpha-six. This site was active. I saw people and vehicles there. This wide-open area here adjacent this X is a poppy field. What is Smith not telling us?"

Ross let the sudden silence hang over them for a moment. In a low voice, he said, "Be very careful what you say about all this. And remember who you work for. Tell me your theories."

"I think Johnson is wrapped up in smuggling himself. He's probably got local tribes doing the harvest and labor. Smith is his enforcer. Minh is probably his main competition, or someone who knows too much. For whatever reason, he needs to be eliminated. He's decided to use us as a death squad to eliminate that competition and do general dirty work."

Ross was staring at the map. "You may have something there. I've long suspected a lot of that. We have to be careful. If they finish this job, if they finish off Minh—or if they suspect we know—we become expendable."

Stanson seemed to skip right past that. "This brings up a lot of questions. What I would like to know... According to Hollister, Minh has other camps. If Smith and Johnson are involved in drug trafficking, is it possible that they have other POWs enslaved in their own camps?" Stanson felt overwhelmed by all the questions swirling in his brain.

"If we take into account," Ross said, "that Johnson wants no more American prisoners resurfacing, since it calls attention to their operation, the next logical step is to try and take out Minh."

"Do we want to be part of that?" Stanson asked.

"We may not have a choice."

Stanson huffed. "What do we do about all this?"

As soon as he said this, Stanson shut his mouth. Beyond Ross, a figure was coming out of the shadows. When Smith stepped up to them, he had the barest hint of a smile. He walked past them and went to the nearby refrigerator, where he grabbed a beer.

Stanson exchanged a nervous look with Ross, and he knew Ross was thinking the same thing he was. How much did Smith hear?

CHAPTER 7

Steve trudged on, enthralled by his mentor's story. Stanson paused, partly to catch his breath and partly just caught up in his memories.

"CIA dealing drugs for profit," Steve said. "Doesn't surprise me."

"I think at the time, it threw me. People have tried over the years to prove that selling drugs is a way the CIA finances a lot of its operations, but no one has ever made a definitive case. Ross became this big-time spook. Every once in a while, he gives me a call to do the Company a little favor."

He fell silent as the march continued. But it gave Steve something to think about. This was why Stanson was the way he was. Just as Steve had been baptized by the fires of war and the betrayal of trusted friends in the Army Special Forces, Stanson became the warrior he was today in the steamy jungles of Vietnam. All the backstabbing from his own people left him the jaded man he was today. But this was the first time he'd talked so openly about his past.

"So, you knew when you saw that card on the body that Smith was the killer."

"Yeah. The suicide king was kind of his signature. He left it on more than one body on those missions. He'd heard about some grunts doing that back in the day. Even years after the war, he thought that was cool."

"It's going to be hard to make a case based on that, but maybe we can get him..."

Stanson stopped abruptly and came in close to Steve. Blazer didn't back down but listened as the Captain made his statement. "Listen to me, son. I came here for one reason only. To kill that son of a bitch and leave his body rotting here in the forest for the animals to feast on. And if that story ever reaches the Police Chief, I will deny it. You can accept that, or you can turn around and walk out of this forest. Go back to your vehicle and go home."

"You called off the manhunt," Steve accused. "That's why there was no police presence in Fort Bragg."

"You should go home," Stanson growled.

"You want to talk about crossing the line," Steve brought up as the march resumed. "This is it. This is the same as it was back then, only now the tables have turned. But you're not the same man you were back then, and you're sure as hell not the same as Smith. Can you accept what you're trying to do?"

"I've said my piece," Stanson growled over his shoulder.

Steve stared hard at his Commander's back. He was starting to see that this was a separate war from anything else, separate from the war on crime, the war in Vietnam. The police captain had been left behind in San Francisco, and the spook John Stanson had come on a special mission. Steve knew that spook well. He'd been trained by that spook. And he knew the game that spook was involved in. Stanson was here to kill a ghost from his past.

As a sworn police officer, could Steve Blazer accept that?

* * *

Steve checked his watch when the Captain brought them to a halt. It was approaching two in the morning, and Steve had been trudging along bordering on exhaustion. Being awake for over twenty-four hours was taking its toll. But then he noticed the faraway look in Stanson's eyes as the Captain surveyed the area. "Smith had a scanner in his truck. He probably knows I moved the police search for him further north. I figure he wants to slip out among all the tourists and leave the area tomorrow. Then again, he probably knows about your firefight in town, and that police are back there. And he didn't seem to be eager to head south, back toward San Francisco."

"Maybe because he killed Bao Lin," Steve suggested. Stanson jerked his head toward him, surprised at this. "That's right. Cameron told me the killer really messed him up. Sounds to me like Smith's torture techniques survived the war."

"So, he's stealing this shipment to sell himself. Which means we have to find him before he slips away. We go silent from here." Stanson pressed forward, walking through the damp grass and the ferns, once again searching the hillside for any sign of a logging camp. Steve listened for his footsteps falling on the damp ground but heard nothing. Another trait learned in the jungle.

The logging road seemed to wind through the forest, cut into the hillside halfway up. Below was a shallow chasm in which a creek babbled its way toward the ocean. The creek would swell soon with the continuing rainfall. They traveled up one slope, hidden by the trees, and then down another.

After another thirty minutes moving through the redwoods, the Captain brought them to a sudden halt with an upraised fist. He went down to his knee, and Steve did the same. Many of the skills he learned in his military schooling were taught by men who'd walked those same jungles. Steve found them applicable to much he did in his life.

Stanson bent over, and Steve saw him examining something near the ground. Blazer leaned in for a closer look, and suddenly realized what the Captain had found.

A tripwire.

Steve immediately took the job of Security, or Cover Officer in police lingo. From his kneeling position, he watched their surroundings. His eyes pierced the darkness, searching for anything that might emerge from the shadows to put a bloody stop to their mission. The terrain had leveled to a plateau here, with the road a hundred yards up a gentle slope. In the back of his mind, he wondered where in the darkness other booby traps might lay in wait for them.

Stanson studied the wire, gauging the pressure needed to trip it. He touched it gently and traced it to a small tree five feet away. There it was wrapped around a small broken-off branch, and it extended up into a split in the trunk. That's where he found the grenade, lodged and ready to spring out onto its victim. The pin had been pulled, so that when the wire pulled the grenade free, the plunger would fly off and the fuse would blow. Steve watched, alert and ready to spring away to a safer distance should the explosive egg suddenly be primed.

Stanson carefully removed the grenade from its resting place, holding the unsafe plunger down to keep it in place. Stanson reached into another pocket and pulled out a small object, which he held up for Steve to marvel at, like he was showing it off. Even in the darkness, Steve recognized it as a cotter pin to a grenade. "I kept this from the bad old days," he explained quietly as he slipped the pin into the proper hole on the fuse. It was secured with an audible snap. Stanson slowly withdrew his hand from the plunger, ready if it flopped away and primed the fuse, ready to throw the whole thing away. It remained secure. He handed the grenade to Blazer, who slipped it into a jacket pocket. "If that had gone off, he would know we were here. I figured this would be a good ambush site, terrain-wise. We're on the right track."

Steve looked around, gauging the terrain in the darkness. With hills on either side and a break in the trees making a natural trail that led into a bottleneck, he saw that the Captain was right. This was an ideal spot to set up a booby-trap.

Smith had to be nearby.

After another hundred yards, the Captain stopped behind a big fat redwood. Steve crouched to look around the other side at what his mentor had spotted.

The forest cleared beyond the tree into a wide-open area covering several acres. Steve noted several features in the clearing. This was some sort of lumber camp, where large diesel rigs were loaded with the trunks of cut-down redwood trees. Three sheds lined the east side of the camp, used for storage and possibly to give shelter to those who worked there at one time. The sheds looked run down and even rotting away. A large pile of wet rotting branches that had been trimmed off of logs, was thrown together near where the dirt road entered the camp. After a cursory examination of the camp, Steve couldn't tell if it was abandoned for the season, to be active once again when the weather permitted, or was simply abandoned and forgotten.

Stanson studied the camp from the cover of the tree as Blazer did. "He's there," the Captain said quietly.

"How do you know?" Steve demanded in a whisper.

"I just know. I see a good place to the north where we can keep watch." He moved out and Blazer cautiously followed.

The moderate rainfall continued to pelt them through the trees. It took ten minutes to circle the perimeter of the camp, and they started up a gentle slope into a sparse section of forest.

Steve saw the observation point the Captain was referring to as it seemed to materialize out of the darkness. It was the stump of a redwood long ago felled by lumberjacks. The stump was three feet tall, eight feet across. The center had been hollowed out by a forest fire dozens of years ago, Steve could see a blackened sheen. From the stump, dozens of small branches had begun to grow upward. Stanson leaped up over the edge between those branches to enter the shelter. He leaned back against one side of the trunk to rest a moment. "I brought Mary up to this area many years ago and we did some exploring. I learned a little about the history of the logging industry in this area. This is called a "goose pen," when a tree gets hollowed out by a fire. But you can't really kill a strong redwood." He traced his hand along some of the newer branches. "These will grow and over hundreds of years create new trees."

He brought out his .45 and aimed it into the distant camp. At this range, none of the small handheld weapons they carried would do much good, but it was good enough to provide some cover for a couple hours until they decided to make their move. Experience told Steve this would happen just before dawn. He slipped off his rucksack, setting it lightly on the ground. He was an experienced soldier in any environment, and he held respect for the kind of jungle fighting Captain Stanson had done. He showed that respect now, trying to remain as silent as possible. He spent a few minutes going through his weapons, the Beretta and the .44 Magnum Desert Eagle he'd brought as backup. He reloaded the Beretta with a fresh clip, checked the three he had left, and mounted the Desert Eagle on his hip. He secured a pouch with three extra magazines for the big Magnum. Stanson rummaged through his rucksack and came out with his rolled-up camouflage poncho. He unrolled it and crawled underneath so it could provide its promised protection from the rain, and Steve did the same.

Through all this, Stanson kept one eye on the camp. He finally rested against the hollowed-out tree trunk, eyes sweeping the clearing for any sign of his target. When Steve settled down, Stanson said quietly, "I ever tell you I was a POW myself?"

This caught Steve by surprise. "No." In the dark, he searched Stanson's eyes, wondering how this could be true.

* * *

1983

They'd designated the next site Alpha-one. Smith advised the group that aerial reconnaissance had shown plenty of activity at the site, including trucks being loaded. Stanson had his doubts about this—it was a little early in the harvest season for the crop to be harvested completely. But the fact that really raised his eyebrow, especially after his conversation with Ross, was the rumors that Minh would be there himself to oversee the shipment.

Twenty-four hours after the briefing, Stanson found himself walking through the jungles of northern Vietnam. According to the maps they were shown, they were just miles from the border with Laos. In fact, they were walking in a northerly direction, moving parallel to the border. The intel that Smith had given them stated that, once loaded, the shipment of opium would be trucked southward along back roads. Eventually, they would connect to the Ho Chi Minh Trail, still very much active a decade after the war. A short distance up the trail, they would hop over the border, crossing into North Vietnam.

Stanson had to fight to keep focused on the mission. They slogged along a trail far from any major thoroughfare. Thick jungle surrounded the trail and had overtaken parts of it. Smith was convinced that this was the best way to get them to the site in a timely manner and undetected. Part of Stanson's focus was on Smith, watching for any signs of treachery. With all that had happened, he had no trust in the man like he did with Ross or Harry. Along with watching Smith, he had to watch the trail. Though the war had ended, there was still a danger there. Numerous times in the past, in their travels through the bush, they had come across booby traps left over from the hostilities. They'd found anything from tripwires connected to aged and rusting explosive devices, to mines buried and long forgotten. Being that he was so well versed in jungle patrol tactics used by troops in Vietnam, Stanson volunteered to take point for the trek. Through it all, he had moments where he felt like he was in the war itself, like he was a soldier there, walking a jungle patrol searching for Vietcong, trapped by circumstances and just trying to survive.

Stanson trudged along the trail, hefting his Colt Commando, a scaled down version of the M-16 rifle. He carried several thirty-round magazines for the rifle. His combat harness also sported several fragmentation grenades, as well as a pistol holstered on his hip. In the last two years training with the CIA, he'd grown to like this particular pistol, a .45 caliber M1911.

He came around a quick bend in the trail, starting down a gentle hill. His senses suddenly screamed at him, wrenching him back to reality from a brief moment in a past he never experienced. He stopped his slow march, threw a fist into the air to signal the team behind him to stop. He went down to a knee to examine the trail ahead. Something was wrong.

Both Ross and Smith came up behind him, joining his crouch.

"What's the holdup?" Smith growled.

"Something is wrong up ahead," Stanson explained. "My gut's screaming at me."

"Take an antacid and let's get moving. We don't have time for your indigestion."

"Smith, hunches like this are what kept assholes like you alive during the war," Stanson said. "Ross, look at the terrain. We'd be walking through a shooting gallery. High ground on either side and thick brush ahead. Maybe it's nothing, but I'd like to get there in one piece."

Ross was studying the terrain as well, and even Smith paused to consider the risk.

"Fine," Smith finally said. "Check it out, get us through it or past it, but let's get moving."

Smith slithered away a few yards, and despite his not believing Stanson about the risk of the moment, he moved up next to a small tree in case he needed quick cover.

Ross stayed with his protégé for a moment, both

of them studying the stretch before them for any sign of danger. Supposedly, they had the element of surprise, none of the local factions knew they were on their way to cause major havoc. There should be no reason for anyone to be waiting in ambush ahead. In another life, Stanson may have been cowed by the big ex-Marine into just going with the program. But his hunch was strong.

Stanson rose to his feet. He stepped into the open, walking slowly, his eyes sweeping over every detail of the terrain.

Stanson suddenly lunged to his left, leapt over a short embankment and plunged into the jungle. Behind him, the squad was caught off guard for a moment, but quickly followed him.

Gunfire suddenly tore the jungle. Ross spotted a muzzle flash ahead of them from a thick area of brush. A line of bullets tore the trail up behind him. He glanced down the line and saw that the whole team had made it to safety. They were now low crawling through the brush trying to get into a good fighting position to return fire. Bullets continued to sail overhead, at times showering them with shredded leaves and branches.

I knew it, John thought as he ducked behind a thick tree. He took a moment to scan the jungle, more with his ears than his eyes. He could tell that his team had reached safety, thanks at least in part to his move that forced the trap to spring prematurely. Just thirty yards off to his right, the team was starting to get organized and throw rounds down range. He tried to figure out the layout of the ambush from listening, but the gunfire was too confused to pick up a pattern.

Stanson jumped from cover, hoping to ambush the ambushers. As he plunged into the open, he caught sight of a pair of Asian shooters jumping to their feet. They saw him as well, and the three raced to see who could fire first. Stanson did, put single shots into both soldiers, and put them on their backs. Movement beyond them drove him to seek cover again. He jumped behind another tree, then leaned out and fired toward the movement in the brush.

To his right, he saw Smith running full tilt in his direction, charging the ambushers. His Colt Commando blasted flame and lead.

Stanson took the opportunity to move. He rolled into the open and sought his next place of cover. He found a downed tree trunk nearby and low-crawled behind it, seeking out the opposite end. In his peripherals, he saw and felt bullets tearing into the top of the log.

When he reached the end, he noticed the lull in gunfire. He popped up with his rifle for just a moment. It was enough to see Smith in action.

The big Marine was running in his direction, presumably to back him up. A group of Asians leapt from an embankment lined with brush, where they'd been waiting. Already running, Smith saw that the first one was still adjusting to the situation. He threw his shoulder into the man and bowled him over. The second was bringing his rifle up to fire. Smith swung his own rifle barrel, knocking the Kalashnikov rifle aside. He then swung the butt of the rifle back around, smacking the Asian in the face and nearly tearing his jaw off. Two other ambushers saw this and scrambled away. Smith opened fire on them. Stanson froze to watch him and saw the effect combat had on him. Smith had an evil grin as he fired on full automatic. He let out a cry of bloodlust as he emptied his magazine into the backs of the running Asians.

Stanson heard shouting beyond them. He could

tell what was going on. The Asians were pulling back to regroup. The team had the ambushers on the run.

John jumped to his feet, scanning the terrain. He spotted a creek bed twenty yards distant and headed that way. He intended to use it to try and flank the ambushers and surprise them. He reached the edge and slid down the muddy embankment, about eight feet to the bottom. He found very little water running through the creek, but plenty of mud from a storm days ago. He could still hear the shouting in the distance, and he headed toward it.

A line of bullets cut into the mud and scarred a tree root to his left. In response, he dove to his right, and nestled himself among the roots of another large tree exposed by the frequent rushing water. He found himself sitting on a root, leaning back to use the cover it provided. He leaned up a few inches, bringing his rifle across his body. He scanned the terrain above, looking for the threat.

It was Smith. He had his rifle sighted on the tree. As Stanson rose into view, the muzzle flashed.

John dropped back, hoping his body was flat enough to fall completely behind his cover. It was. Bullets whistled above him, and one tore into the tree above his waist.

Stanson asked himself a quick question. Was this Smith removing him from the operation, as he and Ross had been afraid of? Or was it possible he didn't know who he was shooting at?

Stanson tested his theory. "Hey!" he shouted, "It's me!" He rose above cover once more. He hoped for a moment to seek out Smith's eyes.

He never got the chance. Smith fired again the moment John was exposed.

Stanson fell back, this time bringing his rifle up. Without exposing himself, he fired off a burst in Smith's direction, just to force him to duck. He then rose and ran. He sprinted down the creek bed jumping rocks and puddles.

Smith didn't take long to recover. Stanson didn't realize how exposed he was until bullets filled the creek bed. Geysers of mud sprouted all around him. He could hear lead whipping past him. But the creek bed had widened at this spot, robbing him of cover.

The gunfire stopped. Stanson did not. He glanced over his shoulder. Smith was running after him on the embankment, changing magazines on the run. He brought the freshly loaded rifle up and let loose another burst.

"What are you doing?" someone shouted. Stanson glanced back to see Ross run up alongside Smith and grab his arm—and get an elbow in the face for his troubles.

Stanson spotted his new goal, a fresh copse of trees with roots digging into the creek bed. He would find cover there. He sprinted into the open now, mindless of the mud pulling at his boots or the physical price of his exertion. He finally leapt behind the first tree there.

Fresh gunfire erupted on the embankment above him. He judged the sound to be coming from a little farther way. The difference in the sound also indicated Kalashnikovs, not M-16s. The enemy had found his team once again.

The Vietnamese soldier came from out of nowhere. One second, Stanson was poised to climb out of the creek bed to join the fight. The next second, a Vietnamese soldier was screaming at him, five feet away in the creek.

Stanson was already crouched, and he launched himself at the soldier. The Asian thought he was ready and backed off a step, but Stanson still managed to power a butt-stroke to the man's skull.

Even as he struck, Stanson heard the clacking

of rifle action, seeming to come from all around him. He found that it was. When he looked up from the man he'd assaulted, he found a dozen AK-47s pointing down at him from both sides of the embankment above.

There was no way he could fight his way out of this situation. He took a quick scan of the hate-filled eyes of the Vietnamese glaring down at him, all of those eyes locked behind the sights of a rifle, ready to cut him down. For just a moment, he thought of raising his rifle, sighting on just one man, knowing they would kill him, and wanting to take just one with him.

The thought occurred to him: no one back home would know that he, John Stanson, just a kid when the Vietnam War raged, would become one of the last casualties of the war.

Instead, he lowered his rifle and dropped it into the mud as he raised his hands.

* * *

John Stanson endured a long truck ride in darkness; at first it was the shade caused by the cover over the back of the Deuce-and-a-half truck bed. The sun occasionally poked through the jungle canopy and in turn through the cracks at the edge of the truck's cover. In that dim light, he was able to see the looks on the faces of the half-dozen Vietnamese guarding him. Their faces ranged from blank stares to absolute hatred. Through the whole trip, every rifle was pointed at him. He'd been relieved of all his weapons, including a knife removed from a scabbard in his right boot. His LBE belt and suspenders lay in a pile at the front of the truck bed, and he knew if he went for it, even for a drink from his canteen, he would be beaten or shot. So, he endured the trip in silence. The ride lasted into the evening, until the light at the edges of the tarp over the truck faded, indicating that the sun had gone down.

He guessed the truck ride to be close to four hours when they finally stopped. Stanson checked his memory of the list of sites that Ross had been intending to check for MIAs. Could this location be one of them? The brief horrifying thought occurred to him: would the team find him here? An even more horrifying question then surfaced: with Smith on the team, and now having tried to kill him, would he let the team even try to find him?

In the darkness with rifles pointed at him, all he could do right now was listen. He could hear activity outside the truck, voices shouting in Vietnamese. They came to a lurching stop. The rear flap was thrown open.

All at once, the guards inside the truck swarmed him. He brought up arms to shield himself, and the guards took this as a moment of aggression on his part. They grabbed for his arms and legs, and a couple of them landed glancing blows to his torso.

Stanson was dragged from the truck. There were several seconds of confusion as he was pushed and pulled to where the guards wanted him. They forced him to his knees and stepped back. The sudden silence and inactivity was like the precursor to horror. He gathered his wits and took that moment to let his eyes dart around the area and scan his surroundings.

The darkness was lit by torches mounted in several places, as well as a central campfire nearby, likely used for cooking. The campfire almost seemed to be the center of the site, with several huts of familiar design laid out around him. Several of them had lights mounted in places. John thought he heard a hum nearby and he deduced that this would be a generator. Locating it could be useful later on.

He was suddenly pinned by a spotlight. His reflexive reaction was to turn and look at it, and he was momentarily blinded. But not before he got a look at the twenty-foot guard tower and the gate he had been driven through. He'd study the perimeter fences more in depth later. For now, he turned away from the light and tried to blink away the shapes burned onto his retina.

He sensed men gathering around him. To his right, Vietnamese soldiers were forming up, and he saw that their ranks had risen to platoon size, at least thirty men. He glanced to his left and was startled by the group assembling there. They wore dirty black pajamas, a "uniform" typically worn by the Viet Cong guerillas that terrorized South Vietnam during the war. But the men wearing the clothes were not Vietnamese.

A rush of emotions washed over him, anger and elation, despair and determination, as he realized he was looking at another group of American POWs.

Stanson sensed a new presence. He saw that he was kneeling before what appeared to be the Command Center, a hut built more secure and even more extravagant than everything else in the camp. There was a balcony walkway that stretched around the raised floor level of the hut. A stairway on either side of him at the corners led up to the balcony. A man had stepped outside onto that balcony. The camp fell quiet.

Stanson stared up at the man, wondering what would happen next. The man, obviously the camp commander, stared back at him.

"You are an interesting anomaly," the Commander began. He spoke good English, and even had a trace of a non-Vietnamese accent. Stanson guessed he had schooled somewhere in Europe. "We haven't seen any new Americans around here for a long time." Stanson couldn't help a quick look over at the white men in the black pajamas.

The Commander stepped closer to the railing and leaned over. "I know why you are here." He looked over to the group of POWs. "There will be no rescue today!" he shouted at them. To Stanson, he said, "I am Colonel Minh Van Vo. You will be joining the other Americans soon. But first...we will talk."

He then barked an order in Vietnamese. The soldiers swarmed toward their prisoners, and they were wrestled and dragged away. With a sweep of his hand, Minh ordered Stanson brought to him.

Stanson was watching the actions of the soldiers as they moved the prisoners, pushed them, prodded them, dragged them, even beat them with bamboo sticks. A moment later, his own captors grabbed him and hoisted him to his feet. He was dragged up the stairs.

Stanson was herded through the door and across a room lit by the dim flame of a kerosene lamp. Stanson glanced around, wondering if he would see instruments of torture that would be experimented with on him. He saw nothing obvious like that. Only a simple table, set up as a desk, with a small shuffle of papers at one side and the lamp at the other. Off in one corner, the Colonel's bed roll lay on the floor.

Stanson was put in a chair that one of the soldiers placed in the middle of the room. Minh himself pulled another wooden chair from behind his desk he set it down across from his prisoner and sat down opposite Stanson. The three soldiers positioned themselves about the room, one at the door, one lounging casually nearby, and one towering over the American.

Colonel Minh's eyes burned into his, examining

him. Stanson glared back at him. He could tell the Viet Colonel was searching for a way into his mind, looking for that one opening that would get him to tell everything he knew. Stanson thought back to his classes at the Farm on interrogation and all they had told him about being held captive by an enemy. He could not simply give them name, rank, and serial number. He knew he was about to be tortured. He knew he would eventually break and give up whatever information they wanted. But he steeled himself. He would not make it easy for them.

The room fell quiet.

"Back during the war," Minh began, "I had the honor of running different camps that held American war criminals. I took it upon myself to gather information for my superiors in Hanoi. I broke many Americans in the process. I would ask them questions like, 'What is your name? What is your mission?' The war is over, so those questions no longer matter. But you, my friend...I think you know things about me. I think you know that I am involved in the opium trade. For several weeks now, my operation has been under attack, my labs, processing centers, distribution centers, even my poppy fields. This is a cutthroat business. I knew of CIA groups who were cutting into the business with networks of their own during the war. It now seems as though one of those networks is back in business. Please tell me your name and who your comrades are."

Stanson said nothing, and the silence stretched for several seconds. Minh finally smiled, giving him a look of pity. "I know you want to be defiant. But you will tell me. Tell me your name."

Several more seconds ensued. Minh smiled through them. Then he suddenly lashed out and slapped him hard across the face. When Stanson looked back at his captor, the smile was gone. "Tell me your name!" Minh shouted.

Stanson stared back, his face becoming harder. He then detected movement behind him and only had a moment's warning before the rifle butt slammed into his side. The pain radiated, causing his breath to catch in his lungs. As it subsided seconds later, Stanson assessed his status. The rifle butt had missed his ribs but may have broken the skin, and he'd have to monitor the bruising for any deeper damage. Then again, the next blow could do more damage.

"What is your name?" Minh barked again. "Who do you work for?"

The punch came from behind again, a simple cuff across the skull. It was not enough to stun or damage him. But then Minh followed it up with a punch to the face. It bloodied his lip.

Minh barked his questions again. Stanson continued to resist. He took another hard punch to the face that opened his skin an inch on his cheek. The guard with the rifle swung again, hitting him in the ribs hard enough to knock him off the chair.

Minh fell silent, as if he felt like he'd gotten carried away. He gestured, and two soldiers picked the American up and sat him back in the chair. Stanson sat up, mustering as much dignity as he could. His breathing was elevated, his vision swam a bit and he could feel a couple of cuts and bruises in some places. He took the momentary lull to seek out the Vietnamese's eyes and stare him down. He braced for more.

"We will talk again tomorrow," Minh said. "But I want you to know something. We knew you were coming. Remember that. You came to our ambush many kilometers from the site you were to attack. We were waiting for you. Someone contacted me and told me you were coming. That someone allowed your men to be killed and you to be captured. That someone sacrificed you. Ask yourself what they owe you. You have been abandoned here to my mercy. Think on my words." With that, he gestured, and the guards picked him up. "You go sleep with your American friends now."

The guards dragged him out. Stanson found his footing and tried to walk on his own. It was difficult, and the guards dragging him faster than he was able did not help. But he managed to stumble along with them. He tried to see where they were going but found this difficult with the dark and the condition of his mind and senses post-beating. He soon found himself in front of a large cage. The cage was constructed of hard bamboo logs lashed together, and much of the bamboo was overgrown with weeds and vines. The guards opened a gate at the end, and he was heaved inside. John landed on a bed of moist dirt. He lay still for a moment to try and let his body recover somewhat.

He heard movement in the darkness. His mind surged with hope and anticipation. Minh had told him that he would be put in with the POWs he'd seen. His mind raced, but for the moment his body would not cooperate. He tensed, tried to push himself to a sitting position. It did not happen the way it usually did.

"Easy, buddy," someone said from the darkness. He felt hands on him, and someone rolled him over. He was soon laying in that someone's lap, and he looked up into eyes that even in the dark appeared sunken. The dirty face was that of a white man.

"Save your strength. You're the new guy, which means your Minh's new toy. They could come back for you any time."

Stanson had lots of questions to ask. But for now, he let his body relax.

* * *

Stanson lay there for close to an hour, gathering his senses and his faculties. The camp fell quiet, and in his many glances at what he could see outside the cage, he'd seen most of the soldiers in the camp gravitating toward one of the huts. He heard the occasional exclamation or laughter from that direction. He could guess what they were doing there to pass time, drinking rice wine, playing cards, telling stories.

"Tell me where we are," he finally said to the man he was sitting with.

The man took a moment to answer. "I'm not sure exactly. For the last few months, we've been moving around a lot. We've stayed at two different camps, like we're switching back and forth. They have us working poppy fields. We've been harvesting them a lot."

"Refining the stuff into Opium and heroin," Stanson said.

"I was seeing a lot of heroin use in the last few months before I was captured."

"What's your name, soldier? When were you captured?"

The man smiled in the dark. "Staff Sergeant Adrian Quintero, Army Special Forces. I was captured in a firefight at the Laotian border, 1970."

"Well, Hooah, Sarge," Stanson said. "I earned the tab too. My name is—"

"No, no," Quintero silenced him. His smile had faded. "Don't give up your name yet." He glanced around at the other prisoners. They had kept their distance for some reason. One was sitting up a few feet away, gazing off between the bamboo bars of their cage. The other two had curled up and were sleeping. "You have to be careful who you talk to.

You're new, you don't know who you can trust." He glanced back at the other three. "There's another prisoner who doesn't sleep in the cage with us. His name is Sergeant Noya. A while back, they broke him and he bought into their line of bullshit. He became Minh's pet. Minh made him a deal, if he signed this bullshit confession to war crimes, Minh would feed him, give him clothes, privileges and then soon send him home. But he's kept the kid around as a propaganda toy. The kid keeps telling us if we just go with the program, Minh would treat us fairly. He's going to have Noya meet with you and try to reason with you. Don't buy into it."

Stanson took this all in. He'd read many accounts, fiction and non-fiction, of life in POW camps. This all corroborated what he had read. But this was all too real.

Quintero's face became distant in the dark. "Tell me... what year is it?"

Stanson's heart broke, hearing the pain in his voice, even pain sprinkled with hope. "It's 1983."

Quintero breathed an unintelligible curse. "Thirteen years. Thirteen years I've been stuck here."

"I have to ask," Stanson said. "I know I'm not supposed to bring up my name, but I've been looking for another American who's MIA. His name is Jed Stanson."

Quintero wrinkled his brow to think. "Can't say I remember him. I've been in a lot of camps, and it's only the last two years I've been working with these guys in the poppy fields." He paused. "You probably can't say, but... I believe you've been sent here to rescue us. I knew we weren't forgotten."

Stanson's heart broke even more. He couldn't bear to tell the man the truth, at least the truth as he perceived it, about how his beloved country felt about MIAs. He obviously couldn't clarify about his own mission—technically to stop the opium, not free the POWs. But this fit with his own personal mission anyway.

A thousand questions swirled in his mind, but Stanson tried to will himself to relax. Rescue likely would not come right away, especially not tonight. He resolved that if a certain amount of time went by and no one came to raid the camp, he would attempt an escape. If he couldn't bring the POWs with him, he would somehow come back for them. Considering what Quintero had said, he felt he had already promised to make that man's hopes reality. He would get them out somehow.

For now, he settled onto the dirt floor of their cage. He tried to sleep, knowing he would need rest. But the security of sleep was fleeting. He kept himself alert in case the guards came to harass them. A light rain began to fall, complicating matters. There was no shelter over the cage, so in minutes they were all soaked. The other POWs were asleep by now, seeming not to care. They were accustomed to this. He lay his head on his elbow and tried to sleep through the rain.

* * *

Stanson awoke with a start. In an instant, he remembered the fresh hell he was dumped into the night before. It was now light in the jungle, the rising sun peeking through pinprick holes in the foliage overhead. He scoped out his surroundings and saw a couple Vietnamese soldiers milling about outside his cage. The rain had tapered off during the night, but his clothes were soaked. He didn't dare sit up yet, lest it attract the attention from their captors he wasn't ready for. He didn't know what the Vietnamese had in store for him yet, but he resolved to follow the lead of the other prisoners, especially Quintero.

Without moving his head, he glanced around his cage. It was constructed of thick solid bamboo, with cross pieces tied tightly in place with leather straps. The cage was built against two side by side trees, which provided minimal shelter from the rain the night before. The cage was large enough to fit the five of them, but it was still cramped.

The Vietnamese soldiers seemed to appear out of nowhere at the door to their cage, shouting and banging the butts of their rifles against the bamboo poles. The four prisoners roused themselves. Stanson rose with them. He went to brush some of the mud off his jungle fatigues, but one of the guards grabbed him and yanked him outside.

What happened next was right out of many of the POW stories he'd read over the years. The prisoners were lined up in front of the command hut, in the same spot he'd been in last night. The garrison of Vietnamese troops made a two-rank formation behind them, and Stanson got a look at how many enemy he was dealing with. He only counted eight men per rank, sixteen total. If he accounted for two, maybe four, as command staff, and anyone who wasn't present because they had stood watch through the night and were now sequestered to sleep... He guessed there were no more than thirty Vietnamese here.

I could kill them all; piece of cake, he told himself.

In the daylight, John glanced around and finally got a good look at the prisoners he'd been put with. All of them wore the black pajama uniforms the Vietcong were known for, but their clothes were filthy, ragged and torn. Their bodies were emaciated from years of malnourishment in captivity, the VC pajamas hung off skeletal frames. All the prisoners had scraggly long hair, lengths varying, and some growth of beard. In particular, he glanced at Sergeant Quintero, standing next to him. His eyes were sunken into his skull, but they were sharp and seemed to pierce his mind.

The camp commander, Minh Van Vo, came out of his command hut, elevated over the camp on its stilts. Stanson saw the commander look pointedly at him. Stanson stared him down. He got a moment of satisfaction when Minh lost the staring contest by looking away first. Minh looked over at a soldier near a tall piece of bamboo set by the corner of the hut. Minh waved, and the soldier pulled a rope there. A flag unfurled as it rose, and Stanson recognized the flag of Vietnam. From what sounded like a record player, maybe built during the 1930s, music began to play. The player must be in the command hut with the volume turned all the way up. With the condition of the record—he could hear how bad the sound quality was, as well as scratches—and the echo of the music off pieces of the camp and the jungle, he could hardly tell what music was playing. He guessed it was a Vietnamese patriotic song, maybe their national anthem.

After their reveille, the troops herded the prisoners to a nearby hut that Stanson soon saw was a primitive kitchen, little more than food storage with a campfire set up in front. A soldier was stirring a pot, and Stanson smelled some kind of stew. However, when the prisoners lined up, they were given a simple bowl of cold rice.

When John's turn came to be given a bowl, one of the soldiers stepped forward and shoved him away with his AK-47. "You no eat!"

Stanson looked at him incredulously, and he again stepped forward to grab some rice. Again, the soldier shoved him, this time hard enough to knock John on his ass. He stared up at the soldier with a deadly glare.

One of the POWs appeared at his side, helping him to his feet. "It's OK," he said to the soldier, then said it again in Vietnamese. The man looked down at them but backed off.

"Come on," Quintero whispered, "come sit with us."

The prisoners had gathered nearby, sitting on the ground. They were gorging on their rice, eating with their fingers and licking every bit of moist crumb from their dirty digits. As Stanson sat down, he saw Quintero glancing around. He then leaned over and slipped a small rice ball into Stanson's lap. John grabbed it and discreetly tossed it into his mouth. He glanced at the guards nearby, who did not appear interested that he might be chewing.

"You'll need to keep your strength up. We'll be working all day, and there will be no lunch. We'll be in the poppy field a couple miles from here. I'll show you how to harvest the sap from the bulbs." He nodded toward the command hut. Minh had come outside and was standing at the balcony railing, looking over the camp. Another man came up next to him. He was short and wiry, and from this distance looked Hispanic. While the other prisoners wore the tattered black pajamas that the Vietcong used to wear, this man wore a khaki uniform like that of the guards, only with no insignia. Stanson pegged him as a man with privilege.

"Meet Sergeant Noya," Quintero went on. "Like I told you last night, he will be paying you a visit. Listen to me. You are going to be Minh's plaything from now on. They've spent the last few years trying to break me, and I've just been toying with them. Now they're going to concentrate on you. Fight it.

We all know each other, but we can't know who you are. Guard your identity. The less they know about you, the better you will be."

* * *

The group was force-marched several miles on a worn trail that had long ago been cut through the thick jungle. During the march, Stanson seemed to notice every bit of movement around him, including wildlife. He saw monkeys and birds in the trees above them, and snakes and lizards on their path before them. Once, the soldiers stopped the column when the bushes moved to their left. Stanson tensed to move in case his rescue was imminent. Instead, a wild boar bolted from the bushes, snorting and squealing to get away from them. Stanson half expected one of the soldiers to shoot the boar to feast on today, but they let the beast go and resumed their march. He also noted that the other prisoners seemed in a trance as they walked, unaffected by the brief excitement.

They followed the trail along a ridge above a rough river. Stanson tried to recall where this river might be on the maps he had pored over back at NKP, but it was in vain.

They finally emerged onto the side of a mountain, where a sloping plain dropped toward more rolling hills. With a shout from one of the soldiers, the prisoners fanned out and began their work. The soldiers spread out as well to form a loose ring around the group. They did not appear concerned about anyone trying to escape. But he did notice that they kept one soldier near him at all times. I'm still a novelty, he thought with an inner smirk.

Stanson stuck with Quintero for most of the

day. The Green Beret showed him how to harvest the poppy, to take the bulb of the flower and scrape the sap off. With a practiced hand, Quintero used a small very dull knife to shave off the substance and scrape it into a small canvas sack. In just minutes, he had completed several dozen flowers and filled his first bag. He gave Stanson a bag and sent him out on his way.

Stanson did his first few poppies to get a feel for the task, and then lapsed into the monotony of the work. He let his mind work on his predicament. He examined the layout of the land, the positions of the guards. He ran over and over in his mind how things would go down if he tried an escape.

The sun rose high into the sky. They were moving from spring toward summer, and though this region had rainstorms year round, there was not a cloud in the sky today. Within an hour, despite the fact that his menial task required no major exertion, he had sweated through his already tattered fatigues. He was also feeling the hunger that a single ball of rice could not alleviate.

Just before lunch time, he noticed newcomers to the party. Two new soldiers had arrived, and Sergeant Noya was with them. Noya had not been with them on the march to the poppy field that morning. He picked John out of the group and approached for the meeting that Quintero had promised would happen.

"How you doing?" he asked. Stanson expected him to offer a handshake, but he didn't. John gave him a suspicious glare.

"I'm Sergeant Noya, from Phoenix, Arizona. What's your name?"

Stanson continued to glare at him.

"Come on, man, I gotta call you something."

"OK, call me John." It sounded anonymous

enough, even if it was his real name.

"Fine. John. Look, I'm supposed to ask you to cooperate with Minh. It will make things a lot easier for you and everyone."

"Is that how it worked for you?" Stanson asked, forgetting his work for a moment.

"Look, things were bad when we first got here, but the last few years, they've settled down. Yeah, they still get out of hand sometimes, the guards go too far. But we're making Minh money, so he's treated us OK for a while. With you here, things are going to get bad again."

"For you, or for everyone? Let me guess. He was a little rough on you in the beginning, but he promised you leniency if you went along with the program. Maybe you get to go home soon? Maybe he treats you better than the other guys? You get more to eat, a roof over your head, make you feel better about betraying your country? Did he make you sign some bullshit statement about your 'crimes' against the people of Vietnam? And if you're so privileged in this camp, how is it you haven't been sent home yet?"

Noya appeared taken aback for a moment, like Stanson had slapped him or given him a shot to the gut. "Look, you have to trust me, it's not the way it looks."

"It's OK, I understand," Stanson went on, now reacting to the pained look on Noya's face. "You're identifying with your kidnappers. It's a defense mechanism. Stockholm syndrome. You have to do what you can to stay alive. Just keep in mind, we all have our own choices to make, including you, the other prisoners... and including me."

Noya took a step back to leave. "I tried," he said. His parting comment was, "Just keep in mind... everything is not as it seems."

Stanson pondered that as Noya walked back

toward his escort. Things were not always as they seemed. This seemed the story of his life. It was like that at The Farm, his CIA training facility. The whole Vietnam conflict was like that. It remained up to those with sharp minds like his to see this and read between the lines. He resolved to keep this in mind and always be ready.

* * *

When they arrived back at the camp just after sundown, Stanson was singled out again. The prisoners were grouped by the kitchen and given their bowl of rice, but he was once again denied food. This time, he had no opportunity to sneak some rice from one of the other guys. The guards took him to the command hut.

Minh waited for him there, along with Sergeant Noya. Stanson tried to interpret the scene. Minh had a slight smile on his face, conveying calm confidence but a slight menace. Noya just looked nervous.

"Please, sit down," Minh directed him.

Stanson was pushed by the soldiers to a chair in the middle of the room. Stanson sat but was not yet tied to the chair.

"I want you to tell me your name," Minh began. When Stanson said nothing, he went on, "You have already told Sergeant Noya your first name, which confirms what I already know. Your name is John Stanson. You work for the American CIA."

Stanson was surprised for a moment, but he should not have been, he realized. Minh likely had good resources in the intelligence community, and he realized that Smith might even be one of them. Minh had already told him that he was tipped off to the raid that led to his capture. Maybe Smith was feeding information in hopes of getting Stanson killed, to eliminate the threat of him exposing the operation he was involved with.

To cover his surprise, Stanson said, "Well, it seems you have all the answers you need, so you don't need me. I'll be in my cage."

He quickly realized that smarting off was a mistake. First, he had been so quiet and mysterious with Minh since his capture, this may expose vulnerability. He never knew if something he said could be checked or used against him. Second, his outburst earned him a stroke to the gut from a soldier's rifle.

"You Americans," Minh laughed. "You have such bravado. And yet you couldn't stomach the fight that you initiated against victorious communists. We drove your decadent imperialist forces from our land and reunited Vietnam. We have created the workers' paradise the leaders have promised. And you still seek to dictate destiny to us."

It was Stanson's turn to offer a cocky smile. "Workers' paradise? Terminology straight from Marx, Lenin and Mao. Is that where the workers are given everything by the state, they want for nothing—except the will to live, and seek their own destiny? You want to talk to me about dictating destiny? Let me ask you something, Colonel. If Vietnam has become such a paradise, why is everyone trying to escape?" He settled back into his chair, caught up in his history lesson. "Take the fall of Saigon. You were there, weren't you, Colonel? You see, I know a few things about you too. You led troops into Saigon in '75. Did you make it to the American embassy? Did you see all the people—Vietnamese people—trying to get into the embassy to catch the next chopper ride out? They wanted out. They wanted no part of your "workers' paradise." Even in the face of "rescue" from "Imperial domination," they saw America as their only hope."

John was watching Minh, and he saw the man trembling like a volcano about to erupt. He couldn't help a smile. "And now that Vietnam is all back together, and all those misguided souls are being reeducated—you don't need to worry about dying in a Communist reeducation camp, Colonel. You serve the party by being stuck out here in the jungle. Of course, you've got your little opium ring going strong. You've embraced capitalism." He leaned forward. "If you want to have a political discussion, we can go there. All the rest of this, you hiding behind politics as you imprison and torture these Americans... that's all bullshit and you know it."

The volcano finally erupted. Minh barked an order in Vietnamese. One of the guards butt stroked the prisoner in the gut again. Before he was ready for it, Stanson found the man in front of him, throwing punches into his face.

"Wait, Wait!" Stanson shouted, bringing the assault to a stop. Stanson took a breath, feeling blood trickling from a cut just under his left eye and on his lip. He looked up at Minh, who was now standing over him, just behind the guards.

Stanson suddenly laughed. "One more thing I know about communists. They all think they're right about everything. But when someone comes along and shows them how wrong they really are... *they tend not to take it well.*"

He laughed again until the next blow hit.

* * *

An hour later, Stanson was barely conscious when they dragged him out to the cage. They dumped him on the wet ground, locked the door and left. Stanson lay there for several minutes, trying not to move. He attempted to inventory the damage to his body, but even doing that hurt.

From out of the darkness, a hand touched his shoulder. "Easy, buddy. Let's sit you up."

Through his daze, he recognized Quintero's voice. The Special Forces Sergeant helped him sit up and lean back against the bamboo bars. In the light from a half moon, Quintero got a look at the bruises and dried blood on Stanson's face. "They worked you over pretty good, didn't they?"

"Here, Sarge," a new voice said. Stanson's awareness was coming back, and he realized that this voice came from *outside* the cage. He swiveled a tense neck around and found Sergeant Noya outside. He was pushing a wet piece of white cloth through the bars. Quintero grabbed it and began wiping at Stanson's face. "I brought him some food too." He pushed another cloth through, which was wrapped around a small bundle of rice. "I told you, things are not always what they appear," Noya whispered. With that, he broke from the cage and disappeared into the darkness.

Stanson's mind flooded with new questions, but he was too stunned and exhausted to ask them. Quintero seemed to sense his curiosity. "Noya was part of my infantry squad when we were captured. He's a good soldier and a good NCO, but he's simply not as tough as some. When they first brought us to Minh, we were beaten and tortured. The war was still going on, so they wanted to know all about our unit and our mission. We were interrogated for two full days, and each night, they would restrain us with our legs tied, and that rope wrapped out around our necks. Laying on your stomach like that, your body shaped like a damn rocking chair... it's a damn sight uncomfortable. After several days of this, Noya saw that I was holding tough—and knew he was not. He came to me and told me he wanted out. I had been working on a plan that if one of us broke, he was to play along, but then help us survive. We went over what information we could sacrifice to make sure nothing too incriminating was divulged. Minh still played his bullshit games. He promised Noya he would be treated well and sent home in due order, if only he would sign a confession of his crimes against the Vietnamese. When we discussed it, I assured him that if he went on trial back in the world, I would stand up for him.

"Well, as you can see, Noya was never sent home. Minh kept him around as a propaganda tool. Noya sleeps away from the rest of us, but he steals food and medicine for us. The others resented him for a while, until they saw what he was doing. Then Minh turned his attention to trying to break me."

Stanson sat still, riveted by the story. Quintero had been mopping his face with the wet rag, wiping away dried blood. Stanson could feel the bruises forming. His torso ached from kicks and rifle-butt strikes, and he hoped there was no organ damage or internal bleeding. Quintero stopped what he was doing, lost in his own story.

"Everything became a mind game. Minh tried everything he could to get me to sign his bullshit confession. He knew that if I caved, the others would break. He did everything he could to turn everyone against me. He even tried to use my family against me. On one particular attempt, he called me into his hut. He was very calm and pleasant. He held up a piece of paper. He says to me, "We have a good network of spies inside your Pentagon and State Department. They have sent me word that your wife is having you declared dead. She has also applied for a new marriage license. She is getting married,

Sergeant. I have decided to extend to you a great measure of mercy. I will release you and send you home to be with your wife so you can save your marriage. If you will only sign my confession, I will immediately send you home.

"I sat there, stone faced, looking at that stupid excuse for a compassionate smile. All I could do was burst out laughing. Once I started laughing I couldn't stop. I just stood up and walked out of there. He didn't even try to stop me. He must have thought I finally went crazy." Quintero couldn't help a low chuckle. "He wanted to tell me I could go home to my wife if I broke my oath? That bitch filed for divorce and left the day I signed up for my second tour."

CHAPTER 8

The longer John was in the camp, the more his fear grew that he would be stuck there for the rest of his life. There were two constant questions on his mind. Would Ross find him, and would Smith even let him try a rescue? The monotony of harvesting poppies allowed his mind to work the scenario over and over in his mind. He worked out multiple possibilities for escape. But each time, he came back to the problem of getting Quintero and the others out as well. During all this, he counted the days, and almost before he knew it, three weeks had passed.

In the first week, he'd been tortured just about every night. It was just simple beatings, causing little more than cosmetic damage to his face, some bruises to his body. They never broke any bones, and he didn't seem to be sick or in pain from any internal organ damage. The torture sessions soon tapered off though. Minh already knew he was John Stanson from the CIA. There was little else he needed. Late one night, Stanson had analyzed Minh's situation with Quintero and Noya. In the beginning, he had tortured the prisoners to gain information on their units and their missions. But now, the war was long over, so gathering information from the prisoners was unimportant. They'd been reduced to slave labor for the lucrative opium harvest by day, and toys for Minh's mind games by night. But lately, in the months before Stanson was taken, Noya told them that Minh was possibly looking for a way to bring himself to the attention of his superiors back in Hanoi and Ho Chi Minh City. Bringing in money from opium sales was not enough to do that. Their fear was that having a CIA man prisoner now would be a new avenue for Minh out of the jungle.

Stanson hit upon an idea one night on how he might use this to his advantage. In an indirect way, it might give Minh the boost he needed, but the true purpose was revenge against Smith. The crazy ex-Marine had tried to kill him and left him to waste away in a Vietnamese POW camp—long after the war was over. John was more convinced than ever that Smith was involved in the opium trade, and that he, Stanson, had been used as a pawn against Minh, a competitor. Smith needed to feel some hurt for what he had done. As an added bonus, it might convey to Ross that he was still alive. Hell, just for his own revenge, Smith might even authorize the rescue. The next time Minh decided to have him roughed up, Stanson would finally break. He would finally give up information valuable to Minh.

He would give them the X on the map.

The next morning, as he woke with the sun, he noticed something strange about Quintero. The man was still asleep, but he was shaking, shivering even in the warm spring air. Stanson checked him over and found large beads of sweat on the man's dirty face. Stanson shook him to wake him.

One of the other prisoners saw this and crawled over. "Damn," the man muttered, "He's got malaria again."

Quintero woke up in time to hear this. "I'm awake. I'll be alright."

Stanson kept watch over Quintero as they started their day. The five prisoners gathered for their morning breakfast of a bowl of rice. Quintero sat hunched on the ground, rocking back and forth for a minute. His hands shook as he scooped his rice into his mouth. Stanson spotted Noya standing nearby and motioned him over. With a glance at nearby guards, Noya approached and crouched next to the Staff Sergeant.

"They say he's got malaria," Stanson said quietly. "He shouldn't work today. Is there anything you can do? Can we get him some medicine?"

"It's iffy," Noya said. "Minh usually keeps it locked up in case his soldiers need it."

In an even lower whisper, Stanson said, "Maybe you can steal some?"

Noya could only shrug. "I'll see what I can do."

Quintero had listened to the exchange. "I'll be OK, guys." He then turned and vomited up the rice he had just eaten.

Stanson looked at a nearby guard, who seemed to be intentionally keeping his distance. "He needs help," he shouted to the guard. "He needs medicine."

The guard could not ignore him anymore. "No!" he shouted. "No medicine. We go now, work."

"I'll be alright, Johnny," Quintero insisted. He got shakily to his feet.

* * *

They were marched the usual route miles down the trail to the poppy field. During the march, Stanson stayed by Quintero's side. He was still shaking and sweating, but he was a Green Beret and tough as they come. He walked on, slumping and shuffling, but moving under his own steam.

During the trip, John learned a new tidbit of information from Quintero. "I heard the soldiers talking last night. We may be moving camps soon. We've almost finished with this poppy field, so they'll want to move us to another."

This was not good news. It meant he might not have the opportunity to implement his revenge plan. It diminished any possibility of rescue. *If* Ross were to come looking to rescue him from this camp, he might not be here.

They began their normal workday, harvesting the sap from poppy bulbs. It was monotonous work, and Stanson had usually kept his mind occupied with observing the activity of the guards or mapping out a possible escape scenario. But one thing he always found a moment of enjoyment in was the view from this hillside. The hill looked out over more rolling hills covered in green. He could make out jungle covering most of those hillsides, with the occasional piece of green and yellow grassland. When he first found himself working this field, he vowed to take a moment to savor the view and take a moment of peace before allowing himself to drift back to his new reality. Today he did the same, he sucked in a breath of moist air and took in the view, relishing a moment of tranquility.

Until he saw the smoke.

In the distance, several hills and several miles away, a brown haze was drifting from a stretch of grassland. He stopped to examine the scene and confirmed that the distant meadow was on fire.

It took the soldiers a few minutes to notice the smoke. For the moment, everyone went about their duties. Stanson turned to Quintero, standing idly nearby. "Sarge, check it out."

As he said this, the guards began to shout and point at the smoke. Stanson watched their actions. Several of the guards galloped into the field, gathering to look at the fire. One of them had a pair of binoculars, and for a moment, they took turns looking through the glasses.

Movement from Quintero's direction grabbed his attention, and he turned to see the Sergeant collapse. Stanson rushed to his side. Quintero had rolled onto his right flank and was completely passed out. Stanson began slapping his face, urging him to wake up.

Fresh shouts from the soldiers reached him, and he saw them running toward where the prisoners were now gathered around their unofficial leader. They shouted in Vietnamese, but one switched to English, shouting, "We go! We go!"

At that moment, Quintero finally woke up. He looked up at his friend. "Hey, Johnny, what's up?"

The prisoners were marched back to the camp. Stanson had to support Quintero during the trip. He felt like he could sense the tough Green Beret getting weaker by the second.

* * *

Back at the camp, the prisoners were tossed into the cage and basically forgotten all day. Stanson stayed by Quintero's side. The Sergeant lay on his side, shivering in the warmth. Stanson could do nothing but watch what he could see of the world outside his cage, and of course feel helpless.

As the sun fell and ushered in the night, Noya approached the cage with two soldiers. "Johnny, Minh wants to see you."

"What about medicine for Quintero?" Stanson asked as they unlocked the cage door.

"I'm sorry, man, I've asked about getting him treated, but Minh is just ignoring my requests."

He was guided into the command hut, where Minh waited. Stanson found himself in the chair once again. The guards stepped back, allowing the meeting to start.

"I'm sure you know by now, John Stanson," Minh began, "that the smoke you saw from the hillside was another of my poppy fields. My men were able to check the field. It was purposefully set ablaze. It seems your friends are unwilling to share the drug trade. The competition is too fierce, and they felt the need to strike at me. I will strike back."

"How very capitalist of you," Stanson muttered. He braced for the blow, and it came from behind, a rifle butt to his rib. But he couldn't speak up. Not yet.

"You are in a position to help me, John Stanson. You have been quiet and enjoyed my generous hospitality up until now. But now, I require you to provide me information." He pulled a large knife from a sheath. "Or I will make things very unpleasant for you. Who are the men you work with, and where can I find them?" He stood and advanced on the American, staring more at the gleaming knife than at his prisoner.

Stanson took a breath. "Look, I can't tell you who the men I work with are."

Minh lashed out, swiping the knife across Stanson's arm. He felt the skin on his left shoulder part, drawing a small stream of blood.

"Wait, wait!" Stanson yelled, "Hold on a second. You're a soldier, Colonel Minh. You must understand that I can't simply give you information that betrays my country. It is my duty to resist that. But there is some information I can give you. I can give you a location to check out." He hesitated for a moment. "But I want something in return."

Minh's usually blank expression turned curious, his almond eyes narrowing. "Go on."

"Quintero is sick with malaria. I want you to treat him, I want you to give him medicine, antibiotics."

Minh considered this. "Show me this location."

Stanson hesitated. He didn't trust the Vietnamese for a second to fulfill his end of the bargain and provide the medicine. But he still needed, wanted, to give his information. If he didn't, he'd be tortured further anyway. "I want your word that Quintero will be treated. One soldier to another."

"You have it." But to Stanson, Minh's lie was obvious.

He pressed forward. "Show me a map."

Minh gestured to the soldiers, one of them pulled a map from a drawer in a nearby desk and spread it across the table. Stanson was allowed to stand and approach. He scanned the map and stabbed a finger at the location he remembered. Minh noted the location, and he stood for a long moment, deep in thought. Then he waved, and his soldiers stepped forward. They grabbed Stanson and pulled him away.

As he was dragged out the door, Stanson called out, "Colonel, the medicine. You promised. You promised!"

His last image there was of the Colonel ignoring him, staring at the map.

* * *

Stanson was shoved back into the cage, and once again forgotten. No one came in the night to administer any medication to the stricken soldier.

Staff Sergeant Adrian Quintero died during the night.

Stanson was awakened by activity in the camp the next morning as the sun tried to penetrate the jungle around them. He crept to the bars to scope out the activity, and he saw soldiers forming up in front of the command hut. This was not a normal reveille. These soldiers were dressed for battle. Each had an AK-47, and a sash filled with loaded magazines. It seemed like the whole cadre for the camp was assembled, and he counted at least thirty men. A platoon sergeant was barking orders at the formation. Three of the four ranks of soldiers were then marched away, right out the front gate. The last rank would apparently stay and guard the camp.

His information was being acted upon. He knew this unit was going to hit the location he'd shown them.

His next thought was to check Quintero. When he grabbed the Sergeant's shoulder, he felt the man's cold skin. He felt for a pulse and found none.

"Hey!" Stanson shouted, trying to get anyone's attention. "Hey! Quintero's dead! He's dead!"

Two guards patrolling nearby looked over at his commotion but walked on by. John followed their movement as they approached the command hut. He saw Minh come out.

"Minh! You bastard! You killed him. I'll kill you, Minh!"

Colonel Minh eyed him from across the camp as the new prisoner continued to yell at him. Then he turned away and walked with the soldiers out the gate.

Out of breath, gripping the bars of his cage, Stanson settled to muttering over and over, "I'll kill you." He meant to carry this out as a promise. Minh, Smith, they would both die by his hand if...*when*... he got the chance.

"It's OK, buddy," one of the other two prisoners

said. "His suffering is over. It'll be OK."

Stanson lapsed into silence. He crawled over to the dead form of one of the toughest soldiers he'd ever known. He said a quiet goodbye, and a quick prayer for all of them. He then curled up next to the bars and began reviewing his plans and ideas for what he now hoped would become a violent escape.

* * *

The prisoners were not let out of their cage all day. At dusk, the guards opened the cage and tossed in a bowl of plain white rice. The three remaining prisoners dug into it. Before joining them, Stanson stayed where he was leaning back against the bars, watching as the guards dragged out Quintero's body. It had remained there in the heat all day, under attack from the insects, and quick decay was setting in. The body was beginning to smell. Stanson lamented the man's lack of any dignity in his final moments on earth. He wondered for a moment what would happen with the Sergeant, if his remains would somehow be returned to the States. He had his doubts, ten years after the war was over. Stanson had collected the man's dog tags, and he would deal with them when he got out of this camp. And he was now more determined than ever that he *would* get out.

The calm over the camp lulled him into an uneasy sleep as the darkness deepened. He was awakened by a commotion. He found the noise coming from the main gate, where the soldiers were returning, marching into the compound with triumphant cries and broad grins. The soldiers who had remained cheered as their comrades returned from an obviously successful mission. Spotlights all over the camp turned on and shifted about in celebration.

John watched all this, trying to interpret what was going on. Minh's raid on the mysteriously active abandoned X on the map must have been successful. What was the outcome, he wondered? Competitors killed? Dope destroyed, or maybe stolen? Would he have personal revenge on Smith when he left this camp, or had Minh dealt that revenge blow already?

Minh himself emerged from the cheering soldiers and strode straight to the cage. A grin stretched his thin lips. He barked an order. Soldiers came forward and unlocked the cage. The other prisoners crept aside as two soldiers stooped to enter the cage. The soldiers grabbed Stanson by the arms and dragged him out the door. It was shut and locked behind him.

With a soldier on either side of him, he was brought before the grinning camp commander.

"I want you to know, John Stanson, that your information was most helpful. We found men preparing a large shipment of opium for transport. My soldiers killed many enemy fighters. We relieved them of the opium. You have made me a rich man tonight." He stepped forward. "Many of the men we killed tonight... they were Americans."

Stanson moved, his actions already planned. With his left hand, he lashed out with a chop that landed at the throat of the soldier beside him. He could not tell if the blow was hard enough to crush the larynx and cause the man's death, but for the moment, it did not matter. At the same time, he lashed out with his right foot, collapsing sideways the knee of the second soldier. As that man sank to the ground with cries of pain, Stanson launched himself at Minh. He wasn't trying to land a blow or a kick. He barreled into the Vietnamese Colonel with his whole body, taking both to ground. The element of surprise allowed him to get hands around Minh's neck. With his enemy on the ground, restrained by the weight of his body, Stanson began to squeeze the man's throat harder and harder.

For a brief moment, he saw actual fear in Minh's eyes.

The first rifle butt slammed in his ribs, and the remaining soldiers began raining blows down on him. He tried his damnedest to block the pain out, focusing only on killing the evil Vietnamese Colonel in his grip. But the moment was taken from him, and the soldiers, shouting orders and curses, finally managed to pull him away from their commander. With soldiers holding his arms, another began punching him in the stomach and chest. He sensed rather than saw that Minh was helped to his feet. Once standing, Minh shoved away the soldiers and straightened his own uniform. He barked another order, and the assault on Stanson ceased. They continued to restrain him.

Minh suddenly smiled. "You have earned a reward for betraying your countrymen." In Vietnamese, he gave an order to the soldiers. Stanson was dragged away, accompanied by what seemed like the entire cadre of Vietnamese. He never saw what happened to the men he had injured.

As their short walk ended, his senses were assaulted by a horrid smell. Through the growing fog in his brain, he saw the pit before him and knew what it was. They had brought him to the camp latrine. Every day, the Vietnamese would urinate here, would dump buckets with their fecal waste, sometimes even the trash from their meals. On top of that the frequent rains often filled the pit, making it a muddy disgusting mess. He knew what they planned to do and he was powerless to stop it.

He was restrained firmly by hands holding his arms, and he was tied by the wrists. For a moment, he did not see where the rope led, but he was suddenly hoisted into the air. He groaned against the strain on his shoulder muscles. He felt himself swinging through the air. He was lowered into the pit full of piss and shit. He sank in up to his neck. Only his arms remained sanitary, stretched overhead as they were by the rope.

To literally add insult to injury, the voices of the soldiers took on a different tone. They were taunting him, he realized. Through the haze of his injuries, he looked up at the soldiers lining the rim of the pit, pointing at him and laughing. He saw one actually open his fly and begin to urinate into the pit.

Gradually, their merriment drifted away as they left to celebrate their victory. He began to drift off, wanting to sleep, but knowing that with his injuries, this was not a good idea.

"That was beautiful, Johnny," came a shout in the distance. Through the fog of pain, he realized that the other prisoners were calling out from the cage, trying to encourage him. "You got him good, you really kicked his ass!"

"Hang in there, buddy," the other prisoner said. It was an ironic choice of words, Stanson thought, but he hurt too much to comment.

Stanson's mind was a thousand jumbled questions, but one thought kept dashing his hopes for escape. Minh had told him that many Americans had died in his raid. His providing information had gotten Americans killed. They could have been rogue CIA, Smith's men, or they could even be expatriates from the war. Maybe they were working the dope trade, but they were Americans. He couldn't help thinking that by giving up the mysterious map site, he had signed his own death warrant. He tried to ignore the stench of the filth he was immersed in, tried to allow himself to rest.

Sometime during the night, he was roused by painful tension in his shoulders. He awoke when he realized what was going on. He was being lifted out of the latrine pit. Instinct gripped him, and he held back cries of pain as he dangled for a moment. He was swung through the air. When he was lowered to the ground, he collapsed.

"Take it easy, Johnny. Lay down. I can't cut you loose, but I can at least get you out of the shit."

He recognized the voice. Sergeant Noya had pulled him out.

"Minh and most of his men are drunk and passed out. Spent the whole night drinking that rice wine they like so much. Let's get you cleaned up a bit."

Mercifully, it began to rain. Stanson lay there for a moment, letting it wash away some of the filth that caked on his body. And maybe a little from his soul.

***

Stanson faded in and out of sleep the rest of that night. He remained tied to the rope that had hoisted him into the latrine pit, though it had some slack, allowing him to move around a bit. The rain was off and on that night, and he lay there through the predawn hours, letting it drench him. He was aware of the sun coming up, and even aware that the soldiers did not rise with the sun. They were all passed out drunk. He couldn't go anywhere, he figured, so he just lay there. He'd begun to shiver a bit from being soaked by the rain, but the rising sun started to warm him.

Well into the morning, he was roused by shouting. He opened his eyes and checked his surroundings. He was some distance away from the command hut, but he caught sight of Minh coming out to his balcony. Seeing none of his soldiers around, he began shouting orders, rousing everyone with his anger. Only now did he see some of the soldiers scattered about the camp, asleep where they had passed out. Some began to rise and wake their drunken buddies.

The soldiers stood up from the muddy camp floor, or came out from their barracks, beginning to get organized. They gathered in some semblance of a formation below the command hut. Stanson smiled at how many were slumped over or holding their heads, deep in hangover.

John then realized that today would be a perfect day to try an escape—or at least kill a few of them before they killed him. If only he could get himself free. He began preparing himself mentally, cataloguing his pains and injuries, and he watched for an opportunity.

Then he noticed Minh staring right at him.

Minh began shouting a long string of curses at his men. He marched downstairs to the muddy ground and up to the formation. Still shouting, he gestured at the latrine. He then grabbed a Sergeant and dragged him toward where Stanson lay. The soldiers followed dutifully. There was no reason to remain on the ground, so he took a bold step and started to stand. The ropes draped from his wrists. He stared Minh down as the Vietnamese Colonel confronted him.

"Who pulled him out?" Minh demanded in English.

There was a moment of silence. Stanson spent the time noting the position of each soldier, and which of them had weapons. His hands were still tied to the ropes leading overhead, but the ropes had plenty of slack. He watched, maintaining a smug grin through the silence, enjoying Minh's look of betrayal.

"I did," a voice behind them said. They all turned

as Sergeant Noya approached. "Leaving him there was cruel and unnecessary, Colonel Minh. I pulled him out to give him back some of the dignity you've taken from all of us."

Sergeant Noya was standing a little taller, Stanson saw. Maybe with the passing of the senior prisoner, Noya was stepping up to fill the gap Quintero left behind.

Everyone stared at Noya for a moment. "Sergeant Noya," Minh began, "You've been my guest for twelve years. I have looked out for you and treated you well. Where is this defiance coming from?"

"You've used me, Colonel. That ends today."

Standing just a couple yards to Stanson's right, Minh's Sergeant slowly drew a pistol. He leveled it at Noya and kept it there.

"So be it," Minh said. "Perhaps some time with your friend in the pit is long overdue."

Stanson felt a moment of despair. If he was going back into the shit, now with Noya next to him, he would have no chance to attempt an escape.

Stanson suddenly caught movement in the jungle. Beyond the wire perimeter fence, he saw someone darting from behind a tree. That someone wore jungle camouflage, but mysteriously for the moment, he appeared not to care if he was seen. He appeared to be heading for the main gate, off to John's right.

He checked the gate, which was fifty yards away. It was manned by two soldiers who had not gotten drunk last night. Their rapt attention was on the altercation happening at the latrine. They did not see the man emerge from the jungle behind them, approaching quietly.

It was Ross.

Two thoughts occurred to John at the same time.

He was about to be rescued.

Smith was most likely in the jungle with a rifle

sight trained on him.

Stanson suddenly lunged at the Vietnamese Sergeant. The Asian was a small man, and Stanson was average size for an American. He was easily able to overpower the Sergeant. With his left arm circling the man's neck, his right went for the pistol. He turned the man's arm until the gun was now trained on Minh. They struggled, and Stanson fought to get a good grip on the man's hand. In moments, he was able to force the trigger finger.

Seeing the struggle, Minh was backing away. The Sergeant's gun went off. Minh staggered back as blood erupted from his flank.

At the gate, Ross took out the two guards. Mimicking Stanson's move, he grabbed one around the neck, and he held the man as he shot the second guard. He then broke the first guard's neck. He ran into the open toward the gathering. "John! Cover!"

As he said this, the camp erupted in gunfire. The Sergeant that Stanson held was hit by a three-round burst that rattled his body. All around him, people moved. Noya hit the deck. Minh turned and ran, holding his wounded side. The hung-over soldiers began to run, but the group was hit by a prolonged burst of rifle fire. Three were cut down, and the rest scattered.

Stanson dropped the dead man and went prone. As Ross reached him, he saw the ropes still tied to Stanson's wrists. He tossed John a Ka-bar knife, and Stanson quickly sawed away the ropes at his wrists. He and Ross then headed for the closest cover, a nearby tree. He scooped up a dead man's AK-47 on the way. The pause nearly cost him his life as bullets tore into the dirt at his heels. He lunged away, clutching the rifle, and he and Ross dived behind the tree.

"What the hell?" Stanson shouted.

"It's Smith," Ross warned, "He came here to kill you. I've been trying for weeks to put together a mission to come here—I knew this was where you'd be. Smith finally put this little operation together in haste because one of his opium sites got hit."

Stanson grinned. "I guess he got my message."

Ross gave him a curious look. "We gotta take him out, John. This has to end now."

"On the same page. Where is he?"

Ross pointed into the jungle. "I left him there, preparing to breach the fence. I broke away when I saw you near the main gate. I couldn't go in the same way with him. I know he means to kill you and probably me. No witnesses."

They heard a distant crack, and they ducked as one of the huts exploded. "That would be Harry," Ross smiled.

"And his trusty blooper," Stanson grinned right back. He pointed behind them. "Ross, up that path is a bamboo cage, with three American POWs inside. They go home with us. I'm going into the jungle. Cover me."

They rose as one. Ross sprayed the remnants of his AK-47 magazine across a section of jungle where Smith was supposed to be hiding. Stanson made a beeline for the camp's main gate. The camp was now echoing with gunfire, but none of it seemed directed at him. He made the gate and plunged into the jungle at the left side.

In the outside jungle, Stanson reverted back to his training. He moved as silently as he could. The rain the night before left the ground soft and moist, easy on his bare feet. The bushes didn't rustle so loudly as he pushed them aside to pass through. Sporadic gunfire and shouting in the camp covered some of the noise of his passage.

He detected movement in a small clearing ahead

and stopped, hidden behind a fern bush, to check the situation. It was Smith. He was crawling backward into the clearing. He would never have a better chance to remove the threat this man presented. He raised the rifle.

Too late, he saw the wire and realized why Smith was crawling backward. The big Marine dropped to the ground and twisted the handle of the detonator that Stanson suddenly saw.

It was a breaching charge, set at the wire and bamboo fence just thirty yards away. The explosion wrenched the jungle, smoke and fire barreling through vegetation. Stanson felt the force of the blast pick him up and toss him back several yards. He landed stunned and for a moment unable to move.

Smith was unaware that Stanson had been behind him. He rose and entered the camp where the charge had torn open the fence.

Stanson rose from the muddy ground where he'd landed. He shook his head to awaken his senses again. He then forced himself to his feet. Hefting the AK-47, he stumbled after Smith. As his senses returned, his mission and his footing became more sure.

Moving in the Marine's wake, he saw one last time how much of a combat animal Smith was. Emerging from the jungle into the camp, Smith opened up on two Vietnamese soldiers approaching from his left. They went down in a tangle of dying limbs. Smith kept firing as more soldiers ran his way.

Stanson moved up silently behind, working his way between two raised huts. He raised the rifle, steadied the sights between Smith's shoulder blades...

Instinct tore him away. Movement above beckoned. As he turned to check three o'clock high, he realized he was right below the command hut. Minh was above him, an AK-47 steady in his arms. The muzzle flashed.

John quickly melted to his right, rolling under the balcony of the hut. Minh was right above him, and bullets from his rifle chased Stanson under the hut.

Stanson landed prone, his rifle seeking out Smith's last position.

"John Stanson!" Minh shouted. "I kill you!"

Smith turned to the voice. He took in Minh on the balcony, his rapt attention on the ground directly below. Minh leaned over the railing trying to fire under the hut. Stanson saw Smith's eyes lock on his position. His face twisted into that familiar grin. He aimed his rifle, not at Minh but under the hut.

Stanson saw Smith's body suddenly rocked by bullets hitting him. Blood exploded from his upper arm, followed by another round tearing flesh and spurting blood from along the front of his torso. A quick glance to his left, and Stanson saw Ross running his direction, firing at Smith. He looked again at Smith. The ex-Marine had dropped to a crouch, but now turned and sprinted away across the camp, weaving between trees and shelters.

A fresh burst from Minh rocked the ground next to him, kicking up gouts of mud inches from his legs. The son of a bitch was again leaning out to try and get a better shot under the hut.

Stanson rolled on his back, the AK-47 sticking straight up at the floor of the balcony. He held back the trigger, letting the rifle on automatic shake his body. His rounds tore up the damp wood three feet over his head, showering him with pieces of that wood. He let the rifle fire for some seconds until the magazine was emptied.

When the breach locked open, it was suddenly very quiet. He saw a stream of blood running through one of the bullet holes above him. The next second, Minh's body toppled from the balcony, landing in the mud next to the hut, just a few feet away.

Stanson scrambled from under the hut. Ross reached him. "Smith took off," Stanson said, "I saw where he went." He started a slow jog, once again in Smith's wake. As he ran, he pointed to the ground. "I got a blood trail."

"I hit him bad," Ross said, three steps behind him, "I know I did."

In the peripherals of his mind, Stanson sensed how quiet the camp was. Apparently, all the soldiers had been dealt with, and Harry Wayne and the rest of the team were nearby mopping up. He'd reunite with his friend later. He followed drops of blood that led between the huts and toward the jungle. At first, the stain was easy to follow, drops in the mud or on bush leaves. He reached the perimeter fence and found a section of the wire that had been sliced open, probably with a bayonet. Blood smeared the ground where Smith had slithered under the wire.

Ross passed him and pulled the wire up for his friend. Stanson scrambled underneath, then held the wire up for Ross. In seconds they were moving through the jungle.

The blood trail disappeared.

* * *

Steve could feel his eyes drooping. He was exhausted, but he was fascinated by the story, patiently waiting for the Captain to finish. When Stanson trailed off, Steve heard the faintest sob—Stanson was once again choked with emotion at the loss of a friend, even so distant in time.

The last few hours were wearing on Steve. But he was gaining multitudes of insight into the world of Captain John Stanson. *And I thought my world was* intense, Steve thought. Stanson had seen more in his life of war than Steve ever thought he could handle.

The sad Captain sat up against the inside of the burned-out tree trunk, reflecting on his dredged up past. Then, as if sensing Steve's exhaustion without even looking, said, "I'll take the first watch. Why don't you get some sleep?"

Gratefully, Steve closed his eyes. In moments, he'd drifted off.

Stanson had the fire of his impending vengeance to keep him awake.

CHAPTER 9

Stanson came instantly awake, his eyes snapping open. To have sat up carelessly would have given his position away. But something had awakened him. He glanced around, oddly expecting to see soldiers and operators from his Thailand unit lounging around nearby, their M-16s ready to take out approaching enemies.

Instead, he saw Steve Blazer out of his poncho, examining the supposedly abandoned lumber camp. He could see the sky through the canopy of redwood branches above him. The rain had stopped, but the sky was still steel gray.

Steve seemed to sense his mentor was awake. They'd each had a mere two hours of rest, but it was enough to keep them going.

Stanson slowly sat up, knowing something had disturbed his rest. He noticed that Steve wasn't just watching the camp, he was staring *at* something in that direction. Silently, the Captain slipped out of his poncho and joined him by the rock.

Someone was in the forest beyond the camp. Stanson watched a young-looking man cross between two trees and disappear. Farther to the west, another was creeping along in the open, finally stopping behind another redwood. He was exposed long enough for Stanson to see he was Asian.

"Those are the same guys that tried for me at the store last night," Steve said quietly. He pointed out one just up the hill, maybe eighty yards away from their position. "That's Danny Dinh. I recognize him from his mug shot from the Bao Lin investigation. He became the leader of Bao Lin's gang, the Specters, by default." Steve paused to note the positions of the whole group as they swept into the camp. "I've been tracking them for the last five minutes. I wish I knew how they found us here."

"I think they're on the same mission we are," Stanson said as he quietly checked his weapons, watching the advancing Asians.

A single gunshot split the morning. One of the Asians had been walking casually between trees. He took the shot square in the chest and dropped dead.

"Where'd it come from?" Steve said, throwing noise discipline to the wind.

In the camp, Smith decided to answer his question. The sudden roar of his truck motor sounded muffled but still echoed across the forest, deceiving those who sought out the noise.

Suddenly the front of one of the sheds exploded in chunks as the truck crashed through it and burst forth into the camp. When Smith found the camp, he found this shed falling apart. It was sturdy enough to back his truck into, and he'd found decayed sheets of plywood to brace over the open front. Those chunks of wood now scattered everywhere. The truck fishtailed into a right turn, throwing up plumes of mud from the trail.

The hit team abandoned their stealthy approach to the camp and the six-remaining rose from cover to try and stop the truck with their firepower. MPKs opened up from the forest, tongues of flame spitting lead at the running target. Several of the shooters broke cover and bolted through the forest in a vain attempt to keep up with the truck.

Smith felt the bullets ripping holes in his truck, and he tried to answer as best he could, left hand extending his .45 out the window to pump out round after round. With his right hand busy fighting the steering wheel, he had no hope of aiming well, so his was merely rapid discouraging fire.

Suddenly both parties had new problems to contend with.

Stanson heard the engine come alive and was up and running the second the truck burst from its hiding place.

Steve had no idea his Captain was going to do this, but he met the new challenge without word or complaint. He was out of their hiding place two steps behind the Captain. He tracked the running Asians with his Beretta to cover Stanson's run. The closest one turned his MPK on Blazer, and Steve loosed two quick slugs. The man went down screaming.

It took Steve a moment to realize that the Asian wasn't just screaming in pain but shouting a warning. As he bolted between two trees, Steve saw three more MPKs turn his way. He rolled through wet pine needles and mud to end up behind a young redwood just ahead of a line of slugs that stitched diagonally across the other side of the tree. Another burst tore into the mud patch just to his right, tossing chunks into the air, showering on him.

Danny Dinh ran up the muddy road with one of his Chinese friends. Their weapons had fallen silent as they chased down the bouncing truck. Steady gunfire behind him registered in his mind, and Danny turned to check the camp. The first thing he saw were the bodies of two of the hitters, men he'd seen alive in combat just moments ago. A new figure commanded his attention, a white man running across the camp in his direction, brandishing a handgun. With a moment of clarity, Dinh recognized him as the tall cop from the convenience store just hours ago.

Stanson cursed his luck as the terrain north of the road sloped upward ahead of him, but he kept his legs pumping, feeling his aging heart pounding in his chest. I knew there was a reason I let myself get promoted, he told himself. All this action stuff is bad for a guy my age. So, in a quick command decision as he traversed the hillside above the road, he tried to cut the chase short. The silver Colt Python was holstered on his hip, but he drew the automatic from his shoulder rig as the truck surged abreast of him below.

Smith tossed the .45 onto the seat next to him and took control of the steering wheel. The road cut into the hillside and curved to the right around it. When he swung into that curve, he felt the back wheels lose traction in the mud and slide to the left. He steered against it to correct. For a second, he thought he saw movement on the hill above him, but when he looked, the roof of the cab blocked his view.

But the next second, bullets began pounding the hood, ripping holes through the metal to get to the engine beneath. The hood popped up in front of him, partially blocking his view. Involuntarily, he jerked the wheel to the left, and at just that moment, the road curved farther to the right. He tried to hit the brakes, but the tires found no traction in the mud. The ground dropped out from underneath him as the truck lunged over an embankment toward the wide-open creek bed below. A tree trunk suddenly loomed ominously before him.

Stanson watched in satisfaction as the truck leapt

from the road and careened down the slope. The truck glanced off a tree and slid around to the left. The slope dropped off here, and the truck found traction enough to tip over on its left side. The bed smashed into another smaller tree, stopping the slide. Something creaked below, and Stanson could tell the truck was in a very precarious position on the edge of another drop-off.

Stanson studied the truck for a moment. A new figure—Danny Dinh—stopped from a run on the muddy road below him. Stanson swung his Colt onto the new target just as Dinh turned his machine pistol on him. Stanson fired his last shot, and the Colt locked empty. But the shot was accurate, and Danny whirled as the large caliber round hit. He landed face down in a puddle of muddy water.

Stanson slid down his slope. He reloaded the empty Colt as he crossed the road and slid it once more into the shoulder holster. The .357 Revolver filled his hand as he hit the drop off and slid carefully down. He was wary of the changing slope, and the drop-off below the still creaking truck. He picked out a smoother path twenty yards to the east. Walking in a slow crouch, he kept wary eyes and a ready weapon trained on the overturned vehicle, waiting for Smith to make his move. He made his way around the front of the truck, where the first evidence he saw made his heart sink and his rage boil.

The windshield was smashed, not just from the crash but actually kicked out, leaving space enough for a man to crawl through.

There was a smear of blood on part of the windshield that was still intact.

When he realized the cab was empty, he alerted and fine-tuned his senses to pick other threats around him. There was only one place Smith could have gone, down, and John dropped to a slide into the creek bed.

Just as he reached the bottom, he detected a presence behind him. He dropped to a crouch and tried to whirl around. The move saved his life.

Smith had risen from behind a giant redwood, like a Phoenix rising from the ashes to enjoy yet another resurrection. He had drawn a bead on the man he recognized immediately, even after thirty years, a man that until just this moment he had no idea was tracking him.

Stanson tried to whirl in his crouch, but a .45 caliber slug burrowed through his left shoulder, knocking him into a sitting position, facing his enemy. For a moment, the two old warriors faced each other, sharing a look that was remembered by both.

Stanson was almost lost in the déjà vu. But the apparent shock of seeing his old comrade seemed to freeze Smith's finger on the trigger, and Stanson used that. He lunged into a dive to his right for cover behind a tree.

Smith's gun followed him, and a slug loosed by the .45 tore into the slope behind the running man. But Stanson made it to sanctuary behind the tree.

* * *

Steve had his own troubles to deal with. He was pinned behind a large redwood. Four gunmen had found cover behind a large fallen tree nearby and were saturating his position with nine-millimeter fire. Steve leaned out and pumped two quick rounds toward the closest one, but as he did, the others opened fire from the stump where the tree had been cut. They surprised him, and he scrambled back to another side of his tree. Another line of slugs pelted his tree, tossing wood and bark chunks across his body. One of the rounds grazed his upper right arm. He ducked back further behind cover and grabbed at the arm. It stung, but he could tell it was not life threatening.

He heard a shout, and glimpsed movement to his right. Two of the men were positioned behind the fallen tree, and they appeared to be moving further to his right. They're trying to flank me, Steve realized.

He did have one edge, he suddenly remembered, and pulled it from his coat pocket, the grenade Stanson had left him. With a glance toward the shooters by the tree stump to his right, he leaned out to his left and fired at the two men moving toward the end of the fallen tree. They ducked behind the log. Steve then pulled the pin on the grenade, leaned back to his right and tossed it at the stump.

The two men saw and heard something land in the ferns just beyond them, but they had not seen what it was. The blast took them by surprise, tossing them against the log as the shrapnel tore their bodies to bloody shreds.

Steve surged to his feet a second after the blast. He crossed twenty feet of open ground and vaulted over the downed redwood. He landed at the edge of the burn scar where the grenade had detonated. Smoke still hung in the air, and debris was still falling to the forest floor. He found himself staring at the bloody remains of the two who'd tried to flank him.

Movement above him grabbed his attention. The third Asian was actually running along the top of the downed log. For a moment, Steve saw the emotion and desperation in the man's face at the sight of his dead comrades and the man who had killed them. He brought up his MPK.

Steve simultaneously engaged him with his

Desert Eagle, fired a .44 Magnum shredder. The powerful round knocked the Asian into the air and he flew several feet to land in a dead heap among a patch of ferns.

The last gunman suddenly vaulted over the downed tree right in front of Blazer. He advanced fast and low. Steve was unable to bring the gun into play in time, and hands wrapped around his wrist, freezing the Desert Eagle in mid-air.

Steve found he had the advantage in size and strength. But the smaller Asian man had drive. They came face to face, and the enemy's snarling visage mirrored his own.

The kick caught Steve by surprise. The Asian brought his right leg forward swiftly, connecting with Steve's knee. But it wasn't enough to do any damage other than a slight jar. Steve seized the opportunity while his opponent was off balance and shoved hard.

The Asian killer was lifted off his feet, and he came down on his back. When he leapt to his feet, he had grabbed a solid two-foot piece of splintered tree branch from the ground. He swung it once, and Steve stepped back, letting the branch sail through the space he'd just vacated. The Asian tried one last desperate attack, bringing the branch down for an overhead strike.

Steve stepped into it, instead barreling his body into the Asian's. Momentum ripped the wood from the Asian's fingers, and he was propelled backward by Steve's lunge.

Steve caught a brief glimpse of where they were headed and tried to stop. He tried to twist off the Asian's body, but they kept going. When they hit the log, a sharp cry escaped the Asian's lips and he suddenly went stiff. Steve stumbled back, regaining his composure. He poised for a strike, to defend against a new attack that never came.

The Asian did not get up, and never would again. This end of the downed redwood, what had been near the top, had frequent branches sticking out from the trunk. A thick two-foot broken branch had impaled the Asian. The body stared up at the gray sky with wide eyes, and after a moment, the eyes had no life in them. The body twitched once and lay still, hanging limp from the branch.

Steve caught his breath, then looked up as two gunshots echoed across the forest.

Stanson's mission was not yet complete.

* * *

Stanson stumbled, giving in for a moment to the pain emanating from his shoulder. He leaned against a tree for a moment to catch his breath. He needed to make his way deeper into the forest surrounding the creek bed, recoup his strength. He knew he was running low on ammo, but he couldn't think of that now.

"John Stanson," Smith called out. Stanson dropped farther into a crouch, checking the forest all around. Smith seemed to be over his shock at seeing him. The voice was coming from back to his left, where he'd left the man near the truck—Smith hadn't moved far. Stanson reached the creek bed and searched for a place of cover to make a stand. He glanced up and spotted one.

"Now there's a face I haven't seen in three decades," Smith continued, and Stanson could tell that now the man was moving. His voice was closer. Stanson tried to track the voice through the forest.

"What you been up to, old buddy? How are you getting along after being in the 'Nam? A lot of old war vets, they went crazy. A lot of them became mercenaries. Me, I went where the money was good. The last I heard, you became a cop."

Stanson could tell the man was baiting him, maybe getting him to give up where he was hiding. He kept silent for the moment.

He was right. For his part, Smith did finally seek cover, and now was scanning the forest with every sense, trying to find his 'old buddy'. "I should have known I'd run into you one of these days. What are you doing running around these woods? Don't tell me you're trying to bring me in." Smith stopped by a tree, listened to the sounds of the forest and the creek. Above the noise he heard a familiar voice try to rise.

"Some things never change."

Smith smiled as he made his way to the creek. "You know, Johnny, that hurt, what you did to me back in 'Nam."

"I tried to stop a killer."

"We were all killers." Smith listened, homing in on the nearby voice.

"You were more than a simple killer. You tried to kill me."

Smith smiled. Stanson was pissed.

"We were there to bring back our guys, pure and simple," Stanson yelled. "But you became a sadist!"

"I'm proud of what I did for that mission!" Smith replied.

"You became a monster."

"I became as they did," Smith barked. Now *he* was pissed. "I did what I had to do to scare the shit out of those people to give up what they knew! We found some of our guys because of what I did! You know that!"

Stanson closed his eyes remembering everything he'd gone through. His head was spinning, from the injury as well as from trying to make some sense out of the thirty-year-old rush of confusion. "So how do you justify what you do now?"

"I gotta make a living." With that, Smith reached the creek bed, aiming his silver Colt down toward the water. He checked up the creek to the east first, but turned back a heartbeat later, sensing sudden danger from the other direction.

Perched eight feet in the air on a tree branch over the bank of the creek, Stanson let two rounds fly. The first missed completely, buzzing over Smith's shoulder. The second tore through that shoulder, punching out a massive exit wound next to a shoulder blade. Smith staggered, then scrambled back the way he came.

* * *

Steve heard the voices down in the thick woods below the road. He slid down the muddy slope, watching his surroundings, until he was nearly abreast of the truck. Moving along the slope, he approached the truck, examining it. He took another treacherous step down and around to the front of the cab, where the windshield was smashed out.

Something caught his eye. Lodged against the windshield was a grenade identical to the one he'd just used up the hill.

Steve reached in through the shattered windshield and grabbed the grenade.

He scrambled back when he heard the truck creak—it was still unstable. The truck slid another inch down the muddy slope, threatening to drop the last twelve feet to the forest floor, but the tree held it fast. For the moment.

A flurry of gunfire sounded from the creek bed.

* * *

John had Smith on the run now. Crouched on his branch, Stanson hopped and landed in a crouch in the grassy sand. He rose and ran in pursuit. All pain was forgotten now, and only one thing existed. The enemy. He no longer had a name, just a designated mission. Kill.

Stanson dodged around a row of bushes, spotted Smith as he bolted between two trees and fired two more shots. Both tore bark off the tree. He kept going, knowing he had to close the gap.

Another sighting. Another shot. This one tore a branch off a tree next to where Smith's head had just been. He kept moving. So did his pursuer.

Smith broke into the open, just twenty yards from the looming hillside, the overturned truck, and the grenade he knew was still inside, the grenade that would give him an edge. It had to. He hadn't had time to search the wreckage for it minutes before, but now he needed it.

He scrambled up the slope, stopped on his knees in front of the broken windshield, eyes searching wildly for the grenade. He fought a wave of dizziness from his wound. He was still losing blood. The grenade was nowhere in sight. He slipped, went down to his hands and knees and crawled closer, desperately hoping maybe this new angle would give him new sight into the empty cab.

A bullet sent up a small geyser of mud next to him.

Stanson fired this last shot from inside the forest. The pistol locked open. But not only was this his last round, it was his last mag. He hit the release to slide the breech closed, disguising the empty gun.

Smith turned as the bullet burrowed into the ground next to him. He let himself slide back down the slope, ending up in a heap on the wet ground. John Stanson stepped from the forest, his dark pistol holding a steady bead on Smith's head. Smith stared at the enormous barrel, and then at the face behind it.

Stanson had changed, he saw, the years had taken their toll. The face smeared with dark streaks of camo paint had a few wrinkles of age. But the eyes were the same. Dead, devoid of human compassion. Just like his own must have been.

Was he seeing only what he wanted to see?

He waited for that gun barrel to spit fire, for that shot he would never hear, for that bullet to finally come for him.

But Stanson stood stock still before him, the gun not even flinching.

Finally, he spoke.

"You greedy son of a bitch. You used us over there as your own drug enforcers. And you tried to kill me to cover it up."

"I was there right beside you in those jungles."

"Don't you dare compare yourself to me."

Smith flashed his condescending grin. "You don't know it, but you're a wanted man over there. There's a price on your head for bringing out those POWs. For escaping from that camp."

"You wanted me to die in that camp. You didn't give a damn about the men we found, who fought and died for this country."

Steve listened intently above them. He'd had to scramble out of there fast when he heard the shots, when he heard Smith running toward him. He took up surveillance from the high ground to gauge the situation below and watch over Stanson. He lay stretched across part of the muddy road just above them, his emotions churning as he heard the words coming from his mentor's mouth. What was Stanson doing? He came all this way to kill this man, why wasn't he firing?

"Maybe you need a taste of your own medicine. Maybe we'll start with the knees. A bullet through each should do the trick, make sure you don't go anywhere and miss the party. Then, maybe I'll take a cigarette lighter, and start drawing a little map on your chest." He smiled a cruel, sadistic smile. "Let's see, then maybe we'll start with the fingers. Do you think I could break each individual knuckle? Maybe if I yank hard enough, I can tear them right off your hand."

Steve continued to listen and weigh his options. But the question nagged at him. Had Stanson gone as mad as Smith, possibly becoming what he most hated? Should he try to interrupt and stop this confrontation?

Smith took a chance. He struggled to his feet slowly. "Look, Johnny, if you're still pissed about things that happened back then, I'm sorry."

Stanson fell back a step, making sure Smith didn't get close enough to snatch his weapon, and ruin the bluff he had going. "Are you? Are you really sorry?"

Too late, Steve noticed what the Captain could not see. Smith had a SIG Sauer automatic pistol tucked into the back of his pants. He drew the gun in a lightning swing. "Actually, no I'm not sorry."

Stanson froze when the gun came up to match his. But with his own weapon empty, there was nothing he could do.

The two stood still, guns fixed on the head of the man in front of them. Stanson couldn't move. If he backed down or pulled his trigger on the empty chamber, his advantage was gone.

Smith grinned. "So, I guess we just stand here until someone decides to pull the trigger."

Steve decided to act.

He pulled the pin on the grenade and rolled it down the hill.

Stanson looked up the hill when he heard the slightest sound of metal knock against the truck.

Smith didn't hear it. All he saw was Stanson momentarily distracted. His grin broadened another millimeter. His finger tightened on the trigger.

The grenade landed near the back corner and bounced into the truck bed. The explosion tore the truck apart, ripping the bed and reaching the gas tank. The rear half of the vehicle became a billowing inferno. Mud, metal, smoke and fire erupted from the hillside. The explosion lifted the overturned vehicle away from its position against the tree, tossing the heavy truck.

The blast took them both by surprise. Smith ducked and turned. Stanson could only watch.

Smith froze at the sight of the fiery pickup dropping toward him from twelve feet up. Before he could dodge away, the nose knocked him down and kept coming, driving him and itself into the wet ground.

The impact echoed through the forest and faded to the crackle of the flames as the smoke and dust billowed away from the wreckage along the ground.

Stanson had been knocked backwards by the blast, and now weakened, he sank to his knees. He wanted to stay on the ground until someone came along to fix him up. Or maybe he'd let the ground just swallow him. But after a moment, he forced himself to stagger to his feet. He took a step toward the truck, which had settled nose first into the ground. The upper torso of Eli Smith poked out from under the crumpled nose of the truck, which seemed to have sliced the man in two. He'd been crushed, possibly even cut in half by the falling truck. The eyes were open, and they stared up at him with an accusatory flare, even in death.

Steve Blazer rose above him, silhouetted against the gray sky as he looked down from the road above. And suddenly he was surrounded by the line of law enforcement vehicles that had rolled down the road and finally reached the camp.

EPILOGUE

In twenty minutes, Stanson was being loaded onto a gurney that would be taken to an ambulance, the last emergency vehicle to arrive. Steve stayed by his Captain's side. He watched over him, the man who had taught him so much over the last ten years, and even more over the last twenty-four hours.

Among the law enforcement officials that showed up at the scene, Agent Kimmins presented himself. He appeared from among the police vehicles that now swarmed the camp. He looked out of place in the muddy forest road in his brown suit.

Steve sighed as the fed confronted them with a blank expression. "Agent Kimmins, however did you find us?"

"Blazer, I've been searching for you since you left San Francisco. I got wind of Cleopatra Point from Inspector Black. I came across the Sheriff's Department wrapping up a massive shooting investigation at a convenience store in Fort Bragg. Interestingly, there were no victims, just one shaken clerk and a whole lot of shell casings everywhere. I had to take a little initiative to get deputies to search the area for your vehicle. It was found at the entrance to this logging road this morning, along with two black Lexus sedans."

"Lieutenant Cameron tells me you suspect me in the Bao Lin murder. The man under the truck down below has a .45 caliber handgun, you might want to check the ballistics."

Kimmins shrugged. "I'll leave that to you local cops." He chose his next words carefully. "You weren't wrong about me, Blazer. I've only been in charge of my section for two years. When I heard that Bao Lin was under my scrutiny and protection, I wanted to cut him off. It's not like he needed us for anything other than to shield him from the law. Bao Lin came to me and found a way to make himself at least seem useful. He's been dangling rumors of plots in front of me since I've known him. Always needs more time or resources to conduct his own inquiries. He played that card to get me to go after you. My bosses wanted me to humor him."

Stanson found this particularly interesting.

"I'm just glad we're all rid of him. Good luck to you both." Kimmins turned away, and in moments, his vehicle left the scene.

After a moment, Stanson looked up at his protégé. "I couldn't do it, Blazer. I couldn't kill him."

"I know, sir. You're not that kind of man."

"You're wrong about that, son. That was the reason I came here, to kill this particular ghost from my past once and for all. When the need arises, anybody can be that kind of man. But I couldn't do it. I ran out of bullets."

Steve's face collapsed into a grin. He'd been worried that the Captain would chew him out for robbing him of the kill. He decided to change the subject. "I promised Mary I'd get you home to her."

Stanson closed his eyes. "How am I going to explain all this to her?" He looked up at his protégé.

"Blazer, thanks for letting me vent. Mary's great, and I love her, but I can't exactly tell her about my day. I couldn't tell her about most of what happened over in 'Nam, so I've carried all that stuff with me for decades." He blinked slowly, still feeling weak. "Son, you're the best therapy I could have had."

Stanson fell silent, for a moment staring out into the forest that had become a hellground. He allowed himself one more memory...

* * *

1983

Stanson returned to the camp with fear in his heart, though he knew it would be his final time there. They'd been unable to find Smith, and Stanson did not like that hanging over his head. He didn't know what his future held with the CIA, but whatever he did with his life, there was always the possibility that Smith would suddenly reappear to seek his revenge. This weighed on him heavily. But at least for now, he was going home.

He and Ross entered the camp from the main gate, rather than return to the breach in the wire perimeter. The CIA team had swept through the camp, cutting down every Vietnamese soldier they found. The bodies lay scattered around the grounds. Stanson saw Harry Wayne with two other members of their team, checking over Sergeant Noya and the three freed prisoners. Harry got up as they approached and threw his arms around Stanson. "Glad you made it, Johnny."

"About time you guys found me," Stanson smiled. "Good to see you, Harry. Can we get the hell out of here?"

Harry looked at Ross. "Huts are all wired and timered. We'll be long gone when they blow."

"We have about ten klicks to hump," Ross said to the group. "Can you guys make it?"

"If it means we're going home," Noya said confidently, "We can make it."

Stanson liked the sound of that and repeated it quietly. "We're going home."

* * *

As they left the camp behind, they were treated to one final special effect. They reached a low ridge just a mile from the camp, just in time to see the series of explosions that destroyed the huts that made up the camp. Stanson smiled when the prisoners cheered at the destruction. But the emotion was bittersweet. One man was not there to share in their joy. The rescue had come a day too late for Sergeant Adrian Quintero.

The hike had been slow, but steady and deliberate. The freed prisoners, and even Stanson himself, were beaten down by their ordeal, but they were determined to finish this final exodus from Vietnam. The team provided them water, and they had food, brought by the team and also raided from the camp storage before they left. As the sun dipped below the jungle, they broke into a clearing at the entrance to a valley. Ross stopped them at the edge of the clearing to keep them under cover as they waited for their chopper ride out.

Stanson stopped to enjoy the sunset, to embrace the moment of peace that he now felt. He would always have a particular ghost stalking him, both figuratively and literally. But he contented himself now to know he was returning to the land of the free.

Returning to what? he suddenly asked himself.

As if reading his thoughts, Ross sat down next to him. "What did you mean, Johnny, when you said Smith got your message?"

"I thought I was stuck there," Stanson said. "I thought I was going to die there. I figured I had one shot to get a little payback on Smith. I gave Minh that site on the map that was supposed to be shut down. I figured Smith didn't want us checking that site because he was running it."

"That's how we found you," Ross said. "I heard about Minh burning that site down and seizing opium. To me, it could only mean that you were still alive. Smith figured out where Minh got his information. He put together the mission to raid the camp. I don't know why he took the team, knowing we would try to rescue you. I knew he would try to kill you, and just count you as a casualty of the assault. When we set up the perimeter at the camp, I was with him. When I saw where you were, I broke away so I could warn you."

"What's going to happen with the team?" Stanson asked.

"I don't know. Johnson hasn't been heard from in weeks. I imagine they'll swoop in and shut us down soon. But my superiors are going to get a full report on what we know about the opium trade here—and the hands of their agents involved in it. What they do with all the information…who knows?"

Stanson paused. "I need out, Ross."

"John, there will be a place for both of us in the Agency."

"No, this two-year odyssey needs to end for me. I believed in the mission, but the mission changed. I believe in America, but America changes too. Sometimes for the better, but not always. I need to adjust and change with it or keep it from changing too much. This is what I set out to do before all this."

"Where will you go?"

Stanson thought on that. "Back to California. I met a nice girl at Berkeley right before you found me. I think I'll go back and look her up. Maybe try the cop thing like I was going for."

"John, you're a damn good agent. Don't let that go." Ross stopped, knowing this was a feeble attempt to keep Stanson in the Agency loop. What he'd said about change made sense. And after what he'd been through, he'd earned a rest. "What about Smith? He's still out there."

"I'm not running away from him. I'll have to always be ready for him to emerge from the past again. In fact, if you ever find him, let me know, and I'll kill him myself."

Ross noted the sudden dark look in Stanson's eyes. "Tell me this," he said. "If your country needed you... if I asked of you a favor... would you answer the call?"

Stanson thought long and hard on that, and almost said nothing as the rattle of a helicopter sounded through the valley. Finally, he smiled and said, "Maybe."

Ross smiled back. He rose to leave the cover of the jungle and motion in the chopper. But Stanson was not through with him yet.

"Ross," he called out before the din of the chopper became too loud. "I've always wanted to ask. My brother was Special Forces. Was he involved with the Agency? Did you recruit me because of him?"

Ross stopped and offered him that coy smile. "All I can say is, you wrote a hell of a term paper."

It was not the answer John wanted, but he couldn't help his smile. He rose with the others as the Huey swooped down into the valley. Back during the war, when soldiers were leaving the 'Nam to go back to 'the world,' they called it the freedom bird, and ten years after the war, in this moment, the title was fitting. He followed the three freed prisoners. They would receive no hero's welcome for their service. Hell, *he* would probably be smuggled home the same way every prisoner they'd freed had gone. It was enough. He felt for a moment what a soldier should feel, the pride that came from surviving battle and seeing a new meaning to words like "duty" and "honor." Those words meant something in America, his home. He would keep these thoughts with him.

He headed for the chopper to leave Vietnam behind, even though he would take some pieces with him. He knew those pieces would always be with him.

* * *

Stanson was finally loaded into the ambulance. Without a siren to serenade the hero's departure, the ambulance pulled away, splashing through puddles of mud and rainwater. Steve laughed at the symbolism that sprung to mind at the sight. It was a more fitting tribute to a man who was a hero from the Vietnam War, even in his own way. In the years that followed, he was a hero a thousand times over. Steve felt humbled by it all. There were thousands of men and women who served their country in that war, faithfully and without question. Many felt they were dumped on, and they were entitled to that belief. They, too, were heroes, locked in that moment in time.

For the moment, Steve just stood there feeling humbled.

ACKNOWLEDGEMENTS

Special thanks to my wife Daria for her editing skills, and for her photography for the cover. Also thanks to Benjamin Walker, Melanie Walker and M.E. Photography for their work on the cover.

A LOOK AT BOOK TWO: BLAZER: RED, WHITE AND BLUE

BLAZER IS DETERMINED TO TAKE DOWN THE CARTEL AND END THEIR CAMPAIGN OF VIOLENCE IN THIS BLISTERING ACTION THRILLER.

Steve Blazer is an honest San Francisco cop—with a reputation for attracting trouble.

While tracking down a Latino gang leader, Blazer comes across a massive cocaine stash where he discovers that a ruthless Mexican Cartel is targeting San Francisco. Any interference with their plans results in violence—turning streets into combat zones. In response, the San Francisco Police Chief reinstates a unit known as Special Forces. It's a risky notion. Special Forces was shut down years ago under a cloud of suspicion. But Blazer, as its new Sergeant, is tasked with keeping the unit honest.

Too bad the squad is immediately involved in the death of a Latino gang member, and accusations and media slanders escalate the city into a race riot. Determined to regain control, Blazer sends one of his men on an undercover operation in the belly of the gang. However, the deeper his undercover agent goes, the more Blazer sees him losing control. With the Special Forces unit in jeopardy of being shut down, the cartel tightens its hold on the streets. But not before Blazer's unit discovers the gang leader's location.

Blazer must now choose between the department and the badge itself. Does he step back and honor the department that wants him out, or push forward shielded by the values of the badge he cherishes and save the city he's sworn to protect?

AVAILABLE NOW ON AMAZON

ABOUT THE AUTHOR

G.C. Harmon became interested in action heroes at a very young age: cops, firefighters, soldiers, even racecar drivers and cowboys. At the age of 10, he discovered writing, and began by creating short stories based on his favorite TV characters. Around the same time, he created the Steve Blazer character, and has been developing the character ever since. As a teen, he discovered the pulp fiction genre, authors writing books with the kind of heroes and stories he aspired to write himself, favorites including the Executioner and Destroyer series. Fresh out of high school and seeking more knowledge on what he was writing about, he joined the Military.

Over the next fifteen years, G.C. Harmon spent time in the United States Army and Army Reserve, first with Artillery as a Forward Observer, then with the Signal Corps. He capped off his military career with a tour of the Middle East in support of Operation Iraqi Freedom. He trained as a cop, graduating from California's Peace Officer Standards and Training Police Academy in 2000. He has worked in the Security industry since 2002, working alongside many police departments.

G.C. Harmon has had many crazy life experiences, some of which find their way into his stories. In 2017, after exploring mainstream publishing and finding no opportunities, he took the plunge and self-published his first Blazer novel, "Red, White and Blue." Through self-publishing, he made new contacts in the publishing business and discovered Wolfpack Publishing, putting out the kind of exciting adventure writing he has done his entire life. He lives in Sacramento, California, and he is always working on new Blazer adventures.